THE MONSTER'S CARESS

A SEVEN KINGDOMS TALE 8

S.E. SMITH

ACKNOWLEDGMENTS

I would like to thank my husband Steve for believing in me and being proud enough of me to give me the courage to follow my dream. I would also like to give a special thank you to my sister and best friend, Linda, who not only encouraged me to write, but who also read the manuscript. Also, to my other friends who believe in me: Julie, Jackie, Christel, Sally, Jolanda, Lisa, Laurelle, Debbie, and Narelle. The girls that keep me going!

And a special thanks to Paul Heitsch, David Brenin, Samantha Cook, Suzanne Elise Freeman, PJ Ochlan, Vincent Fallow, L. Sophie Helbig, and Hope Newhouse—the outstanding voices behind my audiobooks!

– S. E. Smith

Fantasy Romance
THE MONSTER'S CARESS
SEVEN KINGDOMS TALE 8
Copyright © 2020 by S.E. Smith
First E-Book Published September 2020
Cover Design by Melody Simmons

Summary: Tales of his grandfather's amazing journey to another world leads a CIA agent on a quest to discover the whereabouts of the mysterious Seven Kingdoms and the enchanting Empress of the Monsters.

ISBN: 9781952021480 (Paperback)
ISBN: 9781952021473 (eBook)

Fantasy Dragons & Mythical Creatures | Romance (love, explicit sexual content) | Action/Adventure | Contemporary | Paranormal (Shifters, Magic) | Multicultural

Published by Montana Publishing, LLC
& SE Smith of Florida Inc. www.sesmithfl.com

CONTENTS

SYNOPSIS

CIA agent Asahi Tanaka grew up hearing tales from his grandfather about a mysterious realm where magic and monsters are real. His quest for answers takes him back to Yachats, Oregon, his childhood home. His personal investigation of a series of disappearances leads to a break in the case, and he finds himself in a strange but eerily familiar world.

Nali, Empress of the Monsters, will do anything to protect the creatures under her care. When one of her fabled Sea Stags washes ashore grievously injured, she knows the last of the alien organisms that came to her world has made it to her kingdom. Her search for the alien leads to an unexpected discovery—another visitor, this one from Earth!

A perilous journey to find the malevolent alien takes Nali and Asahi across the Isle of the Monsters, leading them to a discovery that changes their perceptions and makes them reexamine their place in the universe. Will the magic that sparks between these two warriors from different worlds be enough to destroy the threat, or will one have to be sacrificed to save not only the Seven Kingdoms but Earth as well?

Internationally acclaimed S.E. Smith presents a new action-packed story full of adventure and romance. Brimming with her signature humor, vivid scenes, and beloved characters, this book is sure to be another fan favorite!

WHO'S WHO IN THE SEVEN KINGDOMS TALES

The Seven Kingdoms

Isle of the Elementals – created first

King Ruger and Queen Adrina

Can control earth, wind, fire, water, and sky. Their power diminishes slightly when they are off their isle.

Goddess's Gift: The Gem of Power.

Isle of the Dragons – created second

King Drago

Controls the dragons.

Goddess's Gift: Dragon's Heart.

Isle of the Sea Serpent – created third

King Orion

Can control the Oceans and Sea Creatures.

Goddess's Gift: Eyes of the Sea Serpent.

Isle of Magic – created fourth

King Oray and Queen Magika

Their magic is extremely powerful but diminishes slightly when they are off their island.

Goddess's Gift: The Orb of Eternal Light.

Isle of the Monsters – created fifth for those too dangerous or rare to stay on the other Isles.

Empress Nali receives glimpses of the future.

Goddess's Gift: The Goddess's Mirror.

Isle of the Giants – created sixth

King Koorgan

Giants can grow to massive sizes when threatened – but only if they are away from their isle.

Goddess's Gift: The Tree of Life.

Isle of the Pirates – created last for outcasts from the other Isles

The Pirate King Ashure Waves, Keeper of Lost Souls

Collectors of all things fine. Fierce and smart, pirates roam the Isles trading, bargaining, and occasionally helping themselves to items of interest.

Goddess's Gift: The Cauldron of Spirits.

Notable Quotes

"It is how we deal with what we are given that defines who we are and who we are to become."

~King Ashure Waves~

PROLOGUE

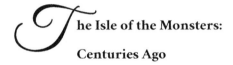 **he Isle of the Monsters:**

Centuries Ago

The tiny Rose Fairies fluttered with excitement. A portal had appeared near the old willow, and through it they could see a view of deep space before a graceful golden woman materialized in the opening. It was the Goddess!

The fairies clung to the branches of the magnificent old willow tree, huddled behind the cover of its many leaves, and curiously peered down at her. The bravest of the slender green fairies flew closer as the woman knelt and gently placed a mound of colorful material on the ground. When the tiny fairy flitted back and forth, trying to get a better view, the golden woman looked up and smiled.

"Watch over her," the Goddess instructed in a melodic voice.

"We will," the fairy promised, landing on the ground next to the brightly colored bundle.

The Goddess smiled. "What is your name?" she asked.

"Rosewood, your Majesty," the fairy replied with a tiny curtsy.

"Thank you, Rosewood," the Goddess acknowledged. Then she faded from view.

Rosewood gaped at the empty space where the Goddess had been a moment ago. Then she flew up and landed on the bundle. She tittered when the creature wrapped inside moved. A chorus of gasps came from the gently swaying branches.

"Be careful, Rosewood," a fairy called out.

"You don't know what it is," another cautioned.

Rosewood impatiently waved the fairies' concerns away. The Goddess had given her a task, and she would not fail.

The creature moved again, and a fold of the material fell aside, revealing an infant's dark, round face and large gold-flaked brown eyes. Black curls peeked out from the edge of the blanket. The infant's mouth opened, her eyes squeezed shut, and her lips twisted. For a moment, Rosewood thought the baby was about to cry. Instead, the infant sneezed loudly and cooed with delight.

Rosewood smiled and confided to the others, "In the palace rose garden, I overheard the Empress and Emperor wishing for a baby, a little girl to name Nali. This must be her. The Goddess has answered their pleas," she announced with wonder.

"What kind of monster is she, Rosewood?" another fairy asked, fluttering above the baby.

Rosewood scrutinized the creature, tilting her head, then shrugged. "Does it matter? She is Nali—our future Empress." Rosewood grinned at the increasing number of fairies crowding around the baby, all curious to see the creature who would one day be the Empress of the Isle of the Monsters.

Yachats, Oregon:

Twenty-six years Ago

Seven-year-old Asahi Tanaka curiously peeked out from where he was crouched behind the long sofa and winced when his father slammed the front door behind him as he left. Asahi had hidden to listen to the conversation between his father and the man who had introduced himself as Aiko, his grandfather.

They had all just returned from Baba's funeral, so today was already difficult without his father's anger boiling over, but the moment Hinata Tanaka had entered the house, he began shouting at Aiko. Their conversation had quickly become heated—mostly because of his father's refusal to listen to Aiko's explanation of where he had been and what had happened to him.

Asahi tilted his head when he heard the tires of his father's sports car burning rubber. Once again, his father had forgotten about him. Baba, Asahi's grandmother, would have been upset if she were still alive. She always complained that his father drove too fast on the narrow winding roads around here.

Tears burned his eyes at the thought of his grandmother. When one escaped from the corner of his eye and ran down his cheek, he lifted his hand and wiped it away. Baba would have scolded him for crying over her.

"Asahi, I know you are there. Please come out," the man sitting in the chair instructed.

Asahi slowly crawled out from behind the sofa and stood up. He stared at the man who looked almost the same age as his father. They looked so alike that Aiko and his father could have been mistaken as twins.

"Come, sit down so we can talk," Aiko Tanaka gently requested.

Asahi stiffened his thin shoulders and lifted his head. He silently walked over and sat in his grandmother's favorite chair. The pristine white doilies she had crocheted were draped over each arm of the green floral-patterned upholstery. He swallowed and remained still as his grandfather studied him.

Aiko sighed and looked down at the picture he was holding. Asahi looked at the photo too. It was an old picture of Baba, his father as a child, and Aiko—and Aiko looked the same as he did now.

"How... can you be the same person?" he asked in a faltering voice.

Aiko smiled at him. "It is a long story, one that I wish I could have shared with your Baba—and one I will share with your father in greater detail if he allows it. I want to share my story with you if you would like to hear it," he said.

Asahi eagerly nodded. "Yes. I love stories. Baba shared lots of stories with me," he shyly answered.

Aiko chuckled. "Your grandmother was a gifted storyteller. She would have loved this one. My story begins on a foggy morning forty years ago...," he began, leaning back in his chair.

Asahi listened with wonder as his grandfather spoke of his unbelievable journey to another world, a world filled with magic, dragons, giants, witches, pirates—and monsters. The marvels of the Seven Kingdoms sparked Asahi's imagination.

Darkness fell while they were finishing dinner. His grandfather paused and stared at him in silence, then twisted in his chair, opened a bag hanging from it, and pulled out an ornate dagger. At the top of the hilt was a small winged lion made of gold. Aiko held it lovingly in his hands.

Asahi stared in fascination at the strange symbols embossed on the thick leather sheath. His grandfather placed the dagger on the table in front of him and nodded toward it. Asahi's attention remained fixed on the richly detailed lion at the top.

"This dagger was a gift from a dear friend. For years, I dreamed of giving it to your father, but I was unsure if I would ever return to Yachats," Aiko softly explained.

Asahi tilted his head. "Baba said that father does not always appreciate the things he receives the way he should. She missed you. I liked when she told me stories about you," he confessed.

Aiko smiled and pushed the dagger toward him. "Then I will give this magic dagger to you," he said.

A knock at the front door forestalled what Asahi was going to say. He waited until Aiko was in the living room before he ran his fingers over the hilt of the dagger. Surprise washed through him when he saw the red-jeweled handle glow. He yanked his hand away.

The sound of his grandfather's hoarse cry of denial drew him to his feet. Asahi walked over to the opening between the kitchen and the living room. He peered around the corner to see who was at the door. His heart hammered in his chest when he saw that a police officer was talking to Aiko.

"Where did it happen?" his grandfather asked in an unsteady voice.

"Along Highway 101. It appears he lost control coming around the curve and hit the guardrail. His car flipped over the edge of the embankment and went off the cliff. Someone reported that they saw it below. He died on impact. I'm sorry," the police officer explained.

"No," Asahi whispered. The tears dripping down his face mirrored his grandfather's. Anger flooded his body.

"Asahi—" his grandfather began.

"It's all their fault," Asahi whispered.

The police officer looked at him and frowned. "Whose fault, son?" he asked.

Asahi looked back at his grandfather. "The monsters. If they had not taken you, then you would have been here for Baba and Father. They should not have taken you. They are the reason Baba and Father are dead," he replied in a low, fierce tone.

He didn't wait for the police officer or his grandfather to respond. There was nothing they could say that would bring back his grandmother or his father. He hurried back into the kitchen, grabbed the dagger off the table and a dish towel from the counter, and exited through the back door.

The tears on his face mixed with the damp mist as he hurried along the uneven path into the forest behind their house. When he was about a hundred yards away, he stopped and took several shuddering breaths of the chilled air. He wiped his face with the back of his shirt sleeve.

There was an outcropping of rocks next to the path where he had often enjoyed playing. He walked over to it, dropped to the ground, and placed his grandfather's dagger and the dish towel on the ground beside him.

It took him a few minutes to clear the dirt he had piled up near one side of the boulders. He felt along the ground until he found the large, loose rock that covered his secret hiding space. He wiggled the rock free, put it aside, and reached into the small crevice. Inside were the treasures he had collected over the past year. He scooped out the rocks, shells, and an assortment of toys he had hidden in the hollow space and tossed them aside.

Asahi carefully wrapped the dish towel around the dagger before he slid it inside the hole. He replaced the rock over the hollow area and concealed it by piling more rocks and dirt on top.

Once he was confident no one would ever find the dagger, he returned to the path. The heavy mist changed to a light rain that soaked through the dress shirt and pants he was still wearing from the funeral. There were dark patches of dirt marring his clothing, but he was beyond caring.

Asahi slowly walked back to the house, shivering from the cold and shock. His grandfather was standing in the doorway waiting for him. He stopped, and they stared at each other in silence for a minute before Aiko stepped out of the house, walked through the rain, and stood before him.

He trembled when Aiko placed a warm hand on his shoulder. "We will start over, Asahi. Yachats has too many memories for both of us," his grandfather quietly announced.

"I took your magic knife and hid it," Asahi confessed.

Aiko nodded in understanding. "Then you will know where it is when you are ready," he replied.

Asahi stepped into Aiko's open arms and hugged his grandfather's waist. Silent sobs shook his frame. He couldn't help wondering if the rain was Baba's tears as she cried with him.

CHAPTER 1

The Isle of the Monsters:

Present day

Asahi roused suddenly from unconsciousness. He frowned when he saw a canopy of unfamiliar trees above him, not the expected Oregon sky. He curled his fingers, noting that instead of beach sand, he touched soft moss. Bright, alien colors filled his vision.

He slowly examined the surrounding area, then forced his body to move. Asahi quickly discovered that sitting up wasn't easy when the world was spinning around him. He rested his forehead on his knees as black dots swam through his vision.

He took several deep breaths until he was confident that he wouldn't pass out. Once he lifted his head and looked around the area, it didn't take long to confirm his suspicion that he was no longer on the beach in Yachats State Park—or on Earth.

"Ruth," he softly called.

He pushed up off the ground, staggering when another wave of dizziness hit him. He bent forward, resting his hands on his thighs, and waited for it to subside. It took several minutes of deep breathing before he was steady enough to stand upright.

The spell had worked. He stood in a strange forest now. Tall trees, many the size of Redwoods and Sequoias back on Earth, were towering over him. Unlike the trees back home, these had long spiraling branches with dark blood-red leaves that grew upward and branched out in huge sections. Their darker red trunks looked like dozens of smaller trees had twined around each other as they grew. The overall effect was breathtaking—and definitely alien.

He had made it to the world of the Seven Kingdoms. However, it seemed that Ruth was not with him. Magna, a former Seven Kingdoms' resident, had given the spell to Ruth, and she had been the one to invoke it, but it was undeniable that Asahi stood here alone.

Blue, green, and yellow vines clung to the tree trunks and some had hanging fruit. He stumbled backward when he saw a small, hairy, bluish-purple mammal dart out from a hole in the trunk and grab a piece of the yellow fruit with two of its six appendages. The hairy creature turned and warily looked at him. It blinked its six eyes at alternate times before it brought the fruit closer to its chest. The animal swished its long, slender tail, which was covered in a series of fluffy purple tufts of hair, and then returned to its nest. Asahi smiled when he remembered the name of the mammal.

"A Purple-Tailed Tree Mouse," he murmured.

He reached into the side pocket of his black cargo pants and touched his journal. It contained the information his grandfather had shared over the years. Looking down at the ground, he breathed a sigh of relief when he saw the black duffle bag that he had been carrying on his shoulder before he appeared here. He hadn't been sure it would make the journey.

He knelt on one knee and unzipped the bag. A quick inventory showed that everything he had packed was still there. The first thing he retrieved was his 9mm handgun and shoulder holster. He secured the holster over his shoulder, then double-checked that the clip was full and the safety was on before he placed the gun in the holster and snapped the strap over the grip.

Next, he reached in and pulled out a white plastic trash bag. Inside the bag was a dirty dish towel wrapped around the dagger he had hidden twenty-six years ago. He unwound the dish towel and stared down at the dagger. It looked as pristine as it did the day he had hidden it.

The sound of chittering drew his attention back to the tree. Nearly a dozen of the Purple-Tailed Tree Mice were now gorging themselves on the yellow fruit.

He scanned the area again, looking for any sign of Ruth. There was no trace of footprints. Even from the brief time he had known Ruth, he was positive that she would have stayed nearby if she were here.

He kept the dagger out, stuffed the towel and the plastic bag back into the duffle bag, zipped it closed, and stood up again.

First things first—he needed to find shelter, take stock of where he was, and decide on his next move. If he was correct and the creatures in the tree were Purple-Tailed Tree Mice, then he was on the Isle of the Monsters. There was a rough map of the Isle in the journal. His grandfather had visited the kingdom once, but he had never ventured farther afield than the capitol city.

Asahi bent down, picked up the duffle bag, and pulled the strap over his head so it crossed his body. Based on the angle of the sunlight streaming through the upper canopy, he suspected that it was just after midday. He would have a few hours to secure a safe place for the night. The temperature was moderate now, but he suspected it would drop when the sun set.

"I think the trees may be out for camping tonight—at least that one," he mused with a shake of his head at the colony of tiny purple creatures.

He closed his eyes and carefully listened to the surrounding sounds. The chirps of birds mixed with the buzzing of insects and the chatter of the Purple-Tailed Tree Mice. Another sound coming from his right filtered through the noise—the sound of rushing water.

Asahi opened his eyes and turned in that direction. Water meant a river or lake that could lead him to either a village or the coast. He unfastened his belt and slid the end through the loop in the dagger's sheath. He refastened the buckle and rolled his shoulders to ease the tension in them before he set off toward the sound of flowing water. If Ruth was anywhere nearby, he hoped she would do the same.

~

Nali's palace:

Underground chambers

"Keep her contained. I want no one except the gargoyles anywhere near her. See if Denae can do anything to relieve her suffering," Nali instructed as she stepped out of the high-security containment room.

"Yes, Empress," Di answered.

Nali looked through the thick diamond plate window. The room had been reinforced and sealed so the alien could not escape. She splayed her hand against the foot-thick steel door as she studied the suffering Sea Stag in the water tank. Two gargoyles monitored the Sea Stag mare.

"Empress, is there anything I can do?" her old guardian asked.

Nali shook her head. "No, Pai. I must do this alone," she murmured.

The hippogriff shook his head and snapped his beak. She looked at him and smiled at his obvious disapproval.

"Your parents...," he began before snapping his beak closed once again.

"...would have insisted that you accompany me. I understand your concern, Pai, but my parents never had to face anything like this before," she said, looking back through the window. "She is being tortured by the alien inside her."

Pai stepped closer, the long talons on his front legs tapping against the polished stone floor. Nali lifted her hand and gently caressed the feathers along his neck. Pai had been her guardian all her life, and she appreciated his many years of unwavering friendship and loyalty.

"I can see to the Sea Stag's execution. I would make sure she doesn't suffer," Pai offered. "It would be more merciful."

She shook her head. "Not yet. Perhaps Denae can draw the alien out of the poor creature without killing her," she murmured.

Nali retraced her steps to the upper levels of the palace. Pai followed her. Gargoyle soldiers stood at attention as she passed. She bowed her head in greeting to each one, even as her thoughts were focused on the problem at hand.

"Nali, if there is another alien, it is best that I help you search. You need my superior eyesight," Pai coaxed.

Nali chuckled and sighed. "You aren't going to give up, are you?" she demanded as she stopped and faced him.

Pai tilted his head as if thinking about her question before he shook it. "No," he teasingly replied.

Her expression softened when she saw the worry that he didn't bother to hide. She also noticed the silvering of his feathers and the slight limp in his gait. Pai's expert skills would be useful, but she worried about his health. He was no longer the spry young hippogriff that he had been a century ago.

"You are aware of what the alien can do. You've witnessed what will happen if it enters your body. We are still not sure how it does that. I hope Denae will be able to tell us. You also know that you won't have the same protection that I do, Pai," Nali warned, already knowing that she would give in to Pai's desire to go with her.

"And what will happen if it takes you by surprise before you can shift? Who would be there to protect you?" he asked.

"You, of course! Do you really think I don't know when you follow me —even against my orders?" she replied with a wave of her hand.

Pai chuckled. "I must be losing my talons," he answered instead. "Where do we start?" he asked.

"We start where the Sea Stag came ashore," she instructed.

Nali soared through a cloud, her long wings spread wide, leaving a faint contrail of swirling mist behind her. Pai flew beside her, his sharp eyes scanning the coast. They were close to the area where the injured female Sea Stag had washed ashore.

"Empress, there is something moving near the rocks half-a-mile north of here," Pai called.

Nali turned north, slowly descending until she had a better view. A line of rocks rose above the surface of the water, protecting one of the many black-sand beaches that lined this part of the coast. Near those rocks, she saw a Sea Stag struggling in the surf.

"Keep a safe distance, Pai," she warned before pulling her wings in tight against her body and diving toward the beach.

She twisted at the last second, landing on her feet. She shifted, her skin and clothing hardening to smooth and supple black marble. Her feet sank into the fine, black grains of sand, her footprints disappearing behind her as she walked over to the Sea Stag. He was lying on the beach, the lower half of his body still in the surf.

She pursed her lips to keep her outraged cry from drawing Pai down to the beach. The Sea Stag was slit from his front fin to the tip of his tail. The wound was large and it gaped, revealing bone and internal organs. It was a miracle that the stag had made it to shore.

Nali cooed softly to the stag as she approached, placing the beautiful creature into a trance. The usually bright-red scales were pale and dull as the life force faded from the beast. The stag turned his head toward her and made a barely audible whinny. She kneeled beside him in the damp sand and gently lifted his head onto her lap.

"I'm so sorry I couldn't protect you," she murmured, stroking the slender jaw.

The stag's eyelids drooped, and he shuddered. Rare tears slipped from the corners of Nali's eyes as she held the dying creature. Only great tragedy and sorrow could bring tears to a gargoyle's eyes. She bent forward and rested her head against the stag.

"Please, I need to know what happened to you before I can let you go," she whispered.

Another shudder ran through the stag at her request. She closed her eyes as images of the stag's last minutes formed in her mind through her bond with the beast. When the creature's fear hit her, she took a deep breath and gently stroked the fin between the stag's ears.

The living black liquid had come up out of the depths of the ocean. Long tentacles had attacked the juveniles before they broke free and escaped. The alien attacked the female first. When the male rushed to defend her, the second alien struck.

The images faded before she could see what happened next. The stag's wounds were too grave, and she sensed him slipping away from her. She lifted her head and looked up at the sky. Above her, Pai kept watch.

Nali lowered her head and tenderly stroked the young stallion before she whispered a simple incantation. Her magic surrounded the Sea Stag, engulfing the body of this once-beautiful creature in a vivid white light. When the light faded, a single brilliant gem was all that remained, and she was alone on the beach.

Nali picked up the precious stone and held it against her heart. She rose to her feet and stared out at the ocean. Pai swept down and landed near her.

"Did you learn anything?" he quietly inquired.

"There were two aliens. We have one. The second one escaped. The stallion—the stallion died before he could show me everything," she replied in a soft voice.

"I noticed tracks leading into the forest. They belong to a troll," Pai said.

Nali clenched her jaw. The two who found the first stag had thankfully kept their distance and sent an alert to the palace, but this troll may not have been so cautious.

"It will be night soon. We need to visit the troll village to find out who was here. We can stay there for the night and then resume our journey in the morning," she said.

"There's smoke rising from chimneys along the river a few miles inland," Pai replied.

Nali nodded. She turned her hand over and looked at the red gem containing the essence of the Sea Stag stallion. Pai silently stood by as she stepped to the water's edge and waited for an incoming wave to roll ashore. She knelt and released the gem into the receding water, watching as it carried the gem back out to sea. With a deep sigh of sorrow, she straightened and faced Pai.

"Let's go. I have an alien to kill," she declared. Her tone was as hard as her ebony skin.

CHAPTER 2

*A*sahi sat on an outcropping of rocks that loomed above the river and watched the first moon rise above the trees, followed shortly by the second. A sense of peace swept through him, and he focused on the emotion, the way his grandfather had taught him. The simple meditation helped keep the residual waves of dizziness under control.

He pulled his jacket out of the duffle bag, put it on, and zipped it up. His thoughts returned to Ruth Hallbrook. He genuinely hoped that she had survived her trip through the portal, if indeed she had gone through the portal at all. Throughout the day, he had searched for signs of her with no luck.

He studied the surrounding area. He had followed the flow of water that meandered southward, hoping that it would eventually lead to the coastline.

As afternoon became early evening, Asahi had started searching for a suitable place to make camp. He had finally settled on the rock platform where he now relaxed. He had needed to cross the river, but that hadn't been an issue thanks to the natural bridge formed by the accumulation of rock and debris that had been washed downstream.

He looked across the river when he saw movement. A dozen small shaggy animals emerged out of the forest.

This spot turned out to be a good place to make camp for the night, he thought.

The yellow and brown striped animals were about the size and build of a wombat, but they had markings like a zebra. Several juveniles grunted with delight and broke for the water ahead of the adults. He chuckled when they began splashing each other.

He slid back and leaned against the rock. A poke in his side reminded him of the dagger at his waist. He adjusted the sheath to a more comfortable position and relaxed. The sound of snapping wood and the warning sounds coming from the family of yellow-striped animals drew his attention back across the river.

A bear-like creature, the size of an elephant, emerged from the forest a hundred yards from the wombat-like mammals. The bear's low growl sent the juveniles dashing out of the water and back into the shelter of the forest, squealing in alarm. The adults took up a defensive stance, but the bear merely shook its head and ambled over to the river. The immense beast waded in and submerged itself in the gently flowing water, propping its head on a convenient rock with a contented sigh.

Asahi laughed softly. It took the striped adults a few minutes to relax. Once they did, the juveniles returned to the river with more caution tempering their enthusiasm.

"This world is amazing, Grandfather," Asahi murmured.

As unusual as the forest appeared during the day, it was even more spectacular at night. Bioluminescent plants and insects began appearing as the evening progressed. He didn't make a fire for several reasons. The last thing he wanted to do was attract attention to his location. He also didn't want anything to affect his night vision.

There was now a chill in the air as the sun settled over the horizon. With a tired sigh, he reached into the duffle bag again, this time pulling out a thin thermal blanket. He zipped the bag and adjusted it for use as a pillow before lying down and covering himself. He was a light sleeper, a habit that worked in his favor because for the foreseeable future, he would have to be on alert.

Lying on his back, he looked up at the moons, and wondered if fulfilling his grandfather's last wish was a wise thing to do. After all, there was no guarantee that he would make it back to Earth, and if he did, he didn't know what year it would be. He had taken precautions, making sure certain items would be passed down as an inheritance. Still, would he be ready to handle a world that would have changed over a forty-year—or more—period? He knew all too well the struggles that his grandfather had faced.

He touched the hilt of his dagger, drawing comfort from it. Intense fatigue dragged at his consciousness. His eyelids drooped. The splashing river below and the chirping insects soon lulled him into a light but restful sleep.

～

The Troll Village

Nali and Pai landed in the center of a ring of massive thatched huts. The small community had clearly been busy with activity a few minutes ago, but the trolls had stopped what they were doing to watch her arrival. She scanned the group. They were several times larger than even her tall physique.

"Empress, what brings you to our humble village?" Zenma, the Elder troll, asked as she stepped forward. She wore a long, beautifully embroidered tunic and carried a long, carved staff.

Nali shifted into her softer form, and greeted the Elder troll. "I fear it is a matter of grave importance, Zenma," she said.

Zenma looked down at her with concern. "Of course, Empress. Please follow me," she said.

"Pai, check the village. If you find anything, do not engage," she cautioned under her breath.

"Yes, Empress," Pai replied.

Nali followed Zenma to a central longhouse. As she climbed the steps, she scanned the surrounding area. Zenma stepped through the opened doors and into the cheerful interior. Three long rows of tables, most of them as tall as Nali, stood perpendicular to a fourth table up front on a low platform. While the tables in the center of the room had bench seats, there were individual chairs beside the table on the platform.

Zenma paused and glanced with concern at the benches and chairs, then at her. It was easy to see what the Elder troll was thinking. Nali gave Zenma a reassuring smile and motioned for the old troll to sit.

"If you sit, we'll be a little more at eye level," Nali suggested.

"Yes, thank you, Empress," Zenma said with a sigh as she slowly lowered herself to the bench. "I'm afraid the years are finally catching up with me."

"How are the trolls doing? Do you need anything?" Nali politely enquired.

Zenma smiled at her. "The trolls are doing well, thank you for asking, Empress. However, I believe your visit involves a more pressing matter. Does it have to do with Elderberry and Dew, the trolls who found the Sea Stag?" the Elder troll asked.

Nali nodded. "Yes. I would like to speak with them, and I believe there is also a third troll. We've discovered another Sea Stag, a mortally wounded stallion. Pai saw troll tracks nearby," she explained.

"I was not aware that there was another," Zenma replied.

The Elder troll lifted her staff and brought it down twice in rapid succession on the hard-planked floor. A guard appeared at once.

"Find Dew and Elderberry, and tell them I wish to speak with them. Also, find out who else has been hunting recently," Zenma ordered.

"Yes, Elder," the guard said with a bow of her head.

Zenma returned her attention to Nali. "Are my trolls in danger, Empress?" Zenma quietly asked.

Nali reached over and laid her hand on Zenma's. She would not lie to the Elder troll. The old troll's hand trembled under hers.

"There is a great danger to our Isle. I believe the same kind of alien that attacked the Sea Witch and the Isle of Magic is now on the Isle of the Monsters. Your trolls were the first to encounter the creature here. It is imperative that I speak with them," she explained.

Zenma nodded. "The trolls will do whatever you require, Empress."

"Elder, Dew and Elderberry are here," the guard announced.

Nali transformed her skin back into the stone exterior of a gargoyle as she turned and faced the two trolls who entered. She searched their eyes for any evidence of the black swirling shadows that she had noticed in Magna's. Twin sets of clear blue eyes watched her with a mixture of awe and nervousness, then Dew ducked his head.

"You wished to speak with us, Elder?" Elderberry inquired.

"Not I but Empress Nali," Zenma replied with a wave of her hand.

"You were the ones who discovered the first stag, correct?" Nali asked.

"Yes, Empress. We planned to fish the cove. Dew was the first to notice the stag. It was struggling in the surf. We've never seen a stag this far north before and never that close to shore. Dew sensed something was wrong with it and cautioned that we should alert the palace," Elderberry replied.

Nali looked at Dew. He was young, and from the way he kept looking down at the floor, she sensed that he was shy. She stepped closer to him, gently reached out, and touched his chin, forcing him to make eye contact. His eyes were clear; she was certain.

"What did you sense, Dew?" Nali gently asked.

Dew looked at Elderberry with a pained, almost pleading expression. Nali refrained from expressing a sigh of impatience. Trolls were clannish creatures, she knew, but this was no time to be keeping secrets from outsiders, so she was grateful when Elderberry silently encouraged Dew to speak with a motion of his hand. Dew looked at her with an expression of resignation.

"I... I... ca-ca-can sen-se th-th-things, like dan-danger. Th-the stag had a-a bl-blood re-re-red aura," Dew stuttered.

"Dew is one of our most gifted trolls. His ability to sense danger has saved many of us from injury or death," Zenma added.

Nali nodded. "There was another injured stag a bit farther north. My guard saw troll tracks leading away from it. Was there another troll with you?" she inquired.

Elderberry frowned and shook his head. "No, it was just Dew and me," he said.

Dew shook his head. "I-I saw... Med-Medjuline in... in the woods earlier," he replied.

Nali looked at Zenma. "Where is Medjuline?" she demanded.

Zenma started to reply when Pai and another guard entered the longhouse. Pai gave Nali a sharp look, indicating that he had found something. The guard bowed low before addressing his Empress and Zenma.

"Empress, Elder, Medjuline is missing. Her parents have not seen her for two days," the guard said.

"Find her," Zenma ordered, rising slowly to her feet.

Nali raised a commanding hand. "No, Pai and I will search for her. It is too dangerous for anyone to be near her until we know for sure what has happened. I will have some of my gargoyle guards come to the village in case she returns. Do not allow anyone near her. I cannot stress that strongly enough," Nali sharply instructed.

"We will do as you command, Empress," Zenma said.

"We will begin our search in the morning. Zenma, do you have lodgings we can use for the night?" Nali requested.

"It would be our honor for you to stay, Empress. Please follow me," Zenma said.

CHAPTER 3

*A*sahi knelt behind a tree and watched as a troll he had come across stumbled and groaned. She was gripping her head and shaking it back and forth as if she were in pain. Then she unexpectedly twirled in a tight circle and ran head first into a nearby tree. Asahi braced his hand against the tree trunk to keep from losing his balance when the ground shook.

He watched in disbelief as she spun in a dizzying circle before her eyes rolled back in her head. She fell backward with a bone-shaking crash. Something was definitely not right. He slowly stood but remained hidden. He was glad of his precaution when, a moment later, he saw the troll's unconscious body suddenly bow upward, and a black, liquid mass oozed from her mouth.

The mass coalesced, its size growing larger until it was about the size of an English Mastiff back on Earth. The liquid blob twisted and turned as if searching for another creature to inhabit. A shiver of unease swept through Asahi when the tar-like mass suddenly twisted in his direction. He remained frozen.

Something large passing overhead cast a shadow on the ground, and he looked up. Through the thick canopy, he saw two creatures flying above. The alien blob suddenly emitted a shriek, whirled, and took off through the forest in the opposite direction.

Asahi crouched down behind a large fan-shaped fern to conceal his presence as the unfamiliar creatures swooped down through the canopy. One, the hippogriff, landed on a thick branch with his wings spread wide to keep his balance while the winged woman landed beside the troll sprawled on the forest floor.

His breath caught when he saw the woman's exquisite ebony features. Her skin was like shining armor, as if she were a beautiful statue cut from the purest black marble. She landed with such grace that there wasn't a whisper of sound.

Asahi studied the female as she cautiously circled the unconscious troll. The woman's eyes were the color of dark brown goldstone and held a shimmering light that made him want to gaze into her golden irises forever. Her face was heart-shaped with high cheekbones, a long, straight nose, and full luscious lips. She was lean, with small breasts, and a commanding stance that spoke of power and confidence.

She knelt beside the troll and gingerly touched the large knot on the giant female's brow before lifting each eyelid. Then the marble woman rose to her feet and looked around with a frown.

"Pai, do you see anything?" she called out.

"There looks to be some fresh damage to the ferns leading northwest," the hippogriff replied. "What about Medjuline?"

The troll softly moaned and the woman stepped back. Asahi stiffened when he heard the low whimper of pain. He watched as a sword materialize in the woman's hand. The troll rolled onto her side and whimpered, lifting a large, trembling hand with thick, dirty nails to her head. The beautiful winged woman took a step toward the troll who was now struggling to sit up.

"Medjuline," the woman said in a soft, reassuring tone.

"Hel-help me, please. Don't... don't let it take me again," Medjuline choked out in a shaky voice.

"Who took you?" the woman demanded in the same soft voice.

Medjuline sat up and looked around her with wide, frightened eyes. She looked back at the woman standing in front of her with her sword at the ready. Medjuline raised a trembling hand to her brow again.

"The creature that... that came out.... The stag... the stag's side exploded and covered me. There was a black glob...," Medjuline exclaimed, her voice growing louder as fear engulfed her again. "It was choking me, and I couldn't get it off!"

Compassion washed through Asahi when the troll began to cry. It was obvious now from her features and the way she spoke that she was young. She looked at her hands and rubbed them together before pushing back her dark red hair as if to make sure none of the residual goo from the black substance remained. She rocked back and forth as she sobbed.

"Where did the alien go, Medjuline? It is important that I find it before it can harm another," the beautiful creature said.

Medjuline wiped her face with her grimy hands, leaving streaks of dirt across her dark tan skin. She looked back at the marble woman, and her eyes filled with tears.

"I don't know. It was hurting me—my head. I had to make it stop. I wanted it out of me. I... I ran into a tree. I don't feel it inside me anymore, but my head still hurts," Medjuline confessed.

The woman lowered her sword and stepped forward.

"Nali!" the hippogriff in the tree growled fearfully.

Nali's lips curved into a smile. It wasn't one of amusement. It was a dangerous, anticipatory smile—as if she were daring anything to attack her. She rested her hand on the young troll's arm and studied her closely. Several tense seconds passed before she whispered something so softly that Asahi couldn't hear it.

He took in a startled breath when the marble woman suddenly changed into a version of herself that was softer, warmer, and far more glorious. Her smooth, light brown skin glowed in the filtered light of the sun above the canopy, making it appear the same color as creamy milk chocolate. Her long black hair hung in tight ringlets around her face and shoulders, reminding him of the ancient Cretan women.

"Pai, the alien has left Medjuline's body. It is safe to come down," she replied.

Medjuline sniffled while silent tears continued to course down her dirty cheeks. Her eyes were now filled with wonder instead of fear. She reached out a hand to the woman.

Asahi tamped down his unease. He had *seen* the liquid parasite leave Medjuline, and this powerful woman was certain that none remained. It was just the horrifying nature of what he had seen that was keeping him on edge. He would surely have nightmares about that parasite for days.

"Nali," Pai cautioned again, "the alien has *never* left a host alive—not without far more force applied than a bump on the head."

Nali's expression softened as she looked at her concerned companion. "I could not say why this time is different, but the alien is gone, Pai. I am certain of it—and Medjuline is hurt and frightened. Please come down."

Nali firmly clasped Medjuline's hand, meeting her eyes reassuringly.

"Empress, I…. It wants to hurt us," Medjuline said.

"I will stop it. Pai, take Medjuline back to her village. Make sure that there are ample guards to secure the area in case the alien tries to circle back," Nali ordered.

The hippogriff landed and pawed at the ground in irritation. He shook his head. "Nali, please tell me that you aren't planning on going after that creature alone," Pai hissed with dismay.

Asahi smirked in amusement when the woman named Nali rolled her eyes before she nodded her head. His amusement turned to concern when Nali helped the troll stand and Medjuline swayed. She was twice the size of the woman who was trying to support her. The hippogriff must have felt the same way because he quietly snarled and pushed up against the troll who leaned on him.

"She cannot return alone, Pai. She's injured and shaken by what's happened to her. Return with her to the village. You can find me after you have made sure she is safe and the village is secure," Nali finally replied.

"I don't like this," Pai snapped.

"I didn't ask if you did," she retorted with a slight bite to her tone.

Asahi's eyes narrowed. This woman was used to giving orders. He studied her features and froze when he suddenly put two and two together and realized who he was watching. She was Nali, Empress of the Monsters. He would never have expected her to be so young—or so beautiful.

Nali waited until Pai and Medjuline disappeared from view before she turned and scanned the forest. She sensed that she wasn't alone. It was unclear whether the unknown presence was an enemy or an ally. She closed her eyes and listened, but all she heard were the sounds of nature—the wind in the trees, the songs of birds, and the faint sound of rushing water from a nearby stream.

She opened her eyes and stared off into the distance. Lifting her hand, she whispered a summoning spell. A small, oval disk made of liquid gold appeared in her hand. The surface of the material flattened and shimmered until it became a polished surface so smooth that it formed a mirror that reflected her image.

"Goddess's Mirror, show me the alien," she murmured.

Her reflection shimmered, changing to show an image of the forest in front of her. The mirror revealed the shadowy form of the alien that Medjuline had described disappearing into the mouth of a cave. Dread filled her, and she looked up. The alien had entered the den of the goblins.

"As if goblins aren't already difficult enough as they are," she muttered. "Goddess's Mirror, show me who watches me."

The image shimmered again. Her breath caught when she saw a man that she had never seen before. His features were obscured by the shadows, giving her only an impression of what he looked like. His eyes were dark brown and his hair short and black. He had a long slender nose, and from the angle of the image, she could see a firm jaw. A shiver of awareness ran through her. It was strange for her to have such a powerful reaction, and it left her with the uneasy feeling that somehow their destinies were connected.

"Where is he?" she demanded.

Nali snarled with impatience and released the mirror when it revealed only the dense forest. The mirror vanished with a sprinkling of gold dust, and she knew that even if she called for it to return, she would learn nothing new. The Goddess's Mirror was a fickle gift, revealing only what *it* wanted, when *it* wanted.

"That damn mirror drives me crazy," she cursed.

There was only one thing Nali could do—draw out the man, discover what he wanted and where he had come from. She didn't have time for games. When—not if—the alien reached the goblins, things could become much more complicated than dealing with a single troll.

"I know you are there. Come out," she called.

A movement out of the corner of her eye caused her to turn and face the man she had seen in the mirror. She took a deep breath and stiffened her shoulders. He was taller than she had expected, and the awareness that she had experienced before became much more intense.

The man wore a pair of black pants with several pockets and a white, button-up shirt with the sleeves rolled almost to his elbows. He carried a long black bag on his back, held there by a thick strap over his shoulder. His features were clear now, and she could see the slight slant of his dark brown eyes. Those eyes held her mesmerized. Her attention moved down to his lips, and a fleeting desire to touch them pierced her consciousness.

"Who are you?" she demanded in a harsh voice.

"Asahi Tanaka," he replied.

She swallowed and remained silent as they warily studied each other. Her gaze slowly moved over him again. A frown creased her brow when she noticed the jeweled hilt of a dagger at his waist. He carried a sorcerer's blade.

"What are you doing on my Isle, Asahi Tanaka?" she demanded.

"I'm searching for answers," he replied.

Her frown deepened. Visitors were not allowed to travel beyond the capital city without express permission. The rule was in place to keep them, as well as residents, as safe as possible. Trolls, goblins, and— well, there was a long list of inhabitants who potentially posed a danger to unwary travelers. What answers would a sorcerer want here?

After a moment of thought, Nali concluded that there was only one reason a sorcerer would be this far north and this deep into the forest. He searched for the magical ore the goblins mined and forged.

"You'll find no 'answers' here," she said to the man standing stiffly a few feet from her. She hissed in surprise when he lunged toward her, wrapping his arms around her waist, and pulling her to the ground. She started to grab his wrist before she realized that she was not the intended target of the dagger he wielded. The dagger's blade became white hot and hummed as it sliced through the long black tentacle that stabbed at the empty air where she had been standing less than a second before.

She rolled over until she was on top of Asahi. Her flesh hardened to stone. Her wings emerged from her back, and she spread them to cover them both as the severed tentacle dissolved around them. She raised her arms, protecting Asahi's head, and pressed her forehead against his, sending her awareness outward to sense the alien's next attack.

They stared into each other's eyes as the seconds ticked by. Their breaths mixed as the silence stretched. Under her wings, Asahi slid his hand across her hip to her lower back. She turned her head just far enough to see the flakes of ash falling around them. She looked down at Asahi with a suspicious expression.

"How did you do that?" she demanded in a hard tone.

"It's all in the wrist," another voice said with a touch of amusement.

"What the—?" Asahi hissed, dropping the blade in surprise.

Nali rolled off of Asahi and rose to her feet. She stood over him, her legs slightly apart and a long broadsword in her hand. After a quick look around, she fixed on the dagger. It was sticking out of the soft ground where Asahi had dropped it. Nali watched with amusement as

Asahi studied the dagger, and the gold, winged lion on the hilt grinned back at him.

Asahi sat up and scooted away from the dagger. The wings on the small lion fluttered and pulled the blade free from the ground. Then the Lion Dagger flew higher, hovering in the air as he demanded, "Is no one going to thank me for saving your lives?"

Nali gently grasped the dagger and held it in front her curiously as she said, "Of course. Thank you very much indeed."

"You're welcome, Empress," the lion said, puffing up with pride. He turned his head to pointedly glare at Asahi who was still gaping at the talking animated object.

"What is that? How—?" Asahi forced out around his astonishment.

Nali lifted a delicate eyebrow. "You are the sorcerer, and you don't know the magic of your own dagger?" she skeptically inquired.

She stepped back when Asahi slowly rose to his feet. He shook his head. His dark brown eyes were assessing her with an intensity that would have drawn a blush to her cheeks if her flesh wasn't stone.

"The dagger was given to my grandfather as a gift. He passed it down to me. It is one of the rare things he refused to say much about, insisting that I discover it for myself. I've never seen it move—or talk before," he replied.

"Perhaps the reason you've never had a chat with me is because you buried me under a pile of rocks and never released me from my sheath," the lion stated with a derisive snort.

Asahi frowned. "I was seven," he retorted before he clamped his lips together.

Nali looked at Asahi and then the dagger before returning her amused scrutiny to Asahi. This time she really registered the differences in his clothing.

"Where are you from, Asahi Tanaka?" she asked.

He stared back at her as if contemplating the risk of sharing the information. The longer he was silent, the more certain she was that she already knew the answer. She held the dagger between them.

"My dear Mr. Gryphon, could you please tell me where you came from?" she inquired.

"Earth," Asahi said before the winged lion could reply. "I was in a place called Yachats, Oregon, in a world known as Earth."

Nali slowly nodded. "You wouldn't perchance know anyone by the name of Ross Galloway or Ruth Hallbrook, would you? Or perhaps, Carly, Jenny, Mike, or Tonya?" she inquired.

He stiffened as she began listing the names. He recognized at least one of them. Perhaps all of them. They had all traveled from Yachats. She gave the dagger a considering look before offering it back to him.

She was concerned that she had briefly forgotten about the possibility of another attack while distracted by the dagger. There was no way of knowing if the alien had left another part of itself behind. She scanned the forest, searching the shadows, but she saw nothing. She turned back to study Asahi.

While she was protected in the form of a gargoyle, Asahi was not—although that hadn't been an issue a few moments ago. Still, she had let her guard down, and that could have been fatal.

Asahi slowly reached out and took the dagger from her, staring at the winged lion that was now absently cleaning one of its paws. Nali turned and surveyed the forest once again.

"Thank you," she murmured.

"What was that thing? I saw it come out of the troll shortly before you arrived," he said.

She looked over her shoulder at him before facing the forest again. "An alien to our world who wishes to destroy it. As far as we know, there are only two left," she explained.

Asahi stepped up next to her. He reached out and offered the dagger to her. She looked at him in surprise.

"Take this, then. It seems to work pretty well at killing them," he said.

"What are you doing? You can't just give me away!" The dagger sounded extremely indignant. "Isn't burying me for centuries enough of an insult? Now you just decide to give me away to the next person like I'm a bloody kitchen knife? No offense, Empress," the winged lion growled with a slight bow of its head.

She shook her head and chuckled. "None taken, Mr. Gryphon," she replied before facing Asahi. "The dagger was created from very old, powerful magic. There are few witches or wizards skilled in such pure magic. I know of only one who had a knack for bringing inanimate objects to life; and, she has passed from this world. Mr. Gryphon was given to you for a reason. The magic held within the jewels, gold, and steel was given to you with love. You cannot pass it on to another unless you give it with the same love," she explained.

Asahi frowned. He studied the dagger and then looked up at her again. "You asked me a few moments ago if I knew Ruth and the others. Do you know if Ruth Hallbrook and the other woman—Tonya Maitland —are safe?" he asked.

Nali's smile grew, and she nodded. "Yes. Ruth is with Koorgan, the King of the Giants, on his Isle. Tonya is probably off sailing the seas with Ashure, King of the Pirates—and getting into all sorts of mischief with him," she said with a rueful shake of her head.

His lips twitched in amusement, though a hint of confusion creased his brow. "That is a relief," he replied.

Her expression sobered. "You've seen what the alien can do. I need to stop it. If you travel east, you'll come to a river. Follow that river south, and you will come to a troll village. Tell Pai to take you back to the palace. You will be safe there," she instructed.

"You plan to go after the alien alone, don't you?" he demanded, looking from her to the woods.

She nodded. "We know from experience that the alien cannot penetrate my skin in this form. Once I have taken care of the alien, I will answer your questions, Asahi, and hopefully you can answer a few of mine," she said, turning away from him. "Remember, east until you reach the river, then south."

She didn't wait for his response. Those few minutes of conversation had already delayed her. Even though she had seen what could happen in the mirror, there was still a possibility of preventing it. She spread her wings and lifted off the ground. Despite her silent promise to not look back, she did when she cleared the canopy.

Asahi had disappeared.

CHAPTER 4

*A*sahi had decided to follow Nali even before her feet left the ground. After she turned away, he silently retrieved his duffel bag, slung it onto his back, and took off at a fast jog. With the dagger at the ready in his grip, he ran along the narrow path, following a trail of broken branches and infrequent glimpses of the Empress through the canopy.

"You do realize that you are going the wrong way, don't you?" the winged lion informed him. "The Empress said to go east. You are going west."

"Yes," he grunted, looking down at the talkative gold lion before refocusing on the path ahead.

He ducked under a partially fallen tree, then leaped over a log. Out of the corner of his eye, he saw another fresh gouge in the bark of a tree. He was on the right track.

"How did you destroy the alien piece that attacked us?" he asked.

The winged lion clung to the dagger's hilt as if afraid he would fall off. It snorted and whipped its tail before wrapping it around the handle again. Asahi was hard-pressed not to stop and watch the mythical beast in fascination.

"LaDonna—my creator—placed a protection spell on my dagger. The spell finds an attacker's weakness and uses it against them. Of course, you probably think being a dagger would be enough to stop someone, but you're not on your world anymore," the winged lion added acerbically.

Asahi ignored the lion's caustic remark. "Can you tell me what the alien's weakness is?" he asked.

The winged lion smirked. "You wouldn't understand. You're not a talking decoration," the creature retorted.

Asahi chuckled, thoroughly enjoying that he was having a conversation with a sarcastic magical dagger on an enchanted Isle filled with mythical creatures while following a beautiful Empress who was about to confront an alien.

He paused when he saw Nali descend through the canopy and land on a thick branch. She crouched on the limb and pressed one hand against the trunk of the tree. Curious, his gaze followed hers.

Through the thick growth of trees and ferns, he could see a pile of rocks and a slight gap that appeared to be the entrance to a cave. The pause gave him time to take several deep, steadying breaths and wipe away the beads of sweat that threatened to blur his vision.

Nali rose from her perch and stepped off the branch. Her wings extended to slow her descent, and she landed as soft as a feather on the ground in front of the cave. Her wings folded behind her, and he watched in awe as they disappeared into her back as though they had never existed.

Even with the distance between them, he could see her skin glistening like polished marble. The knowledge that she was at least moderately safe in this form was reassuring.

"So, what's your plan?" the winged lion quietly inquired as it climbed to the top of the hilt and sat down.

"I plan to follow her and keep her safe," Asahi murmured.

The little lion grinned and shook its head. "That's it? Follow her and what—jump out to rescue the Empress of the Monsters like some amazing hero? I hate to tell you this, but even I, an enchanted object, know it is more likely that Nali will be the one who does the rescuing. I really think you should have listened to her. Besides, do you know what *lives* in caves like that? Goblins! Small, horrible, green, nasty, grouchy goblins," the lion asserted.

Asahi looked down at the lion and frowned. "My presence has *already* helped save the beautiful Empress from a grievous attack. Perhaps you could explain how you know what lives in that cave?" he asked.

The winged lion gave him a pointed look. "Magic, obviously. How am I supposed to help my bearer if I can't tell who is who and what they do? When LaDonna gave me to your grandfather, she knew that he understood nothing about the creatures who lived in the Seven Kingdoms, so she entrusted that knowledge to me," the lion pointed out with a haughty growl.

Asahi looked down at the lion. "My grandfather—there are a lot of things that you will need to explain to me later. At the moment, I want you to be quiet," he instructed.

"Here we go, just like your grandfather. It's obvious that not listening runs in your family," the lion complained.

Asahi gritted his teeth to keep from making a scathing retort. Instead, he slid the dagger back into its sheath. The lion on the top immediately froze in place, now as solid as the gold hilt—as if the last hour had never occurred.

It would appear that the magic only worked when the dagger was free of the leather sheath. Perhaps the strange markings on the sheath's surface were another spell to keep the damn thing quiet.

He took a deep, calming breath and pushed away all the questions crowding his mind. Nali stood at the entrance of the cave. He watched with growing concern when she brushed aside a curtain of tangled roots partially covering the entrance and stepped inside, disappearing from his view.

With grim purpose, Asahi walked toward the entrance to the cave. He didn't understand why the spell had deposited him on the Isle of the Monsters while it sent Ruth—and Tonya—elsewhere. For now, that was not important. Sometimes the reason for an event took time to reveal itself. Asahi smiled, grateful that his grandfather's wisdom was still strong in his memories.

"I am here for a reason, Empress, and I think it has to do with you," he murmured before he pushed aside the cloak of roots and stepped into the darkness.

~

Asahi stood just inside the cave's entrance and waited for his eyes to adjust to the dim interior. Noticing a thin line of glowing green light running along the walls of the cave, he reached out and touched a ribbon of it. He grimaced in disgust when a gooey substance coated his fingers.

"Don't wipe it on your clothing. You'll never get it out," Nali warned, amusement evident in her voice.

He stopped with his hand a fraction of an inch from his trousers. Nali stepped out of the darkness and grabbed his hand, guiding it back to the wall.

Before Asahi's wide eyes, the green glob pulled away from his fingertips and was absorbed back into the ribbon. She released his hand and stepped back. He studied his fingers before looking at the wall. Up close, he could see the green line moving.

"What is it?" he asked, looking back at her.

"A luminescent bacterium that thrives in the cool, dry interior of most of the caves in these mountains," she explained.

"Fascinating," he murmured.

She shook her head. "You must have misunderstood. You were supposed to go in the opposite direction," she stated, her tone disapproving.

"I didn't misunderstand you. I chose to ignore your suggestion," he replied.

She looked at him with an incredulous expression. He smiled. "You chose…? You are a human, correct?" she asked, waving a hand at him.

"Yes," he replied.

She opened her mouth, her eyes glittering with indignation, then she closed it and shook her head in resignation.

"What were you going to say?" he curiously asked.

She shook her head again. "I was going to say you are a fragile species, but—" she laughed, "after dealing with the others of your kind, I know your appearance is deceiving," she wryly replied.

Asahi met her rueful gaze with his own and smiled, his eyes crinkling with self-deprecating humor. As his focus shifted from her expression to her luminous skin, he slowly took a step toward her and lifted his hand to hover hesitantly just above her cheek.

"Do you mind?" he murmured, unable to contain his inquisitive nature now that he was close to her again. Even in the dim interior, he could see the unusual swirl of gold in her irises.

Interest faintly infused her demeanor, and she replied softly with a hint of a dare, "Go ahead."

He gently ran his fingers down the smooth surface of her cheek. Her skin looked like marble, but it was warm to his touch. As she looked deeply into his eyes, she took a tiny, startled breath. He breathed in her exotic scent and felt the rightness of being at her side.

"Deceiving appearances, indeed," he softly agreed.

She pulled away from him and stepped back until they were several feet apart. "There is a lot you don't know about the Isle of the Monsters, Asahi Tanaka. If you are going to join me on my quest, you will need to learn," she coolly stated.

"Then I am your humble student, Empress," he replied with a slight bow.

A wry smile curved his lips when she emitted a low groan and turned away from him. "Come on—and whatever you do, don't touch or kill anything unless I tell you to," she snapped.

Asahi concealed his humor and followed Nali. Her muttered curse warned him that she was aware of his amusement. He adjusted the strap across his chest and decided it might be prudent to stay alert and wait for his first lesson.

The thin strand of green luminescence lit their way, and though the light was faint, it still cast shadows in the underground corridors—shadows for the alien to hide in. Frustration and worry filled Nali.

Remember how resilient humans are! she silently admonished herself. *Well, in their own unique way.*

She grimaced when she remembered everything that had happened since Carly first appeared. There were numerous times when she had either heard of or witnessed humans surviving dire circumstances in unexpected ways during their fight against the alien invasion. Already, Asahi had proven that he could protect himself—and her.

"You said that you had questions. What are they?" she casually demanded.

"You want to know them—now?" he asked.

"Why not?" she asked with a shrug.

He was silent for a moment before he answered. "Perhaps because we are walking through a cave where, I'm assuming from the way you are scanning the shadows, you expect the alien to jump out at any moment," he dryly replied.

She chuckled. "True. I hope you have your magic dagger ready in case it does," she commented.

"It talks too much," he curtly replied.

She stopped and murmured in a distracted voice, "Yes, magical items tend to do the most unexpected things. They have a mind of their own."

"What is it?" he inquired in a hushed voice.

"I sense something," she replied. "Wait here."

"Empress—Nali—" he protested in a harsh whisper.

She looked over her shoulder. "First lesson: Trust me," she said.

Their eyes locked in the dim light. She could see his conflicting emotions. A strange, tight sensation built in her chest at his obvious concern.

"I will wait for your signal," he finally agreed.

She gave a brief nod and turned her head back toward the passage ahead. She stepped forward with determination and continued around the bend. The narrow passage opened into an enormous cavern and revealed a long stone bridge spanning a deep ravine. Far below the bridge, the reddish-yellow glow of molten lava lit the smooth walls of the cliffs on both sides.

The heat from the lava and the rotten-egg aroma of sulfur drifted up from the molten river below. Nali studied the entrance of the goblin stronghold. It was too quiet. The moment she came into view, a horn should have sounded to alert the goblin clan of her presence. She cautiously stepped onto the bridge.

CHAPTER 5

The sound of water and the low rumble from the lava flow echoed through the vast hollow cavern. The bridge ahead was constructed from rough limestone slabs and thick iron plating. Two deep ruts, cut by centuries of heavy carts filled with ore as they crossed over, lay in parallel lines down the middle of the bridge.

Nali cautiously advanced toward the open gate of the goblin fortress, and carefully studied the massive walls. They had been built to withstand even powerful giants, but clearly they had not kept out this slippery alien. A movement along the wall caught her eye and she stopped.

"You won't succeed," she called out.

The alien in a dark liquid form roiled along the wall before it pooled near the entrance of the goblin stronghold. Nali dispassionately watched the creature contort into a humanoid shape. She flexed her fingers and whispered a spell given to her by Gem, Princess of the Elementals. In her palm, a sword appeared, enchanted with the power given to the Elementals by the Goddess herself.

"There is a power in you that is familiar," the alien hissed.

Nali tilted her head inquisitively. She sensed... desperation. A ripple ran through the alien's body, causing the fluid form to move in a mesmerizing wave. She smiled and raised her sword. It seemed the entity recognized the Elemental magic that had killed one of its own.

"I know why you are here. You will fail. I won't let you take over my world," she replied.

The alien's form rippled again. "*Your* world," it laughed, "—is not what you think. Regardless, this and all the others are pawns, put here to feed our whims," the creature replied.

Nali shook her head. "I will not allow you to harm any more of my people," she declared.

She slowly walked over the uneven stones as she spoke, tightening her grip on the hilt of her sword. She was ready when the alien shot out a long tentacle toward her.

She evaded and brought the sword up under the long spiral of thick liquid. The tip of the sword sliced through the tentacle, and the magic embedded in the steel turned the blade a blinding white. Unfortunately, she wasn't close enough to destroy the entire alien, only the tentacle.

She instinctively lifted her arm, protecting her vision. The alien roared a second before another tentacle struck her. The power behind the blow lifted her off her feet. She twisted as she landed, rolling several feet before her shoulder hit the edge of the short wall that bordered the bridge. The sword skidded several feet past her.

Nali glanced at the alien before she looked at the sword. She rolled toward it. Before she could rise to her feet, something cold and wet wrapped around her ankles, drawing her attention to her feet. She hissed in alarm when the alien tightened its tentacle, and pulled her across the worn stone bridge.

She twisted, reaching desperately for the sword. It was then that she saw the thin river of black liquid in the wheel ruts, and realized the alien had distracted her with multiple attacks, sacrificing parts of itself while using the ruts in the bridge to sneak up on her. Nali frantically clawed at the uneven stones, trying to prevent the alien from dragging her.

"Those weak, green creatures that dwelled here were useless, but you —I sense the power of the ancients in you. A power you do not even realize you possess," the alien mocked.

Fury burned through Nali like a wildfire out of control. The urge to transform into a larger, more powerful monster almost overwhelmed her, but she resisted the temptation. In any other form, she would be defenseless against the alien's possession. Even now, she could feel the fluid material of the creature searching for a way to penetrate her skin as it slowly snaked its way up her body.

The sound of metal against stone brought her attention to another long tentacle pulling the sword toward the mass. The creature's mocking laughter sent a chill through her.

For a moment, Nali couldn't help picturing what would happen if she failed. She saw herself possessed, using her powers and the Elemental sword against her own people and the Seven Kingdoms. She banished the thought and tried to roll to her right so that she could grab the sword as the long blade slid past.

She dug her fingers into a crevice between two stones and held on with all her might while she stretched her other arm out, frantically reaching for the sword. A hoarse cry of frustration slipped from Nali when her fingers lost their purchase on the crevice.

A sense of impending doom built inside her. The form that kept her safe would also seal her demise. While the alien could not penetrate her flesh, the gargoyle form limited her ability to fight. Only in her softer form could she use the full power of her magic.

"If you want power, try this," Asahi shouted.

Nali turned and saw Asahi standing in the entrance with his feet spread apart, holding a small weapon aimed at the alien. It was just like the one Mike Hallbrook had used on the first alien back on the Isle of Magic. She flinched at the loud reports when he fired the weapon.

She glanced down at her feet when the creature recoiled with a hiss, loosening its grip on her legs and the sword. She rolled, grabbed the hilt of the sword, and sat up. Turning her head to protect her eyes, she brought the sword up and sliced through the tentacle holding her. With a burst of light, it turned to ash.

Nali stood, holding the sword out in front of her. Asahi continued to fire the weapon at the alien as he strode forward. At his bark of warning, she backpedaled and turned, the sword poised to defend, but this time she couldn't avoid the tentacle that struck her in the side. She stumbled, the back of her legs catching on the bridge's low wall, and cursed when she tilted backward into open space.

Her boot heel was caught in a gap in the bridge and she teetered as she fought to keep her balance. Out of the corner of her eye, she saw another dark tentacle shooting out of the creature toward Asahi. She thrust the sword upward.

The tentacle hit the sword with such force that it knocked the weapon from her hand. Unbalanced by the blow's intensity, she twisted to grab the enchanted weapon just as the bridge shifted. The small movement was enough to knock her over the side.

She spun as she fell and reached for the bridge. Her fingers found purchase in the bridge's rough stone, and she hung precariously by one arm. Looking down, she watched in horror as the magical sword tumbled through the air toward the river of lava far below. Up on the bridge, she could hear the report of Asahi's weapon grow louder as he came closer to her.

With a silent curse, she released her grip on the bridge and focused on the sword. She twisted and flattened her hands against her side to increase the speed of her descent. The heat from the molten river intensified the lower she got.

The sword tumbled a few yards ahead of her. She reached for the hilt when it rotated around in her direction. The tips of her fingers only grazed it, sending it into an uneven wobble. Nali knew she would have to pull up in a few seconds.

"Come on," she hissed as the hilt swung toward her again.

Her fingers slid over the heated metal, and the moment she had a grip on the sword, she called forth her wings, opening them as wide as she could to slow her free fall.

She soared mere feet from the molten river, swerving as a super-heated bubble of lava exploded in front of her. She glided for several yards before she was able to rise on a wave of heated air. It gave her the lift needed without fear of her touching the lava. With powerful sweeps of her wings, she ascended from the deep ravine and turned back toward the bridge. A brilliant, almost blinding light guided her back to Asahi. It took a moment for her to realize that he was holding the winged-lion dagger.

She scanned the area where the alien had been only minutes before. From her vantage point, she could see that the creature had fled but not before leaving a trail of horror behind. Her throat tightened when she counted at least a dozen goblins lying lifeless along the wall and inside the goblin stronghold.

Sword in hand, she twisted in midair, and dropped onto the bridge near Asahi. He slowly lowered his arm as her feet touched the stone. The glow of his dagger faded when he reached out and steadied her.

"Where did it go?" she asked in a voice filled with emotion.

"It disappeared through the larger drainage vent just over the edge of the bridge," he quietly replied.

She walked to the edge and looked down. There was a large pipe with water flowing out of it like a waterfall along the ravine wall. Only the goblins would know where the pipe led.

Nali glanced at Asahi when he came and stood next to her in silence. She took a deep breath to calm the grief rising inside her and turned toward the gates of the stronghold.

"I have to see to the dead—and find out if any of the goblins survived," she said.

"I'll help you," he murmured.

~

An hour later, Asahi gently lay the last of the dead goblins down on the cobblestones. After Nali had left to search for survivors, he gathered all the dead he could find. By the time he finished, twenty dead goblins lay in a row on the path. Now, he stood over the small, armor-clad, green and tan bodies.

He turned away from them, walked over to an overturned cart, and picked up the magical dagger propped there. Mr. Gryphon was keeping a keen eye out in case any part of the alien returned. The animated creature had also filled him in on some of the quirkier details of goblin etiquette while Asahi had completed his gruesome task.

The echo of footsteps, the loud creaking of leather, and the telltale clang of metal on metal attracted his attention. Nali must have been successful in her search. Asahi turned on his heel and faced the approaching group, stunned when he saw that there were already hundreds of goblins gathered at the gates, and more were joining the group every moment.

"Ah, here comes the leader of the goblins," the winged lion murmured, sitting up on the dagger's hilt. "Make sure you show respect or she'll take you down to her level with one swing of her ax

—literally," the lion added with a suggestive swipe of a claw across his front leg.

Asahi distractedly nodded. His attention was focused on Nali. She had returned to her natural form—or at least what he suspected was her normal self. Her creamy skin was the warm color of mocha, and her hair hung about her shoulders in thick, curly waves. She was, in a single word, breathtaking.

He forced his gaze away from Nali and looked at the creature walking beside her. He was surprised when he realized that the leader of the goblins was a woman. The royal goblin stared back at him with vivid green eyes that glowed like the vein of luminescent bacteria in the rocks. She held a short sword in her hand and wore a large, double-headed battle axe slung across her back, much like a Minoan labrys.

Asahi wasn't sure what the proper protocol was for a Goblin Queen since the winged lion hadn't included that part in his ongoing description of the creatures. He tried to remember if his grandfather had ever shared any information that might be helpful, but when he came up blank, he did the only thing he could think of and gave the Goblin Queen a deep bow.

"Your Majesty, my humblest regrets for the horrific loss your people have suffered today," he formally greeted her.

"You are a stranger to our world," the Goblin Queen stated in a raspy voice.

When Asahi heard the rumble of concern that ran through the crowd of goblins, he slowly straightened and looked around at hundreds of eyes staring back at him in curiosity, suspicion, and fear. He returned his attention to the Goblin Queen.

"He is a human from another world," Nali responded, stepping up beside him.

"Another alien!" hissed an old goblin as he pulled his short sword and pointed it at Asahi.

Asahi watched as a wave of alarm swept over the crowd. Suddenly more swords, spears, and even rocks appeared in the hands of the goblins. He warily watched the increasingly upset mob. He understood their anxiety, especially considering the dead lying on the ground behind him.

"Silence!" Nali commanded, lifting her arms.

Asahi looked at Nali in surprise. In the short time that he had known her, she had always been quiet and reserved with a touch of amusement in her tone. She was different now. Her eyes flashed with a silent warning not to disobey her.

There was an immediate compliance to her command. Silence fell over the group, and the old goblin standing next to the Queen lowered his sword. The Queen walked forward and bowed her head.

"My apologies, Empress," the Goblin Queen stated.

Nali looked down at the little Queen and slowly lowered her arms. Her mouth was still pursed into a straight line, but her displeasure dissipated at the apology. She stepped aside and motioned to the row of dead goblins.

"Asahi saved my life—twice. He is not a threat to our people. In fact, the humans who came before him are the reason the Sea Witch is herself again and the alien who controlled her no longer exists. The alien who attacked you is alone now. I must find it before it causes any more deaths," she gently explained.

The Goblin Queen nodded. "You said it went through the drainage pipe beneath the bridge?" she inquired.

"Yes," Asahi answered.

The Goblin Queen chuckled gleefully, surprising him.

"Why is that amusing?" he inquired.

The Queen's thin lips curved upward at the corners, showing off a row of her small, very sharp teeth. Her eyes glittered with devilish humor. The old goblin next to her chuckled sardonically.

"The drainage tunnels are a labyrinth of dead ends and circles. Each passage is enchanted with wards and traps to discourage visitors. The creature will wish it had never encountered a goblin before long," the Queen replied.

"Regardless, we must follow it," Nali said.

The Goblin Queen shook her head. "It would be too dangerous, Empress, even for one as powerful as you. I will show you where the tunnel opens above ground. We will seal the pipe here at this end. Water will soon flood the tunnels. If the alien survives the wards and doesn't drown, it will only be a matter of time before it emerges at the other end," she replied.

"Thank you," Nali murmured. She looked at the row of dead goblin soldiers.

"We will take care of our dead, Empress," said the Goblin Queen.

Nali shook her head. "This is something I must do to ensure that no part of the alien remains," she murmured.

Asahi turned as Nali walked past him. A low hum rose from the crowd of goblins, and he realized that they were singing. The melody was soothing, and the words sounded strange and ancient.

The song's power surged as Nali stepped up to the first goblin and murmured. Startled, Asahi parted his lips and gasped when the goblin's body dissolved. Tiny specks of glowing, colorful lights rose and swirled in the air before they came together, forming into a bright red crystal. She moved down the line, spending time over each goblin. The Queen and several other goblins silently followed Nali, collecting the crystal remains of their brethren.

When she finally completed her sad task, she turned and faced the crowd. A strange tightness formed again in Asahi's chest as he studied Nali. Her face was composed, but he could see the intense sadness in her eyes. One by one, the goblins holding the crystals walked through the entrance and onto the bridge.

Asahi looked down when he felt a slight tap on his finger. The winged lion nodded in Nali's direction. He frowned at the small, gold creature.

"Go stand beside the Empress. She could use a little support," the winged lion compassionately suggested.

Asahi looked up and stared into Nali's eyes. She looked back at him over the goblins' heads. He walked over to her, and she gave him a wan smile of gratitude.

"To the heart of the goblins," the Goblin Queen called out.

"To the heart of the goblins!" the crowd of goblins intoned.

The singing began again. They watched as the goblins dropped the shimmering stones containing the remains of their fallen comrades, one by one, over the side of the bridge. The melody faded as the last of the crystals tumbled into the river of lava below.

"Seal the drainage," the Goblin Queen ordered her goblins as she faced Asahi and Nali. "Now, I will show you how to get to the surface," she added with a hard glitter of bloodlust not quite concealed in her eyes.

CHAPTER 6

"I can almost hear your thoughts," Nali mused, looking at Asahi under her eyelashes.

"My thoughts are that loud?" he teased.

She softly chuckled. "Just a little," she playfully retorted.

They had been walking through miles of endless tunnels for hours. The amount of skill it must have taken to make this maze was astounding. He could spend weeks just studying the artistic designs carved into some of the passages alone. But it was the engineering and the ingenious intricacies of the tunnels that boggled his mind.

They stepped through another narrow, arched opening into a large, circular domed cavern. It was like the others—filled with many tunnel entrances. Only one correct passage would lead them out of the tunnels—eventually. All the others would lead to a dead end or circle back into a tunnel they had already traveled through. Without the map the Goblin Queen had given them, they would have been down here for weeks, months, or even years if they had the resources.

"Which way?" Asahi asked.

Nali lifted her hand and murmured the Goblin Queen's spell. A shimmering map outlined with glowing green threads appeared in the air. He stood behind her and studied the map. He noted a darker green line that was pulsing. The line flowed into the tunnel right next to the one they had just exited.

He steadied her when she quickly turned around to follow the line, unaware that he was standing so close to her. His gaze dropped to her parted lips before slowly lifting back up to her beautiful, Goldstone-flecked eyes. He was two inches taller than she was, and with his head bowed, their lips were almost touching.

She held his forearms, raised her head, and unexpectedly pressed her lips against his. An intense emotion flooded his consciousness, and he tightened his hold on her waist. Their bodies fit together as if made for each other. A tingling awareness of pleasure flowed through him when she slid her hands up his arms and across his shoulders.

He relished the feeling of her lips parting under his. A surge of desire pierced the wall of control he normally kept on his emotions as he deepened the kiss, touching the tip of his tongue along the edge of her teeth. He was acutely aware of her hands sliding along his shoulders until they reached his nape.

A wave of emotions and thoughts crashed over him him—pleasure, desire to take what was between them to a deeper level, a subconscious detailed list of what her lips felt like underneath his, the touch of her skin, the taste of her, the scent of her, and the feel of her body pressed intimately against his.

He experienced a sense of loss when she finally pulled away. They stared into each other's eyes, both lost in their own thoughts before he released her waist, and she stepped away from him. She cleared her throat, the soft sound echoing in the cave's chamber.

"We go that way," she murmured.

He bowed his head and stepped aside for her to go ahead of him. She paused for a fraction of a second—long enough for their eyes to lock —before she shook her head and disappeared into the tunnel. He released the breath he'd been holding.

This changes everything, he thought.

What happened changes nothing, Nali fiercely thought, trying to keep her focus on the task at hand and not the fiery kiss she had shared with Asahi. *It was just a kiss. A nice, hot, incredible kiss.*

She barely smothered her frustrated groan. Turning on her heel, she faced him and thrust out her arm, preventing him from running into her. Her hand splayed against his chest. Her fingers accidentally slid between the buttons of his shirt. She gritted her teeth at the feel of his warm flesh. She would not risk another kiss. Of course, just the thought made her glance at his lips.

"What happened back there—" Asahi began.

"Changes everything," she finished before blinking and shaking her head. "I mean, changes nothing."

A wicked gleam of amusement lit his eyes. "I like your first thought better," he said.

She ruefully shook her head again. "You are a distraction, Asahi Tanaka. That can be dangerous in our current situation," she said.

He lifted his hand and covered hers where it pressed against his chest. "Only if we let it. If we work together, we can be a formidable opponent against the alien," he replied.

With a doubtful, searching look into his eyes, Nali murmured, "Perhaps."

He reached out and gently cupped her chin. "This is your world, Nali, but I'm not completely ignorant of it. We will be successful," he murmured.

For a moment, his words hung in the air, blending with the subtle sounds of the surrounding tunnel. Nali nodded, unable to hide her troubled expression any longer. She lowered her hand and stepped back.

"Thank you. I needed to hear that," she confessed before she looked around. "We should be near the surface. If we are there before the alien, there is a chance we can stop it before it does any more harm."

"How will we know if it's still in the tunnel?" Asahi asked with a frown.

"I have a way," she replied.

She hoped that what she said was true. She had the Goddess's Mirror. Unfortunately, it tended to show her disjointed images that often didn't make sense.

Let's hope this time the mirror will be a little clearer than usual, she thought with a grimace.

"How do you know so much about the Seven Kingdoms?" she asked as she continued walking.

"My grandfather came here. His name was Aiko Tanaka. He passed through a portal into your world while on a fishing trip. He lived on the Isle of Magic for nearly forty Earth years. I never fully understood how he could still look so young when he returned home," he quietly replied.

"I didn't realize that there had been other humans here before Carly. It is possible that we age at a slower rate in this world than in yours. From the conversations that I've had with some of the others, we live much longer than the people in your world."

Asahi looked thoroughly fascinated. "My grandfather said he came here to the Isle of the Monsters once. Over the years, he shared many stories about his journey and the wonders of your world. He put it all in his journal. I have it with me."

Pausing, she turned around and looked at him. "I would like to see it one day," she said with a smile.

Asahi nodded. "Where to now? Did we take a wrong turn?" he asked, realizing that the passage ended at an earthen wall lined with tree roots.

"No. We're here," she said, pointing up.

"So we are," he said, looking up at the vertical tunnel rising a good fifteen feet above his head with a wary expression.

"Do you trust me?" she suddenly asked.

He looked back down at her with a frown. "Yes," he automatically replied.

She grinned. "Then let's see if your grandfather told you about this," she teased.

Asahi wasn't sure what to expect, but what happened next made him say a few colorful words—in his mind. Nali reached out and wrapped her arms firmly around his waist. He reciprocated the move, sliding his arms around her.

The delightful feeling of her arms wrapped around him wasn't the part that made him nervous. He enjoyed holding her. It was what happened next that shook him.

Her body transformed from the waist down. He watched with a mixture of awe and horror as her lower limbs shimmered before changing. Her leather pants turned into thick, black scales—they felt like velvet against his palms.

He hissed in surprise, and he tightened his hold around her waist when his feet suddenly left the ground. She was growing larger—or at least her lower body was growing longer. The upper portion of her body stayed the same.

He stared into her beautiful eyes. They glowed with a golden hue. This close, he swore he could see the universe in her eyes. She blinked several times as if coming out of a trance and tilted her head back. He swallowed and looked up at the opening above.

She moved in an effortless glide up through the opening, rotating in a slow, mesmerizing circle as they passed through. Once they were clear of the hole, she leaned over the edge and released him on solid ground.

He took a stumbling step backward and watched as she rose farther through the opening. She coiled the lower half of her body around and around, pulling free of the pit.

The black scales that covered her from her waist to the tip of her tail shimmered in the late afternoon light until she twirled, her arms outstretched like that of a ballet dancer, and what had been the long tail of a snake disappeared in a cloud of golden sparkles.

"And… we are out of the tunnel," she said with a smug grin.

"How—how did you—?" he asked, waving his hand up and down in her direction.

"Magic," she cheekily replied.

"Magic," he repeated with a shake of his head before he looked around.

"So, will your magic tell us if we made it here before the alien?" he asked, meeting her eyes.

She sighed. "I hope so."

He walked around the hole, looking down inside it as he did, then stopped next to her. She had turned away from him, but not before he saw something appear in her hand. He frowned when he noticed that it looked like a mirror.

"What is that?" he asked.

She glanced at him before refocusing on the mirror. "A gift from the Goddess," she quietly replied.

"It's beautiful," he responded, looking at it more closely. "On Earth, the Japanese believe that Amaterasu, the Sun Goddess, gave her grandson, Ninigi, a mirror when he descended to Earth. Ninigi gave the mirror to the first emperor. The mirror has been passed down to each emperor since," Asahi said.

She looked at him, intrigued. "The Goddess gave this mirror to the Empress of the Monsters long ago to guide her through the challenges that she would face," she said.

Asahi nodded. "'Within the reflecting surface of the Sun Goddess's mirror is something beyond normal understanding,'" he quoted the ancient Japanese legend.

He stepped behind her and slid his hand over hers. She started a little at the closeness, then leaned into his warmth. Together, they looked at their reflection in the mirror. He smiled when he saw her looking at him with curiosity.

Deciding not to comment on their current position, she replied, "Yes, what we will see—if the mirror cooperates—is both real and unreal at the same time. The mirror creates an interface between the physical and the spiritual realms."

As she spoke, the image in the mirror became ominous, as if someone had blown smoke in front of it. The smoke gradually cleared, but the image no longer showed their reflection—it showed the alien, and the creature immediately struck out at the glass. Asahi tightened his grip on Nali's hand when she suddenly jerked backward.

"This is not possible," Nali hissed in shock.

The creature struck again, only this time it did not stay within the mirror. The glass stretched outward as the black liquid hand tried to grab Nali.

"Watch out!" Asahi warned.

He yanked the mirror out of her hand and turned it toward the ground, quickly pulling his dagger from its sheath and swiping it across the protruding hand. The alien in the mirror howled in pain as its severed limb writhed on the ground.

"Asahi, step back," Nali ordered.

The mirror disappeared from his hand as Nali came forward and wrapped a granite hand around the alien limb. It slithered around her arm, trying desperately to penetrate her stony flesh.

"I'd kill it now," Mr. Gryphon suggested. "If anyone wants my opinion."

"Not yet," Nali hissed. "How were you able to come through the Goddess's Mirror?"

The alien chuckled with malevolence. Asahi wasn't sure which was more troubling—that the creature came through Nali's magical device or that such a small part of the alien had the potential to become a separate living entity. He tightly gripped the magic dagger when he noticed that the struggling black extremity was turning to liquid. She grabbed the entity with her other hand to keep the creature from falling to the ground.

"*Liqcora solidify*," Nali commanded.

Magic crackled in the air as the spell washed over the alien, causing it to harden—for a moment. A loud crack shattered the silence of the forest, and the alien mass broke free from Nali's grip. In a split second, the creature had wound itself around her throat.

She stumbled backward, clawing at the alien band choking her. Tiny fissures appeared along Nali's throat. Eyes wide with horror, Asahi pursed his lips in determination and moved with the skill of a surgeon, slicing through the alien appendage with the magical dagger. A brilliant light, so intense that it nearly blinded him, briefly flared as it consumed the severed section of the alien. The creature's screech lasted less than a second before the limb turned to ash.

Nali took loud, hissing breaths of air. She violently trembled and sank down to her knees as she fought to pull oxygen into her lungs. Asahi knelt on one knee next to her and touched her throat, trailing his fingers along the cracks in her hardened skin.

"Are you alright?" he murmured with concern.

She lifted her hand to her throat. "Yes," she hoarsely replied as she lifted her head and looked at him.

He saw the alien's reflection in her eyes as they widened with alarm. A larger section of the being emerged from the tunnel behind him. Asahi wrapped his arm around her shoulders as it flew past them. He winced when the entity struck his shoulder a glancing blow as he rolled to the right—pulling her with him. He caught a brief glimpse of the fleeing form as it vanished into the forest.

"Let's go," he growled.

He released her and surged to his feet, his eyes on the forest. He reached out a hand to help her up. She grabbed it and stood.

"I will take to the air and follow it," she said.

He turned toward her when he heard the raspiness in her voice, and he noticed that the fine cracks on her throat were already healing. She would be safer in the air than on the ground until they were healed completely.

"I'll track it on the ground," he said.

"Be careful," she warned.

In seconds, her long wings appeared, and she lifted off. He watched her clear the canopy, then he looked down at the dagger. The small, winged lion was sniffing the air.

"Can you track it?" he inquired.

"Do flies like dung?" the winged lion retorted.

Asahi chuckled. "I'll take that as a yes," he replied.

"That way," the winged lion snorted, pointing a front paw to the north.

CHAPTER 7

*A*n hour and a half later, Nali dipped under a branch and swerved to avoid a tree before gliding over a thick covering of ferns toward Asahi. She pulled up a few feet from him, retracted her wings, and landed on the soft soil with the ease of a swan landing on a calm lake.

"It's as if the alien has just vanished," she commented.

"My guess is that it went into hiding. It *is* injured," he responded.

Mr. Gryphon snorted. "That *thing* isn't the only one feeling injured! You would think that after dismembering and disintegrating part of the fiercest foe the Isle of the Monsters has ever seen, my nincompoop wielder would give me some well-deserved rest, but oh no, here I still am, being brandished through an endless forest like I'm some common pitchfork!" the Mr. Gryphon irritably complained with a shudder of distaste.

Nali raised an amused eyebrow.

"Perhaps you could try talking to him, Empress," the disgruntled gryphon continued. "I've tried to explain to him that even magic needs time to recharge, but oh no, what would I know? I'm just an enchanted dagger made by a powerful witch who *appreciated and understood magic!*"

"Calm yourself, Mr. Gryphon. Asahi knew it was important to destroy the alien before it infected any of the forest creatures. He couldn't have done that without you. Asahi, you should be able to sheath Mr. Gryphon now. We will stay alert, but the dagger does need to recharge. It will be dark soon, so we should find shelter for the night," she suggested.

"Thank you for your help, Mr. Gryphon," Asahi said ruefully before he sheathed the dagger. The small winged lion was already curled up on the hilt with his head buried under one wing, sound asleep.

Nali reached out and gently touched the golden figure. "The magic embedded in this dagger is impressive. LaDonna was a powerful witch," she reflected.

"My grandfather spoke highly of her," he said.

She smiled and looked up at the sky. "There is a Manticore village near here. I want to warn them of the alien. We will request lodging there for the night," she said.

"Manticores? Will it be safe?" he asked with a hesitant expression.

Nali chuckled and peered at him with a grin. "The only one you may not be safe around is me, Asahi. Haven't you learned yet that I am the most frightening of all the monsters?" she teased.

"If that is the case, then I have nothing to fear, for I know you would protect me," he calmly responded.

Nali softly smiled and caressed his cheek with the tips of her fingers. He spoke with such calm conviction. Her powers intimidated most of the men she knew. The shape she had converted to earlier—half woman, half snake—would have horrified all but a few close friends and the rulers of the other Kingdoms who all had their own unique talents. Even the monsters she cared for and protected were leery of her.

Her life was blessed and cursed at the same time. The monsters on the Isle, from the smallest to the largest, filled her heart with joy at their unique beauty. However, Nali wasn't just a monster—she was the very essence of all monsters. She could assume the form of any of them and even create new forms. She belonged to all monsters and still none. Yet, Asahi accepted her for who she was—without fear or any qualms at all. It was refreshing. Only with Ashure had she ever felt this measure of acceptance.

With a shake of her head, she turned away. "You have given me a gift, Asahi Tanaka. I will treasure it, always," she said.

Asahi clenched his hand around the dagger's hilt. The desire to kiss her when she touched his cheek had been powerful. He drew in long, deep breaths and released them slowly to regain his sense of balance as he silently followed her.

She was currently in her marble form, walking at a brisk pace. The fabric of her clothes and the strands of her hair moved as if they were merely an illusion. He lifted a hand and touched his cheek where she had caressed him. Her fingers had been warm against his skin and her caress had left a tantalizing sensation against his cheek that lingered long after she had turned away.

He lowered his hand and became lost in thought as they continued along the barely discernable path through the forest. The memory of a conversation with his grandfather Aiko suddenly came to mind. Incredibly, he could remember the day as if it were only yesterday. Each detail was as clear and crisp as if it had just happened.

They had been in his grandmother's car on their way to California, the back seat filled with treasured photos, clothing, and a small box of old coins that had once belonged to his great-great grandparents. When his grandfather, Aiko, said they would start fresh, he had meant it. Aiko had sold everything else or given it away.

∼

Twenty-six years ago:

Driving along Highway 101 in Oregon

The morning rain cleared as his grandfather drove over the Oregon state line into Northern California. Asahi looked up at the sky, squinting when the clouds parted, and the sun temporarily blinded him. He grabbed a pair of sunglasses that had belonged to his dad. As he slipped them on, Asahi had an idle thought that it was as if Baba's tears couldn't follow them into their new life. Even the sky proclaimed that it would be different now. He didn't believe it though. His mind and heart were still aching from the loss of his beloved grandmother and his father. Aiko's decision to leave everything behind as if it never existed made the pain worse for Asahi.

His grandfather had been silent throughout the morning drive, so it was a surprise when he suddenly started talking. Asahi turned in his seat and faced his last remaining family member.

"There is always a reason something happens, Asahi," Aiko quietly explained.

"How could there be a reason for you disappearing and Baba and father dying?" he sullenly muttered.

Aiko slowed the car and turned on the blinker. He turned into a scenic overlook and pulled in between a group of motorcyclists and a Tour America RV with the imprint of a Golden Retriever looking out of the door. He shifted the car into park, but left the engine running as they looked out at the ocean. They sat quietly for a couple of minutes before he softly sighed and answered.

"I have asked myself that same question many times. Then I consider what happened and asked myself, 'what if I had not returned when I did—or if I had never left in the first place?' You cannot change what happened in the past, Asahi. Your father was always a headstrong soul, even before my journey to the Seven Kingdoms. It was who he was, and I must believe that my being here would have done little to change his destiny. For whatever reason, whatever force that exists in the universe, I am supposed to be here now—for you. If I had never left, I would now be an old man—if I were even still alive. Your father had many issues, Asahi, but the one thing he did right was having you," Aiko said.

"My mother didn't want me—neither did Father. The only reason he kept me was because of Baba. I knew that," he said in a small, sad voice.

Aiko looked at him and smiled. "You are wise for your age, Asahi. You brought great joy to your grandmother. I saw her love for you in the photos she kept of you. You gave her something to live for—something neither your father nor I could do," he said.

"I don't understand why we had to leave everything behind. Why couldn't we start over in Yachats?" Asahi asked, looking up and peering into his grandfather's eyes.

Aiko reached over and gently removed Asahi's sunglasses. They stared at each other for a long time. His grandfather's eyes reminded him of Baba's. Her eyes always held a calm understanding in them as if she knew what he was feeling but was waiting for him to figure it out.

"Are you afraid that you might disappear again?" Asahi whispered, trying desperately to understand.

His grandfather sighed again, this time letting out a heavy breath, and handed him the sunglasses. Asahi took them, his attention still on his grandfather's face. Aiko turned his head and stared out of the windshield.

"Not afraid—but cautious. We fear what we do not understand. I have seen and experienced things others can only imagine," Aiko explained.

"I don't understand why we had to leave then," he muttered.

"You will in time, Asahi. All I can do is ask you to trust me—and listen carefully to everything that I will share with you. I believe my journey to the Seven Kingdoms, and subsequent return, happened for a purpose," Aiko replied.

"What purpose?" he asked with a puzzled frown.

"My time there has ended, but I believe that yours will one day come," Aiko said before he shifted the car into reverse and backed out.

∽

Present Day

Isle of the Monsters:

Asahi looked around, studying the forest and the woman in front of him. For most of his life, his grandfather had prepared him to thrive here in the Isles. Aiko had shared all his knowledge, making sure that he carefully documented every vital piece of information in a journal. They had spent many hours studying ancient myths and legends at the library and online.

Aiko had recorded a lot of information about the Isle of Magic, the Isle of the Giants, the Isle of the Sea Serpent, and the pirates. His grandfather also shared what he could about the Isle of the Dragons and the Isle of the Elementals, but very little about the Isle of the

Monsters—except that it was ruled with an iron fist and savvy compassion by each Empress.

Nali came to a stop at the edge of a cliff, and he stood at her side. Below was a long and lush valley dotted with houses and farms. The view reminded him of some of the valleys nestled between the mountain ranges in Washington State. He studied the enormous boulders tucked in among tufts of tall, thick blue-green grass.

"The centaurs and manticores live and work here," she explained.

"Centaurs—I thought they lived at the Palace," he said with a frown.

She regarded him with a raised eyebrow. "How do you know about my guards?" she asked.

"My grandfather—he visited your kingdom once, a long, long time ago," he reminded her.

"Ah, yes, and he put it in the journal," she mused.

"Yes. I added more to the stories he wrote. Little details that he didn't bother to write down seemed more important when he shared them," Asahi reflected.

They studied the four large manticores, heavily armed with long, wide swords, as they rode toward them on animals that looked like huge dogs with tusks. One manticore growled something to his mount in a language Asahi didn't understand, but he knew it was a command. The canine underneath him shook its head, but followed the manticore's order, slowing to a stop.

Asahi warily watched as the manticore dismounted. Long, thick claws protruded from massive lion paws. This manticore had a tail with foot-long spikes on the end. The others had scorpion tails. Dark brown leather pants covered the Manticore's densely muscled legs and a tan cotton shirt, open halfway down his chest, was tucked inside them. His head was in the shape of a lion, with a thick, brownish-black mane curling down and forming a vee under his chin.

"Empress, my apologies, but we need to be sure that you are not infected," the manticore said.

"There is no need to apologize for protecting your people, Reese. I understand. We came to warn you of the danger presented by the alien, but I see word has already reached you," she said.

"Yes, Empress. Pai arrived early this morning to see if you had passed through the valley yet," he explained.

"Pai! That is good. It grows dark soon, and we will require lodging," she replied.

"Of course, Empress. Forgive my inquiry, but who is this with you?" he cautiously asked.

Nali clasped Asahi's hand. "This is Asahi Tanaka. He is a human from another world. He is no threat—except to the alien," she reassured Reese.

"Human—we've heard of them. The Dragon King is married to one," Reese said with a nod.

"As is the Sea King, the King of the Giants, Princess Gem, and Ashure," she chuckled.

"Ashure Waves? The Pirate King is married?" Reese exclaimed with an expression of astonishment.

Nali laughed in delight at Reese's reaction. "Yes, Ashure Waves has finally met his match," she said with amusement.

Reese shook his head, then looked back at the other three manticores, and motioned to them. They guided their mounts closer and dismounted. Asahi nodded to them in greeting when they looked at him in curiosity and at Nali in awe. He grinned when Reese told the others about Ashure Waves marrying a human. He didn't know who the man was, but Ashure's marriage was hilarious to the men.

"I apologize again, Empress. We've had a bit of fun betting on whether a woman could ever capture that rogue—I mean—the Pirate King's heart," Reese said, wiping a tear of laughter from the corner of his eye.

Nali laughed again. "Yes, believe me, I understand."

"If you'll follow us, we'll take you to the village. The hippogriff will be happy to see you," Reese said with a wave of his hand toward the village in the center of the valley.

CHAPTER 8

$\mathcal{I}$sle of the Pirates

"What is it? You've been lost in thought and distracted all day," Tonya Maitland-Waves said.

Ashure Waves smiled when she wrapped her arms around him from behind and rested her chin on his shoulder. He should have known that she would realize that something was bothering him. He looked at the woven bracelet he was rolling between his fingers. Originally the three beads were white. Now, one had turned completely red and a second one was half red. The dark red color stood out starkly against his wrist.

"It is Nali. She—had an encounter that did not go well with the alien creature I told you about," he replied.

"Is she okay?" she asked, her voice filled with concern.

Tonya walked around the chair he was sitting in and sat down on the footrest in front of him. He gently stroked her cheek.

"I think so. I'm worried though. One bead has turned red and another is partially discolored," he replied with a worried frown.

"Hey, don't you have this really cool mirror that will take you to your heart's desire?" she suggested, biting her lower lip and looking back at him with an expectant expression.

"Yes—and no. I told you that Nali thinks it is best that she handles this alone," he responded in a disgruntled tone.

Tonya sat back and raised an eyebrow at him. "Since when has anyone ever stopped you from doing what you wanted to?" she dryly inquired.

A wave of pride and anticipation washed over him. The indecision and frustration that had been building inside him since Nali returned to her kingdom melted away. He leaned forward and pressed a kiss against Tonya's lips.

"Nali's going to be furious," he murmured, pulling back and looking into her eyes.

"She loves you. She'll get over it," she reassured him with an encouraging smile and a little shrug.

"I love you. I don't want you to—" he began.

Tonya pressed her fingers against his lips and leaned into him. "I love you, too. I'll monitor things here. You never know what Dapier might decide to give away. Just… just promise me that you'll be careful and come back to me safe and sound," she whispered.

"Always," he vowed.

~

Valley of the Manticores and Centaurs

. . .

"Pai," Nali called out when she caught sight of the old hippogriff talking with a centaur.

Pai turned around, his sharp eyes scanning her before he responded. "Empress, it is good to see that you are still in one piece," he said.

"You sound almost disappointed," she dryly replied.

Pai snapped his beak and shook his head. "I'm surprised," he retorted before his sharp eyes rested on Asahi and narrowed. "Who is this creature?"

Nali cast a sharp glare of warning at her old friend. "Pai, meet Asahi Tanaka," she said with a wave of her hand at Asahi.

"Pai. I saw you in the forest. You helped the injured troll. I hope she is recovering," Asahi said with a polite bow of his head.

"You saw—How could I miss him? I don't miss anything!" Pai grumbled.

"If you remember, we were caring for Medjuline and dealing with an alien," Nali reminded Pai.

Pai shook his head again and glared at Asahi. "I still should have seen him," he grouchily muttered.

"Let us find some food. It has been a long day," Nali said with a tired smile.

"If you would please follow me, Empress," Reese said.

Nali nodded. She glanced at Asahi. Pai had skillfully inserted his immense body between his Empress and Asahi. From the amused expression in Asahi's eyes, he knew exactly what her second-in-command was doing.

I am centuries old, and Pai STILL thinks I need a chaperone! she thought with wry humor.

～

"Where were you—in the forest—exactly?" Pai demanded.

Asahi looked at the strange creature. Pai's eagle-eyes were focused on his face. The sharp beak showed signs of age with hairline cracks and small chips along the edges. The vibrant colors of his feathers on his cheeks were streaked with gray along the vanes.

"To the east of where you were standing, about twenty feet away, behind a tree surrounded by tall ferns. There was a dead tree lodged against it, allowing for plenty of cover from the air and the ground," he replied.

Pai grunted. "Excellent choice. What did you see before we arrived?" the hippogriff continued.

"I came across the troll approximately five minutes before you arrived. She was agitated and muttering under her breath. I assumed that wasn't typical behavior. She ran headfirst into a tree, knocking herself unconscious. I saw the alien emerge from her mouth. It is incredible that she survived," he said.

"Why didn't you come out when we arrived?" Pai suspiciously demanded.

Asahi stopped and looked at the hippogriff. "If you were in my position, would you have come out?" he asked.

The old guard snapped his beak and shook his head. "No, I would have remained hidden and observed what happened next," he grudgingly admitted.

"Pai, if you've finished interrogating Asahi, we are going inside for a meal," Nali said as she stood in the broad doorway of an extensive structure.

"I've eaten. The fishing is good in the river," Pai commented. "I'll do a flyover of the valley with the manticore guards and meet with you afterwards."

"Be careful," Nali said, her voice reflecting both concern and affection for the giant hippogriff.

"You worry too much about others and not enough about yourself," Pai muttered.

Asahi could see the twinkle in the old hippogriff's eyes before he trotted away. He shook his head in wonder and looked at Nali. She was silently watching him.

"Pai's very protective of me," she defended.

"I can understand why," he murmured. His eyes connected with Nali's intense, vulnerable gaze.

"Empress," Reese called from inside the building.

She blinked, as if coming out of a daze, and turned away. "Thank you, Reese," she answered.

Asahi released the breath he hadn't realized he was holding. He understood Pai's feelings of protectiveness toward Nali. He also recognized that his own feelings were on a different, more primitive level than the hippogriff's. Pai wanted to protect Nali like a father would protect his child. Asahi wanted to protect Nali as a man for a woman.

He followed her through the door into the spacious interior of an inn. It was easy to understand why each building they had passed in this valley had either oversized double doors or a single large one that was twice the size of those back home. They matched the colossal size of the manticores and the centaurs.

"Can I take your bag upstairs for you?" a young centaur inquired.

Asahi tightened his grip on the strap before he nodded and lifted it over his head, wincing when a shaft of pain ran through his shoulder. After holding out the bag, he watched the boy trot up a wide set of stairs.

"The food smells amazing!" Nali said with a sigh.

He absently nodded. At the moment, he was trying to process and categorize everything he was seeing. Long tables, spaced far apart, had an assortment of bench seats. Some seats were curved, allowing the centaurs to sit down, while others were flat.

Enormous platters, the size of a turkey platter back home, were used as regular dinner plates. He blinked in wonder when he saw fauns moving throughout the room serving drinks or carrying heavy platters filled with food. The noisy room gradually became silent, and a wave of hushed whispers announced their arrival.

As if in slow motion, young and old alike— regardless of what type of creature they were—put down their cups and silverware and rose to their feet in respect for their Empress. Nali stood poised and regal. Her gaze swept over the room as if she silently greeted each creature.

"Thank you for your welcome. The food smells delicious, I look forward to enjoying it with you," she declared with a smile.

A centaur, his head bald and his neatly trimmed beard gray, lifted a tankard from the table in front of him and held it high in the air.

"To Nali, our Empress! May the Goddess be with her and the Isle of the Monsters!" he proclaimed in a deep, booming voice.

Others swiftly reached for their drinks. Fauns scurried to refill the empty ones as the diners all turned and faced their Empress. Asahi took the cup a female faun shyly held out to him. Reese handed Nali a tankard.

"To Nali!" the crowd roared.

Nali motioned to those before her with her tankard before she took a sip in tribute to her people. Laughter filled the air, and within minutes, everyone was back to enjoying their meal. Asahi moved up beside her.

"Does this happen everywhere you go?" he curiously asked, sniffing the drink in his cup before sipping it.

She laughed and shook her head. "Not everywhere. The centaurs and manticores enjoy their ale. They'll toast almost anything if it means getting a refill," she teased.

"If you'll follow me, Empress, I have a table set up for you and your guest away from prying eyes," an older female manticore said.

"Thank you," Nali murmured.

Asahi could sense the curious gazes following them as they weaved their way to a secluded corner. There was a half-wall separating it from the main dining room. A set of double doors stood open to a small patio. There was a large double window that looked out at a walled garden. Their manticore hostess must have ordered the table moved outside to give them additional privacy.

They silently followed their hostess to a table, set for an intimate dinner for two. The sun had set, and the stars were becoming visible. The manticore picked up a large candle, briefly turned away, and blew a stream of fire, lighting it before replacing it in the center of the table with a sincere smile of pleasure.

"My name is Kora. My daughter, Darla, will take care of you tonight, Empress. I will make your room ready while you dine," Kora explained, holding out a large menu.

"Thank you for your hospitality, Kora," Nali replied.

"What would you like to drink?" Kora asked.

Nali sighed. "You wouldn't have any bourbon, would you?" she wistfully inquired.

"Only the finest the pirates had to offer," Kora chuckled.

Nali laughed. "Then make it a bottle," she declared.

Kora grinned. "With pleasure, Empress," she said before turning to Asahi. "Would you like something else?"

"Bourbon is fine," Asahi replied.

Within minutes, Darla returned with a bottle of bourbon in a large decanter and two glasses. Darla poured the bourbon into the glasses while Nali ordered for both of them since she was more familiar with the cuisine offered. He picked up his glass and sat back.

This was a lot different from their meal and accommodations the night before. Except for brief breaks every couple of hours, they had kept going. Fatigue was wearing him down, and he knew that Nali must be as exhausted as he was, if not more so, after her battle with the alien.

"Tell me more about the Goddess's Mirror," he quietly requested.

She looked at him with a startled expression before she sat back in her chair and looked up. The sky was now dotted with stars that glittered like billions of brilliant twinkling lights. His breath caught at the beautiful swirling river of colors flowing across the heavens.

"It is said that the Goddess who created our world wanted a place where magical creatures could exist in harmony. To do that, she created the Seven Kingdoms. Each Kingdom held a piece of her essence. The Dragons received the Dragon's Heart while the Sea People were gifted the Eyes of the Sea Serpent. The Elementals were given the Gem of Power—which turned out to be more different than any of us expected," she mused. She took a sip of her bourbon before she continued. "The Isle of Magic was given the Orb of Eternal Light, a gift that Magna, the Sea Witch, was able to unlock through the spell she cast on the King of Magic. She used the power to kill the alien that had possessed her body. The Giants were given the Tree of Life while Ashure—" Nali stopped and looked down at her glass with a half-smile. Asahi experienced an emotion that surprised him. It almost felt like—jealousy. She sighed and looked up at him with an amused expression as if she could sense his conflicted emotions.

"You said that he and Tonya are together," Asahi remarked.

"Yes. It is good to see him happy—not that he didn't appear to be before. Ashure is a complex man. His mother was from the Isle of the Monsters and his father was a pirate. Neither one of them deserved a son like Ashure. In fact, neither one of them should have become a parent at all. The only good thing they ever did was create Ashure, though of course they didn't *intend* to do that. They died when he was very young," she explained.

"You love him," he reflected, watching the play of emotions that crossed her face as she spoke of Ashure.

She smiled at him. "Yes, very much. I never had a sibling, but Ashure is as close—and as irritating—as any brother could be. He is the King of the Pirates and protector of the Cauldron of Spirits," she said.

"That sounds ominous," he replied.

Nali's grin hinted at her dangerous side. "Only for those who cross the line. You aren't in your world any longer, Asahi. Here we are each made of a magic that goes all the way to our souls. The magic doesn't die when we do."

Asahi was quiet for a moment as he absorbed that information, then he asked, "And what is the story of the Goddess's gift to the Isle of the Monsters?"

She glanced at him before looking up at the sky again. "It allows me to see the future—when she wants to share it with me. The mirror warns me of harm to my people—or any of the Seven Kingdoms—and can guide me in protecting them… sometimes," she softly replied.

"But…?" he prodded.

She looked at him with a rueful expression. "But—it is often not very clear," she admitted.

He leaned forward and rested his elbows on the table. "Did anything like the incident with the alien earlier ever occur before?" he asked.

She shook her head. "Never," she said.

Asahi saw Nali look behind him and heard Darla approaching with their meal. He sat back and silently waited as the young manticore placed their dinner on the table. He murmured his thanks to her and waited until she left them alone before he spoke again.

"The mirror is too dangerous to use again. Somehow, the alien can connect with it," he stated.

"I've warned Reese about the dangers. He, the other guards, and Pai will keep watch tonight. Pai and the manticores have excellent night vision. There is also the possibility of using the mirror to our advantage now that we are aware of the entity's capabilities," she countered.

Asahi nodded and began eating. The delicious flavor of grilled fish seasoned to perfection flooded his taste buds. Nali's soft groan of pleasure covered his stomach's growl of delight.

"This is delicious," he commented.

She nodded. "I didn't realize how hungry I was—or how tired," she confessed with a rueful grin.

CHAPTER 9

*N*ali bit her bottom lip to keep from laughing at the myriad of emotions flitting across Asahi's face. Kora had led them to the nicest room in the inn. Neither of them had expected the room to have only one enormous bed. It was obvious the manticore assumed they were together.

"I hope you'll be comfortable, Empress. This was the last room available because of the Valley Festival that starts tomorrow," Kora said with a slightly anxious note in her voice as she nervously wrung her hands together.

"It is perfect, Kora. Thank you," Nali politely assured her.

Kora beamed and nodded. "Enjoy. I'll have food packed for your journey tomorrow. Sleep well," she said with a nod before backing out of the room.

Asahi looked at the bed before he scanned the room. She didn't miss the way his eyes briefly lingered on the cushion in the window seat. She chuckled, walked over to him, and gently patted the center of his chest.

"Don't even think of sleeping in the window seat or on the floor. We are both exhausted and mature enough to keep our hands to ourselves. We will need a good night's rest if we are to stay strong and alert. I'm going to get cleaned up," she stated.

She knew he was watching her when she grabbed the soft forest green silk robe that Kora had laid out at the end of the bed. She strode across the room and then paused at the door, looking at him with a sexy smile. Her heart hammered when she saw intense desire glimmering in his dark eyes.

"Of course, you could always wash my back if you want to save time," she suggested rather provocatively.

Nali internally groaned. That was *not* what she had planned to say. She wanted to blame her ill-advised choice of words on the look in his eyes, but that would have been a lie.

"Be careful what you wish for, Nali," Asahi warned, slowly advancing on her, his eyes never leaving hers.

She parted her lips and lifted her chin in a silent challenge. "Be careful what offers you accept," she countered when he stopped in front of her.

He lifted his hand and caressed her cheek, then he tilted his head forward and paused. Their eyes locked, and she could sense the intense anticipation building between them. She leaned forward and pressed her lips against his.

The robe in her hand fell to the floor. As she slid her hand up his arm to his neck, she caressed his bottom lip with her tongue. In one fluid movement, he grabbed her waist, pulled her into his arms, and deepened the kiss.

Their breaths mingled, becoming one, as their need for each other ignited a fire that could only be quenched with their union. She tilted her head back when he threaded his fingers through her long dark curls. He kissed her with his eyes open, and she did the same. A powerful wave of pleasure filled her when she noticed the play of emotions in his eyes as their tongues danced in a primitive mating ritual. She reluctantly ended the kiss to take a breath.

"Are you sure?" Asahi said, his voice raspy with desire.

Nali gave him a confident smile and slid one hand down between them to cover the telltale bulge pressing against her. He deeply inhaled and tilted his hips forward as he exhaled with a low groan. Excitement zinged through her.

"How do you like the water?" she purred.

"With you in it," he murmured, placing another kiss on her lips.

Asahi couldn't drag his eyes away from Nali. She turned on the water to the shower unit before she started to undress. She removed her boots while he removed his shoes. They set them aside and turned toward each other.

He reached up and slowly unbuttoned his shirt. They both removed their shirts and dropped them to the floor. He moved his hands to his belt and waited until she did the same. Together, like mirrored erotic dancers, they continued undressing until they stood before each other —unshielded by clothing.

"You are a very... impressive looking man," Nali said.

He closed the distance between them. Impressive didn't even begin to describe the woman standing in front of him. Her long black curls hung down her back and over one shoulder, the curly swath stopping just shy of the dark areola surrounding her taut nipple.

Her skin was the color of rich mocha, and he wanted a taste. He trailed the back of his fingers up her arm to her shoulder. His body reacted to her softly inhaled breath.

"Soft as the petals of a rose," he said.

Nali lifted a knowing eyebrow and gave him a wicked smile full of promise. He shook his head in grudging concession when she slid her hands around his waist, splayed them across each of his buttocks, and pulled him into the shower. Her parted lips met his as she switched their positions and pushed him back against the wall.

Asahi threaded his fingers through her hair and gripped her hip with his other hand. She ran her tongue along his bottom lip before gently sucking on it. After a few seconds, she reluctantly tilted her head back to look into his eyes.

"I'm glad that you didn't listen to me when I told you to go east," she admitted.

He cupped her cheek. Water droplets clung to her eyelashes. She pressed another fervent kiss full of promise on his lips and then stepped back.

He grabbed the bar of soap, and with tender strokes and attention to detail, he washed her. He wanted to take his time to memorize her luscious body. Her muted moan of pleasure made him smile.

His smile faded when she took the soap from him. The touch of her hands gliding over his body created mental images of her lips following every stroke. When she dipped her hands lower and stroked his cock, he gritted his teeth to keep his control, but he loved the pleased expression in her eyes when she felt his immediate response.

He slid his hand down her arm and wrapped his fingers around her wrist. If she continued caressing his cock this way, he would come. He took the soap from her and placed it on the shelf. Then, applying gentle pressure, he turned her until her back was to him.

"My Enchantress," he said, kissing her shoulder.

She leaned back and rubbed her buttocks against his erection. "I want to create magic with you, Asahi," she breathed.

He reached out and turned off the water. Together, they dried each other. They caressed and fondled each other as they moved back into the bedroom, skimming their hands over skin in an erotic foreplay that increased their hunger.

He wrapped his arms around her and pulled her down on top of him. She straddled his hips, the soft curls covering her mound rubbing against his engorged shaft. He cupped her full breasts and captured her nipples between his talented fingers. She leaned forward, caged his head with her forearms, and slowly licked his parted lips.

"You make me feel alive," she said.

She balanced on one arm while she moved her hand down between them. Firmly gripping his cock, she guided it to her soft folds. The soft hair covering her mound brushed against the bulbous head of his manhood before the sensation of liquid heat surrounded him.

"Nali," he groaned, lifting his hips as she sank down on him.

She arched her back and rode him. Emotion overwhelmed Asahi as he watched the expressions of pleasure cross her face. Her eyes were closed, her lips parted, and her head tilted back. He pinched her taut nipples, drawing a passionate cry from her. All the while, each stroke of her sweetly heated channel was a pleasurable torture. His balls were rock hard and a tingle low in his spine spread until the dam of his control felt like a fragile web caught in a hurricane.

He leaned up and captured one of her nipples between his lips, sucking it in deep. She responded with a cry and rotated her hips, brushing her swollen nub against him. Her feminine depths fisted him like a glove. He sucked harder, thrusting his hips as she gripped his upper arms.

"Yes! Oh, yes!" she cried out as she violently shuddered with her orgasm.

He dropped his head back against the pillow and reached around her. With a quick flip, he turned them over until he was on top. He didn't give her a chance to recover. He tightened his arms around her and pumped his hips faster as he drove deep inside her. Her cries grew louder and she clung to him. He uttered a low, guttural groan as the dam burst, and he emptied wave after wave of hot cum inside her.

He lowered his head to her shoulder as pleasure and contentment swept through him. She held him, caressing his lower back. Another shudder ran through him when her channel squeezed his cock.

He nuzzled her neck. "You are my rose, Nali. You are my sun, my moon, and my magic," he murmured near her ear.

She drew in a deep breath and released it on a sigh. "You don't mind that I'm a monster as well?" she asked.

He leaned back and tenderly brushed her hair away from her face, then gently cupped her cheek, stroking her smooth skin with his thumb. She gazed up at him, her beautiful eyes searching.

"Your ability to transform is part of who you are. You are a monster and an Empress, but more importantly, you are a beautiful, compassionate, and intelligent woman in any form—one for whom I have feelings and deep respect," he said with great sincerity.

Her eyes glittered with emotion. She leaned up and captured his lips, deepening their kiss when he parted his. She caressed his back, moving along the curve of his buttocks. His body responded to her loving touch, and he knew in that moment that he wanted to feel Nali's touch for the rest of his life.

My beautiful, passionate monster, he thought, losing himself in her kiss.

~

Isle of the Pirates

· · ·

Ashure leaned over and brushed a kiss across Tonya's lips. She sleepily murmured and rolled over onto her back before blindly reaching up and cupping his cheek. He tenderly smiled as he looked down into her sleep-filled eyes.

"Are you leaving already?" she murmured in a voice still thick with sleep.

"Yes, love. The sooner I leave, the sooner I can come back to you," he affectionately teased.

She scooted backward until she was leaning against the headboard. "Do you have the sword that Magna enchanted?" she asked.

"Yes, it is safely hidden," he replied.

"Do you have the mirror and the bag I packed for you?" she continued, pushing her tangled hair back from her face.

Ashure chuckled and gave her a lingering kiss. "I have everything. Food, clothing, swords, the magic wards Marina gave me, and the human weapon Max insisted I take," he promised.

"Oh, okay. I just wanted to make sure you didn't forget anything. Promise me again that you'll be careful," she whispered, staring at him with huge, worried eyes.

"I promise," he said with a groan when the desire to hold her close was almost too strong to resist. If he gave in, it would be hours before he was ready to leave again. "I can't let Nali do this alone. I hope it doesn't take long to capture or kill the alien."

"I know. This thing—this alien—Magna told me about it and how dangerous it is. I know that I would only be in the way if I came along, or worse, a distraction. You need someone like Magna, or Max, or Mike Hallbrook," she said.

"And that is what I love about you—you understand. I'd better go now, otherwise Nali will be having all the fun," he muttered before he leaned in and kissed her hard one last time, then stood up and backed away.

She touched her lips and sent a warm look his way. "I love you," she murmured.

"I love you, my beautiful pirate," he softly replied before he held up the mirror.

He firmly gripped the mirror. The items he was taking with him were tied to him through magic, kept safe in the magical realm of the Cauldron of Spirits until he called on them. He took a deep breath and stared at his reflection for a moment before he spoke the incantation.

"Oh, magical mirror, grant my wish, take me to Nali, the Empress of the Monsters," he instructed.

He slid his finger over the rose thorn to activate the magic. He looked down when the portal's swirling colors appeared. A look of dismay crossed his face an instant before he fell through.

Oh, boy, Nali will really be pissed at me this time, he thought with wry amusement.

CHAPTER 10

*A*shure fell through the air until his feet hit the soft surface near the foot of the bed. He pinwheeled his arms as he fought to keep his balance on the unstable surface. A sudden movement behind him caused him to fall backward on the bed. He bounced on his back several times between the pair of startled and distinctly irate lovers. He grunted in relief when his head landed on a soft pillow.

While the landing had been soft, it was probably the worst place and time to suddenly appear. He gave an apologetic smile to soften the impact of his intrusion. Given the heated glare he was receiving and the dagger brandished in his direction, his effort wasn't working.

He swallowed when he felt the dagger's tip press against the soft tissue at the base of his throat. The appearance of a tiny, animated gold Gryphon on the hilt of the dagger caused him to blink in surprise. The diminutive winged lion shook his head in disgust and snorted at him before it looked up at the man who was holding the dagger.

Ashure's smile turned into a grimace, and he sent a beseeching look to his beautiful but equally furious friend. She had scrambled out of the bed and was tying the belt of a dark forest green robe around her slender waist.

"Ah, good morning, Nali," he mumbled, trying not to move his throat as he spoke. "Do you think you could ask your lover not to skewer me, please? I promised Tonya that I would return unscathed."

"Asahi, you can release him. He is not a threat. Ashure, what are you doing here? I told you not to come unless all three beads turned red," she angrily hissed.

Ashure breathed a sigh of relief when the man above him pulled the magical dagger away from his throat. He curiously followed Asahi's movements as the man rolled off the bed. Amusement struck him when Asahi walked naked across the room, picked up a black duffle bag from a chair near the bathroom, and disappeared out of sight.

He lost his enjoyment in the situation when he glimpsed the worried expression in Nali's eyes as she, too, watched Asahi disappear into the other room. Deciding that sprawling in the center of the tousled bedcovers would not help, he sat up and scooted to the edge. Nali turned to face him. He stood and gave her a slight bow and his best contrite expression.

"Nali—" he started.

She waved her finger at him. "Don't you 'Nali' me, Ashure! What are you doing here?" she growled.

He looked over her shoulder when her lover silently stepped back into the room. He relaxed when he caught the amused expression on Asahi's face. Nali's low growl warned him that the mood she was in was not as understanding.

"I was worried about you. When the first bead turned red, and then the second started turning, I wanted to help... and... I... um, I had no idea that you were... you know..." He waved a hand at them. "The mirror didn't show me.... I apologize," he said with a remorseful expression.

"Mirror?" Asahi and Nali exclaimed at the same time.

He grinned and held up the mirror that he was still holding. "Yes. This thing is utterly amazing, Nali. I discovered that it not only shows my true heart's desire, but it will take me to it, if I prick my finger. Tonya and I finally figured out how the magic works—quite by accident," he admitted.

"Ashure, can I see the mirror?" Nali asked, walking around the bed.

"But of course," he said.

"What if the alien can do the same thing with this mirror as it did with yours?" Asahi asked.

She glanced at him before looking at the mirror. "I don't know," she murmured.

Ashure looked back and forth between them with a frown. "What mirror? What happened?" he demanded.

Asahi looked at him. "Nali was using the Goddess's Mirror, and the alien came through it," he explained.

Disbelief swept through him. "Came through... Nali, how is that possible?" he exclaimed.

She shook her head. "I don't know," she impatiently hissed. "How does this thing work again?"

Ashure shook his head. "Give the mirror back to me. I will do it," he grimly replied.

"Ashure," she growled.

He shook his head. "Perhaps you should get dressed before we do this," he suggested.

Nali glared at him before she turned away, grumbling that she could kill aliens half-naked if she felt like it. Instead of going into the other room, she snapped her fingers. The forest green robe vanished and was replaced by midnight blue trousers and a matching silk blouse underneath a black leather vest. Black knee-high boots completed her outfit.

"Happy now?" she asked with a raised eyebrow.

He grinned at her. "Well, I was hoping you would show me your lovely ass to replace the memory of Asahi's—but... Yes, this is nice," he hastily finished when she twitched her fingers in warning.

"The spell to work the mirror, Ashure—now," she growled, snapping her fingers.

He gave Asahi a pained look. "She can be grouchy when she is rudely awakened," he observed before he grimaced at Asahi's frown.

"You are about to join the world of the Bogleech if you aren't careful," she retorted.

Asahi tilted his head inquisitively. "The world of the Bogleech? That doesn't sound pleasant."

Ashure grimaced and nodded. "She excelled at transformation spells when we were kids, and she procured some exceptionally good ones from a few witches on the Isle of Magic," he replied.

She gave him a sardonic smile and wiggled the mirror in front of him. "Would you like to find out?" she flippantly inquired.

"Say the words 'Oh magical mirror, grant my wish, show me...' and whatever it is your heart desires. Just be careful not to prick your finger on the rose thorn on the back. A drop of blood will open a portal, and you'll drop right into the alien's lap," he warned.

Nali turned the mirror over and saw the thorn he was talking about. Her breath caught when she saw the embossed decoration of fairies and the old willow tree. She brushed her finger along its raised contours before she remembered his warning and nodded.

"Asahi, be ready with Mr. Gryphon. Ashure—stand back. I'd have you leave the room entirely, but we may need you for something," she said with a worried expression.

"Ouch, Nali, that's harsh, even for you," Ashure dryly remarked.

She gave him a pointed look. "Remember what would happen if the alien were to inhabit your body," she gently reminded him.

His eyes glittered with a warning. "Then I will make sure that doesn't happen," he retorted.

"You have a reason to live now, Ashure," she reminded him. "Someone to live for."

He reached out and gently caressed her cheek. "So do you, love," he replied, glancing at Asahi, who was watching their exchange in silence. "Say the words. We'll be ready should anything happen."

She nodded and held up the mirror while Ashure pulled out his gift from Magna, the blade resonating with imbued power. Asahi nodded at him, stepped up next to Nali, and gripped the Gryphon dagger's hilt.

Nali looked at both of them before she spoke. "Oh, magical mirror, grant my wish, show me the alien," she murmured.

They watched warily as the image in the mirror swirled. Confusion coursed through Ashure when he saw a row of golden statues.

"I don't understand...," he said, his voice fading as one of the golden statues screamed in agony as a dark entity entered the scene and destroyed it.

~

A galaxy far, far away

. . .

"Phoenix, what is it?" Spring Reykill asked.

Phoenix turned and looked at her twin sister, older by just a few minutes. Spring's long blonde hair was pulled into a high ponytail. She had streaks of dirt on her nose and cheeks—nothing unusual for the petite blonde who loved to spend time outside in the garden or burrowing underground in her dragon form.

They were as opposite in their coloring as they were in their personalities. Spring was the day while she was the night. Phoenix also knew that she differed from her sister in other ways. In fact, Phoenix was different from everyone on Valdier—including her parents.

Phoenix didn't consider herself special. Instead, she believed she'd been given a gift from the Goddess. She had been chosen, but she didn't understand why or what the future held for her. Her eyes were the same golden color of the symbiots they had each received shortly after their birth.

Even her dragon differed from the others'. While her body was in the shape of a dragon, her head, wings, and tail had the likeness of a bird. It reminded her of the beautiful bird on her mother's back. Her parents had even named her after the mythical creature. She liked to think her dark coloring came from those ashes, but she knew she had inherited it from her father.

"Phoenix, did you hear me? Is everything alright?" Spring asked again, wiping her hands on her pants.

Phoenix smiled and nodded. "Yes… yes, everything is fine. I think I'm going to go for a flight. I'll meet you back at the palace," she said.

"Do you want me to go with you?" Spring asked.

Phoenix shook her head. "No… no. I'll have Stardust with me. You should focus on finishing the garden. It is looking beautiful. I'll try to find some more seeds for it while I'm out," she promised.

Spring grinned. "Oh, that would be lovely! Thank you! If you can find more starflowers or night moons, that would be fabulous," she breathed.

"I'll see if I can find some," she replied, half her attention on the whisper drifting through her mind.

"Are you sure everything is alright? You've been so distracted the last few days," Spring commented, studying her sister with a frown.

She smiled. "I'm fine. I'll be back later," Phoenix promised.

"Okay, be careful," Spring said.

Phoenix gave her sister a reassuring smile that faded when Spring turned away. She could tell that Spring's thoughts were already back on the new garden that she was creating. Spring had inherited their grandmother Morian's touch with plants. Her mom called it a 'green thumb'.

She stiffened when the odd feeling that she had been experiencing flashed through her again. She bit her lip in indecision and looked questioningly at her symbiot, Stardust.

Stardust must have felt the same odd foreboding because her coat was agitatedly shimmering with different colors. "I wish Aikaterina were here so I could ask her what I should do," she whispered to Stardust.

She shook her head to clear it and started running along the stone path away from the palace. Up ahead, she could see where the gardens met the cliffs. She shifted into her dragon form ten feet from the protective rock wall and soared into the air. Her long, feathered black wings shimmered for a moment before she vanished.

CHAPTER 11

"I don't understand. What were those golden creatures? What does it mean that the alien destroyed one of them? Who were the others? Did you recognize the cavern?" Ashure impatiently grumbled.

Nali shook her head and lifted her shoulders in a delicate shrug. "No, I don't know what any of it means. It's your mirror—and no, I've never seen a river of gold like that on the Isle of the Monsters," she replied.

"It seems there is more to the alien than meets the eye," Asahi said, drawing the attention of his companions.

The mirror had shown them a dozen scenes, each appearing and disappearing like a mirage in the desert. The montage had ended with an image of their enemy curled up in a fetal position in a dark, unde-fined space. Unfortunately, with no clear landmarks, it would be impossible to know exactly where the alien was hiding without using the portal to take them directly to it, and if they did that, they would be vulnerable when they emerged—if Ashure's sudden appearance this morning was anything to go by.

Asahi's eidetic, or more commonly called photographic, memory slowly replayed the scenes from the mirror in his mind. The first had been in a cave with a dozen different golden statues standing on pillars. A long river of gold flowed through the center of the cavern. At one end, there were steps carved into the stone leading to an archway.

They had watched in horror as a malevolent shadow struck one of the statues—or what they had thought was a statue until the golden figure suddenly moved and writhed, screaming in agony as thick black bands wrapped around it. As a nearly inaudible hum of distress filled the cavern, the river of gold rose as if it were alive. Asahi was shocked at the powerful wave of grief that had filled him when the statue exploded into a million pieces.

The scene that stood out the most was the one that followed. It had shown them a battle. On one side was a man who turned into a dragon. He had ordered the destruction of the golden entity. The dark creature at his command seemed to be just like the alien the Seven Kingdoms had been fighting, although clearly less powerful given that it was taking orders. The dark creature's master fought against adversaries that included a man he called 'human'. There were several dragons fighting alongside the human, but Nali said she didn't recognize any of them as residents of the Isle of the Dragons. She would have to ask Drago. Asahi looked up when Nali laid her hand over his.

"What is it, Asahi?" she asked.

He frowned as he processed the information into something that made sense, rotating the cup of hot tea in his hand as he thought.

"Given the lower status of the alien," he began, "the way it obeyed that man, I think the attack in the cavern was in the past," he asserted. "You asked the mirror to show you the alien—so what if it *did* show us the alien in that very first scene, the part before the dark entity showed up? What if at least one of those golden creatures is part of the alien now? This battle could have been essential to how it gained power, to how it... evolved. What if the alien *consumed* that shattered golden entity—absorbed its power—and became the version that we are familiar with today? Is that a possibility?" he hypothesized.

Nali paused with a thoughtful expression. "We know the alien can split into parts that move and speak. Theoretically, if this golden entity could do that also, then instead of dying when it shattered, all those pieces would continue to hold power and life—and they could be acquired and used, similar to how Magna was used by the alien. Given Magna's experience, it would be reasonable to assume that the dark alien would need this golden entity to be conscious in order to derive the most power from her, so perhaps the pieces of the living statue were at least partially reassembled into larger pieces within the alien and this entity is now locked inside as captive fuel? We never spotted evidence of this golden species in any of the other aliens, though."

"Maybe it was only in this one," Ashure suggested.

Asahi lifted his shoulder in a shrug. "I don't know what happened with the other aliens. Perhaps you destroyed them without realizing the golden entity was a prisoner within, or perhaps the other forms didn't contain any of its—essence. This one appears to be heading in a specific direction with a definite goal in mind. It hasn't tried to return to the coast or deviated to throw us off its trail. It is heading North-west. Is there anything in that direction of potential interest to it?" he inquired.

Nali's lips parted on a soft gasp even as Ashure's eyes widened with a similar epiphany. They stared at each other in silent communication while Asahi studied their expressions. He leaned forward.

"What is it?" he softly inquired.

"I'm not sure if there is a connection, but—" she paused, deep in thought.

She looked around the empty patio where they had enjoyed dinner last night and started pushing their breakfast dishes aside. Ashure quickly helped her clear an area in front of her on the table. She waved her hand over the table, and a contour map of the Isle of the Monsters appeared.

"The first stag was discovered here. The second came ashore here," she said, pointing at two coastal locations on the map. "From there, it moved inland. We located Medjuline here."

"I first saw her somewhere around here," Asahi added, pointing to an area on the other side of the river.

"She was traveling north, away from her village," Ashure concluded.

"Yes, but why would the alien leave her body without harming her, unlike the Sea Stag that it killed?" Nali pondered.

"Perhaps it didn't want to destroy the only viable body available until it found a replacement," Asahi replied.

Nali nodded. "That makes sense. It killed the Sea Stag because Medjuline was there and the alien could take over her body," she said.

"But—why did it leave Medjuline?" Ashure asked.

"The troll knocked herself unconscious," Asahi answered.

Nali paused, tilting her head. "I've seen one of the other aliens using a *dead* host… someone much smaller than a troll. Perhaps size makes a difference when controlling a host that is not conscious."

Asahi's eyes lit up with this new theory. "That makes sense. So, then the alien attacked a nearby goblin fortress."

"Goblins!" Ashure commented with a look of surprise before he chuckled. "I would have loved to have been in the alien's head when that happened. At least with a troll, it is bigger and stronger. Goblins —well, they'll kill you with their nasty tempers."

"More than two dozen perished fighting the alien, Ashure," Nali gently chided.

Ashure's expression was instantly contrite. "Sorry, I still remember them suspending me—never mind," he muttered.

Nali looked at Asahi and gave him a slight grin. "Ashure upset a group of goblins once. They might have put him in a cage and hung him over the cliffs," she explained.

Ashure picked up a piece of fruit and waved it at Nali. "There was no 'might have'—the beastly, dirty creatures not only did it, they made sure it was placed at the entrance to the harbor so that every arriving ship saw me hanging out like a piece of laundry to dry in the wind," he growled.

"If I remember correctly, there was no clothing involved. They left him as bare as the day he was born. You shouldn't have argued with them," she said with a shake of her head and another grin before looking down at the map again. "The alien came out here from the tunnels and headed in this direction."

Asahi followed the direction she was tracing with her finger, and focused on a mountain, the top obscured by clouds.

"What's here?" he asked.

"A very special place. It isn't on ordinary maps," she confessed.

"Well, the alien appears to be heading in that direction. What's so special about it? Is it possible that the alien could know something about it?" Asahi pressed.

"I don't know how it could. Few of the locals are even aware of it," she said, looking at Ashure again.

"There is Fairy magic protecting it," Ashure added.

"Yes, and my own. Only those true of heart can scale the mountain, and even then, there is no guarantee they will survive," she explained.

"You still have not told me what is there," Asahi calmly pointed out.

Nali sighed and ran her finger over the cloud cover on the mountain. "Unicorns," she murmured.

Asahi blinked, frowned, and shook his head. "Did you say—unicorns?" he asked.

Ashure nodded and grinned. "Yes, unicorns—with a very playful sense of humor," he confirmed.

"Unicorns?" Asahi repeated with a skeptical look at the map.

"Unicorns," Nali and Ashure confirmed at the same time.

The four of them left the village an hour after sunrise. Nali, Ashure, and Asahi planned to search for signs of the alien at ground level while Pai flew overhead. After a brief discussion, they had decided to follow a winding road that passed through the valley and mountains.

Reese had provided a transport powered by one of the Thunderbird feathers. Ashure took the wheel before Nali could get to the driver's seat. She silently chuckled at the excitement on Ashure's face. When it came to anything of Nali's that could move fast—be it this electric transport, one of the many airships, or her fire-breathing horses—he wanted to try it.

The vehicle had a convertible top. It hovered two feet off the ground and could easily pass over most obstacles. Asahi stored his duffle bag in the aft storage area. Nali added Pai's smaller sack before she walked around and slid into the passenger seat. Asahi sat in the seat behind Ashure. Pai set off into the air.

"I talked to Reese while you were retrieving our belongings," Nali said as she twisted in her seat and faced Ashure and Asahi. "He has set up extra security with multiple teams to keep an eye out for the alien. If the alien stays on the course we suspect it is traveling, we can move ahead of it and make sure the residents have ample warning to evacuate."

"I hope they will be safe," Ashure replied. "Ross Galloway, a human from your realm, said the alien inhabited *spiders* on the Isle of the Elementals. I would rather not have to deal with what it could achieve with some of the unique insects, arachnids, or reptiles on *this* Isle," Ashure muttered.

Nali's expression darkened at the looming threat to her monsters, but she quickly schooled her features and changed the subject. "Ashure and I were discussing the reason his mirror worked without triggering the alien compared to the Goddess's Mirror," she said.

"What was your conclusion?" Asahi asked.

"His mirror uses a magic spell, whereas mine—mine comes from the Goddess herself," she softly replied.

"So perhaps there is a connection between the Goddess and the alien. This Goddess—has anyone ever seen her in person? Has anyone ever seen what she looks like?" he asked.

Ashure glanced uneasily at Nali before looking back at the road in front of them. Nali knew he was mulling something over, and she waited for him to speak. After a moment, he breathed a lengthy sigh.

Nali had a feeling that she knew what he was about to share. Neither he nor Tonya had fully explained what had happened when Tonya lay on the brink of death—mortally wounded by Bleu LaBluff. He had been Ashure's right-hand man until Bleu betrayed him. Nali knew the experience had been very traumatic for her dear friend and had never pressed him for details. In the end, the how wasn't important. What mattered the most was that Tonya had survived.

"Tonya described the Goddess who saved her. She looked—yes, she looked like the entities in the caverns," Ashure soberly replied.

"Then it would appear," Asahi said grimly, "that it was your Goddess that the alien consumed. If not your *exact* Goddess, then one of her species—and now it can access objects created with your Goddess's power."

Nali nodded and remained silent as they continued along the road. She stared ahead and absently caressed the silver mirror that Ashure had handed to her earlier while the men continued to talk.

Turning the mirror over, she studied the old willow tree and the fairies. Her fingers trembled when she saw something that she had missed before. Partially obscured by the hanging branches of the willow was the figure of a woman. Nestled in her arms was a swaddled baby, and behind her—a portal opening to the universe.

Tears suddenly burned Nali's eyes. She held the mirror closer so she could see the minute details of the infant. While the face and body were obscured, there were curly locks of hair peeking out from underneath the blanket.

She touched a strand of her long, curly hair, and suddenly she felt a bone-deep knowledge, a realization that had always been waiting for her in the depths of her magic. *She* was the infant depicted. The images carved into the mirror—they were about her arrival.

"Are you alright?" Asahi murmured near her ear.

She looked over her shoulder at him. He tenderly caressed her neck, and she gave him a distracted smile.

"Yes, I'm thinking about what you said," she replied.

"Pai is landing," Ashure warned, slowing the transport.

Nali pulled her gaze away from Asahi's and nodded. Ashure eased the transport up alongside the hippogriff.

"What is it?" she asked Pai when they stopped beside him.

"There's a Daktyloi longhouse ahead. I don't see any signs of life," Pai warned.

"Scout the surrounding area, we will check the longhouse," she instructed.

Pai nodded and stepped back from the transport. "Don't forget to shift," he grumbled before taking off.

Ashure shook his head. "I notice he hasn't changed much. He still likes to order you around," he commented with a humorous grin.

"His heart has always been in the right place," she absently murmured.

CHAPTER 12

ifteen minutes later, Ashure turned onto a short driveway off the major road and stopped the vehicle. Asahi leaned back and pulled the gryphon dagger from his sheath. The animated creature yawned, stood up, and shook, causing his golden mane to fluff out.

"What is it?" the lion growled.

Asahi kept his attention on the long, rectangular hut before them. "We aren't sure yet," he said.

"It helps if I know what I'm about to encounter," the gryphon pouted.

"That would help me too, Mr. Gryphon," Asahi replied.

He followed Nali as she exited the vehicle. Her body shimmered with a golden hue as her flesh hardened, and a sense of déjà vu struck him for a moment. She motioned with her hand for him to stay back. He paused, monitoring her progress before he glanced at the winged lion that was tapping on his hand. He realized that Mr. Gryphon was still waiting for more information about their location.

"We are in front of a Daktyloi longhouse. Pai thinks something may be wrong. What can you tell me about them?" he requested.

The gryphon scratched behind his ear. "Well, the Daktyloi are a strange bunch, even for monsters. They live together in groups of three to five. They are brilliant in areas like mathematics, metalworking, and healing magic. They are also obnoxious. They think Daktyloi are better than everyone else, and each Daktyloi thinks he or she is the best of their own kind. That's why they live apart from everyone. No one can stand them. They can barely stand each other," the gryphon said with a dry chuckle.

"I'll remember that," Asahi murmured.

Nali paused at the front door and frowned. She looked over her shoulder at him, gave him a brief nod, then turned and knocked on the door. Under her fist, the door popped from its latch and came to a halt just past the door jamb, hiding what lay beyond.

Ashure pulled a sword out from under his coat and signaled that he would take the back. Asahi nodded and followed Nali.

He drew the 9mm handgun from the holster under his jacket, released the safety with a quick flick of his thumb, and strode forward, stopping next to Nali.

"Something's wrong," she said. "I smell blood."

"I'll look inside first," he said in a barely audible voice.

She nodded. He stood with his back against the outside wall. Reaching out, he pushed the door open with the barrel of his gun. He peered inside.

Dim light flickered through the windows, giving the interior a surreal, horror-movie appearance. Dust particles floated in the stream of light. From this angle, he could see an overturned chair and a bunch of papers scattered on the floor.

He looked over at Nali and shook his head. Her eyes darkened with concern, and she nodded her understanding. He silently stepped across the threshold, aiming his pistol with his sight line as he carefully scanned the room. He focused on the shadows in the corners, looking for movement. Nali followed him, searching the area.

The room was long and narrow with three openings—one on each end of the room and one in the middle. He moved in a crouch to the left while Nali went to the right. He tightened his grip on the gryphon dagger as he slowly stepped into the next room.

It looked like a university library. After examining the area from left to right and back again, he felt confident that the room was empty, and he moved forward. This room also had three entrances—the one he had stepped through, one at the opposite end of the room, and an opening in the back wall.

A long table was positioned in the middle of the room. There were five chairs around it, two on each of the longer sides and one at the far end. On the table were many books stacked high in neat piles and several beautiful black metal racks filled with scrolls. Each rack had a unique decoration.

There was an ink well and a quill placed in front of each chair. Mixed in among the papers and books were a variety of mathematical tools. Three of the walls contained floor to ceiling bookcases filled with leather-bound books. An enormous window was precisely centered in the fourth wall. On each side of the window there were two large transparent display screens filled with mathematical equations that he didn't attempt to analyze closely. He was no mathematician.

The room was immaculate except for a tipped over inkwell. Ink had dripped onto the floor. He stepped around the table and walked over to the chair positioned slightly further from the table than the rest.

A dark imprint from a small shoe stood out on the polished wood floor. The dainty footprints circled around, crossing over others before they disappeared into the next room at the opposite end.

"Maybe you should let me go ahead of you," Mr. Gryphon suggested in a barely audible voice.

Asahi looked down, startled. He had forgotten about the animated creature. He frowned when he realized that the magical lion could be parted from the hilt of the dagger.

"I'll follow the footsteps. Can you search the other room?" he murmured.

"I can. I wasn't created just to look pretty," Mr. Gryphon retorted.

Asahi shook his head at the lion. The dagger's creator must have had one hell of a sense of humor. He waited until the winged lion had taken flight and disappeared through the side entrance before he continued following the footprints.

Asahi paused at the doorway to the next room and pressed his back against the wall. A dainty slipper lay upside down, the sole covered in ink. He bent forward and peered around the corner. Out of his peripheral vision, he glimpsed a woman's small, bare foot in a position that indicated she was lying face down.

Automatically executing FBI procedure, he methodically scanned the area before he entered, slowly twisting in a tight circle as he backed toward the body. He skirted the edge of the couch, looking in each corner of the room, then crouched down next to the woman's body. She was lying on her stomach with her head twisted to the side. A flash of grief seared him when he noticed the glaze of death in her eyes. There was a small pool of blood near her mouth.

He rose to his feet, holding his gun at the ready and his dagger firmly clenched. A sound behind him caused him to twist around, gun aimed. Ashure raised his hands in the air, and Asahi silently cursed, lowering his gun.

"I found two dead. One in the kitchen, the other in the bedroom," Ashure said.

They both turned when Nali stepped into the room. "I found another body in the den," she said, her voice tight with strain.

"I found this woman; no others," Asahi replied.

"That makes four. There should be five. There's a portrait on the wall of them all together," she said.

"Mr. Gryphon hasn't returned from the other room yet, but if he had found another body, he would be here. He is probably checking the surrounding area outside. Ashure and I will search the house," Asahi said with a look at Ashure to see if he agreed. Ashure nodded.

"I'll search from the air and check in with Pai to find out if he has located the one who is missing," she replied.

He stepped back when her wings suddenly appeared. She looked up at the ceiling sixteen-feet above their heads before she shot upward. He widened his eyes, wondering how she was going to get out that way. There was a sturdy ceiling above them.

He understood a second later when a large hole magically appeared, revealing tree branches and the blue sky above. The hole closed the moment she passed through. He looked at Ashure with a confused expression.

Ashure gave him a grim smile. "Remember, my friend, you are no longer in your world. Nali is much more powerful than she appears— and I suspect more than even she is aware of," he added.

"I see," he distractedly replied.

"We would have heard a scuffle if Mr. Gryphon encountered anyone. He will likely meet up with us soon. We need to discover if this is the alien's work. It rarely happens, but there has been the occasional murder among monsters," Ashure said with distaste.

Asahi frowned. "What happens in that case?" he asked.

"Then they get the unfortunate opportunity to meet me," Ashure commented.

Asahi drew in a long, hissing breath when their eyes connected. It was as if Ashure had removed a veil of pretense from his eyes, revealing the dark and dangerous man hidden behind his charming facade. Deep in the recesses of Ashure's pupils, Asahi could see shadows, and it felt as if he were being drawn into an endless abyss.

"The Cauldron of Spirits," Asahi remembered.

"And the Keeper of Lost Souls," Ashure added. "There is a special place for magical souls who have turned bad. Magic does not die when the shell that contained it fades away."

"What happens to the friendly souls?" he asked, looking down at the dead woman.

Ashure's gaze followed his to the body of the woman. A sad but peaceful look came into Ashure's eyes before he concealed it. The shadows were once again shielded from prying eyes.

Ashure looked back at him with a sardonic smile. "You'll have to ask Nali that question. I've only been gifted with knowing what happens to the rotten ones," he replied in a deceptively light tone.

Asahi silently followed Ashure when he stepped around the woman's body. They took their time, examining each room in the house. They did not find Mr. Gryphon.

"They killed themselves and each other," Ashure concluded as he looked at the stab wounds on one of the men. This was the second man with stab wounds, and the injuries on both of them gaped far more than they should have.

Asahi nodded. "If I had to guess, the killer entered through the front door. It took over the oldest victim in the front room while he was studying. The Daktyloi male in the bedroom saw what happened. A fight ensued, and the oldest Daktyloi was killed. The alien tried to take over the victor of that fight, but the man ended his life before the alien could use him. Next, the alien went after the woman. Given the defensive wounds on her arms and hands, she resisted, and during the struggle she died from strangulation."

"That leaves the man in the kitchen and the one that is missing—unless the missing one is our killer," Ashure added with a sigh.

Asahi nodded. They walked into the kitchen. The back door was wide open. The third man was lying on his side on the floor. Unlike the others, a green-tinted foam ran down the man's cheek. His glazed eyes were bloodshot, and there was a slight odor to his skin.

"Poison," Ashure muttered, nodding to a torn bright-blue mushroom lying in the man's curled, stiff fingers.

Asahi squatted next to the man. He used the tip of the dagger and gently touched a black smudge on the man's bottom lip. He jerked back when the smudge shrieked and writhed at the touch of the dagger's point. The magic in the dagger turned it a brilliant white, which then faded. The residue left by the alien turned to ash.

"I guess we now have a definitive answer on what killed them," Ashure murmured.

Asahi heard a faint flutter of wings, and stood up, facing the back door. He held out the dagger, hilt pointing up, for the lion to land on. Mr. Gryphon shook his body from head-to-toe and wingtip-to-wingtip before folding his wings against his body and sitting down.

"Did you find the missing man?" Asahi inquired.

Mr. Gryphon shook his head. "No, but I found footprints leading into the woods. I followed it as far as I could. I'm tethered to the magic in the dagger, so unfortunately, it wasn't very far," he added with an indignant sniff.

Asahi looked through the doorway. Nali was landing just outside. She strode across the yard and into the kitchen.

"Did you discover anything?" Ashure asked.

She shook her head. "Nothing significant. Pai is still searching," she replied.

"We know for certain it was the alien. There was black residue on one victim's lip," Asahi said with a nod toward the body.

"I found footprints leading into the woods," Mr. Gryphon stated.

"I'll—" Nali began before they heard their transport's engine start up.

"By a Sea Monkey's tit," Ashure cursed.

Asahi was already speeding through the other rooms, heading for the front door. He pulled it open in time to see the back of the transport fishtailing as the missing Daktyloi stole their mode of transportation. Nali pushed past him, lifting off as she ran. He started after her, but Ashure reached out and gripped his arm.

"Ashure," he growled, trying to pull his arm free.

"Something is not right, my friend. Besides, you couldn't catch up with either of them on foot," Ashure muttered with growing unease.

Asahi pulled his arm free and looked around. There was a strange chill in the air.

"Step back inside," Ashure murmured.

Asahi slowly moved back into the longhouse. Ashure followed him, shutting the door and sliding the thick iron bar across to secure it. Ashure signaled him to close the window to the left while he took care of the one on the right.

"We need to secure the rest of the house," Ashure said.

"I'll take the front. You take care of the back. Make sure you start in the kitchen. The door was still open," Asahi grimly agreed.

They split up. Ashure disappeared through the doorway leading to the back of the dwelling. Asahi secured the living room area before retracing his steps through the front room to the library. Upon entering the room, he hastened to the windows, closed the heavy iron shutters, and locked them.

The Daktyloi had cleverly engineered slats with tracks at the top and bottom. Polished wooden shutters folded away into the window frame when they were not in use and were easy to close when needed. On the right side was a recessed set of vertical slats which slid across the windows while the left portion threaded a set of horizontal slats through grooves in the first set. This unique crisscross pattern locked the iron shutters and eliminated any weak areas in the event of an attack.

Asahi stepped into the room where he had found the dead woman. He glanced at her before he focused on sealing the windows. He was almost finished pulling the vertical blinds closed when a swarm of bright red beetles hit the window, cracking the thick pane of glass.

To his horror, more beetles appeared. They slammed into the glass, uncaring that the impact cracked their hard bodies and exposed their vulnerable internal organs. He understood why when a stream of black matter oozed from each dead beetle and was eagerly absorbed by another.

Asahi yanked the shutter closed and secured it. Sconces around the room, fueled by magic, illuminated the darkness. He backed away from the window.

"Ashure!" he yelled.

"I saw them," Ashure grimly replied behind him.

"I suggest that we pick a room and barricade ourselves in," Asahi asserted.

Ashure nodded before he stiffened and paled. Asahi turned to see what Ashure was staring at and stumbled back into the pirate in horror.

Standing in the doorway was the dead body of one of the male Dakty-loi. Asahi's mind flashed to the zombie movies and television programs he had avoided as a child. He had an intense dislike of horror films.

It took him a split second to realize that the blackness in its eyes was the reason it was moving. He muttered a curse. They should have inspected all the bodies for residual alien matter. They were trapped inside the house with zombies, and the longhouse was under siege by the alien-possessed beetles.

"I hope Nali and Pai are safer than we are," he breathed.

"Dead Daktyloi to the left," Ashure grimly answered.

"Do you have your alien killer handy?" Asahi wryly asked.

Ashure uttered a sardonic laugh and pulled his sword out. "I never leave home without it," he replied with a malevolent smile.

"You take the one on the left, I'll take the one on the right," Asahi muttered, surging forward with the gryphon dagger in one hand and his pistol in the other.

CHAPTER 13

*N*ali swerved to miss a tree branch when the electric transport disappeared into a tunnel of trees. Her eyes narrowed in determination. She wouldn't let the Daktyloi driver get away that easily.

Pai noticed what was happening and flew ahead to block the driver's exit. Nali frowned when she noticed the vehicle was swerving left and right, possibly trying to make it difficult for her to land.

"Challenging but not impossible," she muttered to herself as she followed the transport.

She closed the intervening distance, retracted her wings, and landed in the transport's cargo bed. The vehicle fishtailed, almost toppling her. She reached out and grabbed the headrest of the seat in front of her to steady herself before she swung into the back seat.

The transport jerked hard to the right, and she slid at the sudden movement, grunting when she slammed into the door. She grabbed the front seat to keep from being flung out. With her feet against the floorboard, Nali wrapped a stone arm around the Daktyloi's neck and applied pressure.

"Stop the transport now," she ordered.

Horror gripped her when the man's head dropped back, and she saw empty sockets where his eyes should have been. She released her hold and fell back against the seat.

The transport picked up speed, heading straight for the edge of the road and the ravine beyond. The front of the vehicle clipped the top of an enormous boulder, and the transport flipped in midair. Nali felt the sickening sensation of weightlessness.

The alien spewed from the dead man's mouth, disappearing down into the ravine. Briefly pinned to the seat by the centrifugal force of the spinning vehicle, she fought to escape before it crashed. The transport rotated again, and she pushed off the seat when it was beneath her, rising into the air as the vehicle continued to drop like a stone.

Their baggage was flung upward, too. At the edge of her peripheral vision, Nali glimpsed an enormous shadow. It raced by her, plucking the two bags out of the air and tossing them back up onto the solid rock along the cliff's edge. Before she could call forth her wings, the speeding shadow swooped underneath her. She twisted to meet him when she recognized the smell of her favorite hippogriff.

She landed on Pai's back, just in front of his shoulders. Leaning forward, she gripped the feathers surrounding his neck and frantically searched for the alien creature.

"We have to find it," she shouted.

Pai shook his head. "The alien will have to wait. We have a more immediate issue to deal with," he replied, veering back in the direction of the longhouse.

"What's wrong?" she demanded.

"The alien left a gift," Pai grimly replied.

Just then, Nali glimpsed smoke rising from the longhouse—and the surrounding mass of small red insects.

"Goddess!" she hissed in horror.

"What are these things?" Ashure snapped, tossing a bucket of water on the door of the bathroom to extinguish the small flames that were appearing.

"Fire Beetles," Asahi replied.

Asahi ignored Ashure's wince when he fired his pistol, stopping several beetles that were entering through a hole burned through the heavy iron door. He hated using his ammo, but it wasn't like he had a lot of options available at the moment. The damn things had melted the iron like butter in a microwave.

He grimly smiled when Mr. Gryphon snarled and pounced on the tiny droplets of alien DNA that were trying to escape. They had quickly discovered that the Gryphon's sharp teeth held the same magical properties as the dagger.

"Is there any other way to kill them than with that noisemaker?" Ashure growled.

Asahi lifted one shoulder in a shrug. "Do you have a better idea?" Asahi retorted.

Ashure responded with his own shrug. Clearly, he didn't have a better plan. Asahi raised an eyebrow in surprise when Ashure pulled a 9mm handgun from his coat pocket. Ashure fired several shots and touched the beetles' remains with the tip of his enchanted sword.

Asahi stared at Ashure with an inquiring expression. Ashure waggled his eyebrows in return and shot him a grim smile.

"Tonya's father is a police detective on Earth. After he heard how Mike's weapon helped save the day with Magna, he decided it might come in handy for me too. We like going to the shooting range when we visit her parents," Ashure replied.

"Well, unless there is a load of magical clips to replenish the spent shells, we are going to be in some serious trouble very soon. I only have three bullets left," he stated.

"Unfortunately, no. I have two clips minus what I have used," Ashure responded.

Asahi was about to reply when a molten drop landed on his shoulder, sizzling through his shirt and burning the skin beneath. He instantly sidestepped and looked up. Hundreds of tiny holes were appearing above their heads, dripping molten droplets of melted roof. He frantically looked around for a shield.

Ashure cursed when a droplet hit him. They backed as far into the corner as possible to get away from the rain of liquefied metal. Asahi fired his last two rounds and Ashure emptied his clip. It made no difference. They would be lucky to have an additional thirty seconds before the room was swarming with the insects.

"Tonya will be furious with me if these things somehow kill me—and that is after Nali gets done with me," Ashure muttered, looking at him with an expression of resignation.

"Hold on," Mr. Gryphon ordered.

"To what?" Ashure snapped.

Asahi frowned. "What do you mean if they are somehow able to kill you? Can't you die?" he asked.

"Cauldron of Spirits, Keeper of Lost Souls here. Death has a slightly different meaning for me," Ashure wryly replied.

"Hello, Asahi, will you hold on to me? Ashure, you'd better hold on to Asahi. I'm not sure this will work," Mr. Gryphon interjected.

"Not sure what will work?" Asahi asked with a confused frown.

"I'm going to release a burst of magic and try to fly you two out of here. It will be a miracle if it works, but hey, it's worth a try," Mr. Gryphon said.

"By all means, please try," Ashure fervently encouraged.

Asahi reached out and grabbed the small winged lion by the feet at the same instant that the roof collapsed. He closed his eyes and hissed in surprise when a brilliant light flooded the room, and his feet left the ground. He opened his eyes and looked down when he felt Ashure's firm grip on his ankles. The light was so bright, it limited their vision, but it seemed to be keeping the beetles from incinerating them as they escaped. Asahi hung on for dear life as they soared through the gap in the ceiling.

Once they passed through, they continued climbing higher and higher. Below them, millions of beetles fell into the bathroom like Lemmings falling off a cliff, and he gaped in alarm when he saw a mushrooming, orange-red glow rising from the hole.

"Ah, Mr. Gryphon, I think it might be wise to get us away from the house—NOW," he shouted, lifting his head toward the tiny golden lion struggling to stay aloft.

"What do you think I'm trying to do?" the gryphon snarled.

Out of the corner of his eye, Asahi saw a movement in the distance. He sighed when he saw Nali riding on Pai's back. Worry for her briefly overrode his current predicament. It wasn't until he felt a wave of heat rising from the longhouse, heard the tremendous explosion, and felt the resulting shockwave that he realized death might still have a better grip on him than Ashure did.

"No!" Nali's cry was swept away in the wind.

She slid off of Pai's back and fell several feet before she called forth her wings. Shooting forward, she flew as fast as she could until the superheated shockwave knocked her backward. She tumbled several times before she righted herself. Pumping her wings to stay airborne, she stared in horror and fear at the smoking remains of the Daktyloi's longhouse.

Blackened framework, glowing deep red from the heat, reached up from the ground like skeletal fingers begging for help from beyond the grave. The explosion, initiated by the Fire Beetles and intensified by the chemicals stored in the house, had flattened an area of over a hundred yards in every direction. Tall trees lay like matchsticks in a circle around the house. Small fires burned in pockets of the debris. The metal roof lay in twisted sheets, buckled and distorted by the intense heat. The few surviving Fire Beetles sizzled and popped as they exploded in the remains of the once beautiful home.

"No," Nali whispered. "Pai—"

Pai paused beside her, his eagle-eyes searching the ground for Asahi and Ashure.

"He can't be dead, Pai. *They* can't be," she said, her voice catching at the thought.

"Hello! Uh, a little help here, please!" Ashure wildly called out. "Asahi! Nali! Pai!! Is anyone there? I'll even take help from Mr. Gryphon! Anyone?"

Nali took a shuddering breath and swiveled in the direction of Ashure's voice. She was half-laughing, half-crying when she saw them in a tree at the blast zone's edge. Ashure was hanging upside down by his knees with his coat caught on a broken limb, making it impossible for him to pull himself up. Asahi was standing on the stump of a limb that had been sheared off by the explosion. He clung to the tree's trunk. Below him, about twenty feet of the trunk had been stripped of its branches.

As Nali flew straight for Asahi, Pai grumbled, "No worries, Empress. I'll save the King of the Pirates—you know, one of the rulers of the Seven Kingdoms and your long-time friend—even if I *am* only saving him from his jacket." Pai snorted.

~

Nali wrapped her arms around Asahi, holding him like she would never let him go. That was a splendid thing considering that the force of her embrace had knocked him off his narrow perch and she was now the only thing keeping him from falling to his death. She kissed him hard. Her kiss conveying her relief.

When she ended the kiss, she gazed into his eyes. His expression was soft, filled with concern and another emotion that she wasn't ready to deal with at the moment. Her heart was still pounding from fear. She leaned her forehead against his.

"I thought I had lost y—" she whispered, her voice breaking on the last word.

He gave her a quick kiss on the lips. "I did, too," he confessed before he grimaced and peered around them. "Is this—? How long—? Mr. Gryphon!" he bit out.

~

"Yes, I'm fine. No, it was no bother to rescue them and deplete the magic inside me. Thank you for *not* asking. After all, who cares about a poor animated magical object that just saved *the King of the Pirates—* and a human—from certain death?" Mr. Gryphon loudly proclaimed his litany of grievances.

"You will be fine, Mr. Gryphon. Though you really should be resting," Nali soothingly said with a shake of her head.

Mr. Gryphon gave Nali a pained look. "That's fine for you to say, Empress. You have the powers of the Goddess on your side. Me—I'm doomed to a life of pain and suffering because I was given to an unappreciative—"

The unceasing complaints had started nearly a half hour earlier when Asahi found the winged lion stuck in a rivulet of sap oozing down the tree trunk. Asahi finally sheathed the magical dagger despite Mr. Gryphon's vehement protest that he was fine and wanted to remain unsheathed until he knew the threat was over. The resultant silence was blissful.

"Thank you," Ashure muttered.

"You're welcome," Asahi replied with a slight smile.

"So, why are we walking?" Ashure inquired.

"Because the entity destroyed the transport, and Pai is getting too old to carry anyone a long distance, much less both of you," Nali retorted.

"Pai is hardly a frail old hippogriff, Nali. As long as he takes reasonable breaks, I'm sure he could carry Asahi and me in a pinch. If he did, we might get to the mountain in time to save the lives of the unicorns. Could you at least ask him?" Ashure asked.

Nali glared at Ashure. "No, I won't. You know what Pai would say. He would boast how he could carry all three of us with one wing tied to his side. I won't endanger his life any more than I already have," she growled.

"Well, we can hardly walk the entire distance," Ashure reflected.

"We won't. Additional assistance is coming," she replied with a wave of her hand to a group of approaching riders.

"What do you... oh! Those are some of your prized Fire-Breathers! Oh, sweet Goddess, just look at them," Ashure practically drooled.

Nali shook her head and rolled her eyes at the envy in Ashure's voice. "Don't even think about it, Ashure," she warned as they came to a stop and waited for the approaching riders.

Out of the seven horse-like creatures, four had riders. Each horse was far more massive than the largest Clydesdale. The beautiful beasts were midnight blue with long black stripes. Their red eyes flashed as they tossed their heads, and when one of them snorted, small flames flared out from its nostrils. Each horse wore a bridle of ornate silver with matching armor covering their foreheads and chests. As they got closer, Asahi noted that all the riders were male—and they were heavily armed. He blinked in surprised when he noticed his black duffel bag strapped behind an empty saddle on one horse.

They were an intimidating group. Their size and dangerous appearance was so distracting that one of the *last* details Asahi noticed was that each man had a single eye in the center of his forehead. While Asahi knew from his grandfather that cyclops existed, the impact of seeing them in person still sent a shockwave through him. The lead cyclops bowed his head in greeting, his attention focused solely on Nali.

"Severene," Nali greeted as she reached up and tenderly stroked the lead horse's muzzle.

"Greetings, Empress," Severene replied. "Pai arrived with the grave news about the Daktyloi and conveyed your urgent request for transportation."

Severene dismounted and signaled the others to come forward.

As the other men dismounted and stood by their steeds, Nali replied, "Yes." There was a world of grief infused in that single word.

She affectionately stroked the horse's neck. As she did, Asahi noticed how its hair glowed.

Ashure leaned closer to him. "They are magnificent beasts. Strong enough to carry the weight of a cyclops, faster than any land transport, and deadly in battle," he murmured.

"You appear to know a lot about them," Asahi noted.

Ashure breathed a long, envious sigh. "Oh, yes. I had a dozen of the beautiful creatures in my stable for a few months. They are as mean as Drago, the Dragon King, but so amazing that I had to have a few. The damn beasts kept burning down the stable, but it was worth it. I swear, if you harness a dozen of them to a carriage, you could cross the largest isle in less than a day," he said.

"What happened to them?" he curiously asked.

Ashure gave him a wry smile. "They were part of Nali's prized stock. Some rather unscrupulous characters had taken them, so I re-appropriated the steeds, but alas, she requested that I return them to her," he replied.

"Along with a case of his finest brandy as a 'thank you' for allowing the temporary use of her beasts," Pai added behind them.

Asahi turned in surprise. He hadn't heard the hippogriff land. Pai's dark eyes twinkled with amusement.

"She should have been thanking *me* for saving the poor beasts from a miserable existence. I was going to return them to her—eventually," Ashure grumbled.

"There is a quote back home that says, 'no good deed goes unpunished,'" Asahi shared.

Ashure scowled at him. "That is a horrible saying. I hope whoever came up with it met a dastardly demise," he retorted.

"The quote was attributed to several people, including Oscar Wilde, who died a miserable death," he dryly replied.

"Thanks to Severene's gracious assistance, we can now continue on our way more rapidly," Nali cut in.

"My men and I can journey with you if you need our support, Empress," Severene offered.

Nali shook her head. "Thank you, Severene, but what we face is something that not even the might of the cyclops can stop. Please send riders north to warn our people of the danger. The alien is exceedingly powerful and deadly. It would be best if they evacuated to the east until I give word that it is safe to return," she instructed, gripping the reins of a beast.

"We will not rest until everyone has been warned," Severene replied, mounting his steed. "May the Goddess be with you," he added before nodding to the other men.

Asahi walked over to the horse and took the reins Nali held out to him. He looked up at the magnificent beast. The stirrup was almost shoulder high. There was no way he could climb onto it.

He looked around for something to help him mount the beast when the creature tossed its head and knelt. In this position, the stirrups were within reach, barely. He placed his foot on the ring, stepped up, and slid his leg over the back of the magnificent steed.

When the beast rose to its hooves, Asahi's knuckles turned white as he gripped the reins tightly. He felt like a child perched on an elephant. The sound of a soft, sympathetic chuckle caused him look up.

"Have you ever ridden before?" Ashure inquired, guiding his beast over to Asahi.

Asahi pursed his lips and shook his head. "No, not unless you count a Merry-go-round," he curtly answered.

"The ride is as smooth as the wind. If they gallop, lean forward and hold on. There is little else you can do," he advised.

"Ashure, do you have the mirror?" Nali inquired.

Ashure shook his head. "No, it was in the transport," he replied with a grimace.

An expression of disappointment swept over her face. "Then we'll do this the old-fashioned way. We follow the cliff above the ravine and see if we can discover where the alien emerged. Even if we think we know where it is heading, we cannot be sure. I don't want to risk it harming anyone else," she said.

Asahi thought of the horrible death the Daktyloi had faced and how the alien had taken over the Fire Beetles. He touched the sheath at his waist and traced the hardened form of Mr. Gryphon. The dagger—and especially the tiny animated winged lion—was more than an inanimate object. Asahi's most treasured mentor had given him this legacy, and he felt his grandfather's spirit strongly as he followed in Aiko's footsteps. With this dagger, it was almost as if Aiko himself were protecting him in this beautiful, strange world. The thought gave him a measure of peace.

His steed started forward, following Nali and Ashure. They left the road a short distance later, wending their way around the rocks and dense clusters of trees on the slope until they came to the same deep ravine that had swallowed their transport and the alien. Nali turned her steed north along the cliff edge. Asahi looked down. Far below, the rushing river cut through the rock. Somewhere down there was an alien waiting to kill again.

CHAPTER 14

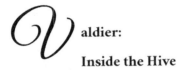aldier:

Inside the Hive

Phoenix paused just inside the cave entrance and wiped the moisture from her face. An exhausted golden seagull landed with a plop beside her and lay on its back, panting. At least they were out of the freezing wind and rain.

She looked over her shoulder. The driving rain, crashing waves, and a thick fog concealed this island off the coast. She shivered and rubbed her arms. It would have been smarter to shift back into her dragon form, but her dragon was more exhausted from their journey than she was.

She breathed a quick sigh of relief when Stardust, the living gold symbiot that was her constant companion, rolled over and flowed upward, wrapping around her shoulders like a shawl. The warmth from her symbiot helped a lot, but they both needed some rest and a chance to get dry.

We not supposed to be here, her dragon nervously whispered deep inside her mind.

"I know, but we had to come. You know that. We have to find out what is causing me—us—to feel...," she shook her head. "How can we understand anything if we can't even describe it?"

Mom and Dad be worried, her dragon muttered.

"I know," she repeated with a sigh.

Well... we here, her dragon grouchily relented. *I cold. Fix it.*

"Stardust, help me gather some driftwood, please," she instructed as she caressed the shimmering swath of gold enveloping her.

Her symbiot reformed as a petite Werecat. Phoenix smiled and began gathering pieces of wood dry enough to catch fire. She would put any that were still damp on top.

It didn't take long to make a nice fire ring of rocks. Stardust padded over, a three-foot piece of driftwood in her mouth, and dropped it on the pile they had collected. Phoenix lined the bottom with several dry pieces of wood before she took the remains of a bird nest that she had found in the cave and broke it apart. She made a loose pile on top of the wood. Next, she took a few pieces of wood in various sizes and created a square around the pile, adding several layers and topping it with a teepee of smaller pieces.

She shifted into her dragon form and blew a long, fiery breath into the center. The remains of the bird's nest quickly caught on fire. In a matter of minutes, she had transformed again and was sitting on a log with Stardust curled up next to her. She absently stroked the exhausted symbiot's head.

"Thank you, Pop," she whispered as she stared into the flames. Her grandfather, Paul Grove, had taught all the dragonlings how to survive in the wild.

Phoenix curled her fingers into Stardust's soft warmth. She hadn't wanted her symbiot to follow her. A part of her had been afraid that something might happen to it on the journey—or worse, something might happen to it here.

The Hive was a special place. She was one of the few who could locate it. Phoenix's grandmother, Morian, was the Priestess of the Hive, and her Uncle Zoran was the ruler of Valdier; they also knew where the Hive was. Most of the others were symbiots. The Hive housed the river that the symbiots came from. All of them would one day return to it.

Phoenix, well, she was a child, and she didn't understand how she knew what she knew or how she did some of the things that she did. Her grandmother thought she was destined to be the next Priestess, but Phoenix didn't think that was the reason. There was something else—something deeper, but she didn't have a name for this feeling that was thrumming inside her.

"Sometimes I feel like I'm going crazy," she whispered, staring at the driving rain outside the cave.

Stardust lifted her head and rubbed it against Phoenix's chest, right over her heart. Inside, she could feel the flame of her dragon trying to warm the chill from her bones—and her spirit. She hugged her inner dragon close to her heart and wrapped her arms around Stardust's neck, burying her face against the symbiot.

"I'm never alone when I have you two with me," she murmured, rubbing her cheek against Stardust. "Let's rest for just a little while before we search the cave."

Stardust melted in her arms and reformed as a sleeping bag next to the fire. Phoenix giggled when the top layer lifted invitingly. She pulled her boots off and placed them next to the log. Surely getting warm, dry, and taking a brief nap after the exhausting flight wouldn't hurt.

It will only be for a little while, she promised her dragon, who was already sound asleep.

She snuggled down against Stardust, lovingly rubbing the soft flow of energy. Her eyelashes fluttered and she yawned. She just needed a few minutes, that was all, just a few minutes of rest.

Aikaterina? she silently called, searching for the Goddess. She hadn't seen her for a long time, and Phoenix was worried.

A soft sigh escaped Phoenix when there was no reply—again. She frowned when she felt a distant tug on her subconscious. Someone was calling for help.

I'm coming. I'll help you, she promised, hoping that whoever it was could hear her.

◟◞

Isle of the Monsters

"We should stop for the night. This is as good a place as any," Nali said as she reined in her beast.

"It isn't the Manticore Inn, but I guess it's better than nothing. It will rain tonight," Ashure said.

"How do you know?" Asahi asked, looking up at the clear sky.

"All pirates are a living barometer. If Ashure says it will rain, it will to rain," Nali said with a sigh.

Ashure grinned. "It helps to know the weather when your life depends on it at sea," he acknowledged.

"In that case, the hut looks very inviting—as long as the roof is still structurally sound," Asahi replied.

"It will be if the dwarves built it," Nali said, dismounting when her steed kneeled.

"I'll take care of the beasts," Ashure volunteered, dismounting.

"Asahi and I will check out the hut to make sure there are no unwanted visitors inside," Nali distractedly replied.

Asahi held on to his steed's thick mane as it lowered itself to the ground. He slid off, quickly untied his duffle bag, and stepped away. Ashure gave him a sympathetic glance when he winced at the sudden discomfort in his thighs and buttocks.

"Ahh, the joys of riding. I suggest asking Nali to give you a massage, otherwise tomorrow morning you may be in worse shape," Ashure quietly suggested.

Asahi tried to forget the suggestion, but couldn't completely erase it from his mind, and it tempted him into a full-blown fantasy. He distracted himself by pulling the duffel bag strap over his head and opening one of the zippered side pockets. He ejected his spent clip, placed it in the bag, and grabbed a full one.

Out of habit, he checked to make sure the clip was full. Satisfied that it was, he slid it into the pistol and double-checked the safety. He holstered the gun and pulled the other empty clip from the cargo pocket of his trousers. Later tonight he would take some time to refill them and do an inventory of his supplies.

"Is everything alright?" Nali inquired, noticing the gun in his hand.

He looked up and nodded. "Yes, hopefully we won't need it," he said.

She nodded. "Yes, perhaps I should...." she said with a wave of her hand at her form.

He nodded. "Excellent idea," he agreed.

The rippling effect of the change sweeping over her no longer surprised him. Truly, it highlighted her beauty. He reached out and caressed her hardened cheek.

She covered his hand with hers and pressed her lips against his fingers. Ashure's humorous monologue with the fire-breathing horses intruded on their intimate bubble, and they both looked over at the Pirate King. He was telling the three beasts about the grand stables that he would build for them and the magnificent fields that would be reserved for their use.

"I better monitor him when this is all over or he'll have half my monsters eating out of his hand and following him home," she said with a rueful shake of her head.

"Ah, he is the Pied Piper of Monsters," he commented.

"Pied Piper?" she asked.

Asahi chuckled. "A children's tale of a man who played a magic flute to lure all the rodents out of town. When the townspeople refused to pay him as promised, he used the same flute to lure their children away," he explained as they walked toward the hut.

Nali frowned. "So, what happened to the children?" she asked.

Asahi shrugged. "There are several versions. Some accounts say the children were never seen again. Other versions state they were returned after the town's people paid the Piper more than the original sum. I'm afraid I don't remember anything else about the tale's history," he said.

"Well, it serves the townspeople right for not paying him his due, but I would have slit this Pied Piper's throat if he had hurt one of them," she replied with an indignant sniff.

"I'm sure he would never have dared to cross you, my beautiful Empress of Monsters. Wait," he said, reaching out and touching her arm before she could push open the door.

She waited for him to pull Mr. Gryphon from his sheath. The winged lion was immediately alert, menacingly circling the hilt of the dagger. The gryphon sniffed the air before he looked up at Asahi.

"What is it this time? Bone-melting slugs? Hostile bees? Monster-eating grasshoppers?" Mr. Gryphon demanded.

Asahi shook his head. "Hopefully, none of those. We are stopping for the night at an abandoned hut. We would appreciate your vigilance as we make sure the hut is safe," he explained.

"Oh, okay," Mr. Gryphon replied with an enormous yawn.

"Are you sure? I mean, if you are still tired…." Asahi dryly inquired.

"I could save you with one eye still closed," the Gryphon retorted with a nonchalant wave of his paw.

Asahi sent a commiserating look toward Nali. "He saves our lives once, and now there will be *no* living with him," Asahi teased.

"Once, *recently*. And it was a truly spectacular save. I outdid myself!" Mr. Gryphon preened.

Nali smothered her laughter with a delicate hand over her mouth. "I'm not stepping into an argument between you and a magical dagger," she teased.

"Can we please get serious?" Asahi chided.

"Somebody's in a foul mood. I'll keep both eyes open," Mr. Gryphon grumpily acceded. "Do you want me to go in first?"

"How about we do this together?" Nali countered.

Asahi pursed his lips. Sometimes he loved this dagger like a long-lost family member, and *sometimes* he wished he had left it glued to the tree sap, thrown it in the ravine, or given it to those ill-tempered, creative goblins! The memory of the Daktylois' horrendous deaths was enough to refocus his mind on the task at hand.

Taking a deep breath, he gripped his newly reloaded pistol in one hand and the dagger in the other. Nali placed her hand against the door and waited for him to give her the go-ahead. He gave a brief, sharp nod and stepped through the door when she pushed it open.

He ducked when several birds, startled by his entrance, swooped toward the open door. Nali ducked too, her hand shooting out to slam the door against the wall. Once the birds were gone, they were able to get a good view of the cabin. It was very rustic, with leaves and the remains of vermin nests scattered across the floor. It contained one sizeable room and a small bathroom off to one side.

"Well, I think we can safely assume the alien did not find this place," he said, holstering his pistol.

"No, but it looks like every rodent known to monsters has," Mr. Gryphon remarked with distaste.

CHAPTER 15

*T*wo hours later, Nali sat in a rocking chair and eased it back and forth in a calming rhythm. Ashure had repaired the rocker with a simple fix-it spell, making it as good as new. A fire, created by magic, burned in the fireplace. Asahi sat next to her in a sturdy chair he had found when they cleaned up the hut. Ashure questioned Mr. Gryphon at the table. The pirate was eager to learn about the golden lion's abilities. All of them, except Mr. Gryphon, had steaming meals in front of them, thanks to Asahi's travel food packets.

As Nali slowly stirred and scooped up a spoonful of chicken and dumplings from the pouch in her hand, she casually remarked, "You know that Ashure is trying to decide if it is worth the trouble to steal Mr. Gryphon from you, don't you?"

He chuckled and looked over his shoulder. "I suspected, though with Mr. Gryphon's caustic personality, he'd probably return the dagger just as quickly," he replied.

He turned back and smiled at her when she softly moaned with pleasure at the taste of the meal, not bothering to hide her enjoyment as she savored the burst of flavors. She hadn't realized that she was famished until the warmth of the concoction hit her empty stomach.

"What is this food called again?" she asked, holding up the pouch in her hand.

"An MRE, Meals Ready-to-Eat. They're not the same level of quality as the food from the Inn, but they are edible," he replied.

"I think they are delicious," she responded with a sigh.

They both looked up at the roof when a flash of lightning lit up the room, followed by the rumble of thunder. Ashure had been right—they were in for a storm. She hoped the fix-it spell Ashure had used on the roof lasted through the night, or they were all going to be cold and wet.

"Ah, only one thing is better than a magnificent storm," Ashure called from behind them.

"What's that?" Nali inquired.

"Dreams of being in my bed with Tonya in my arms," he replied.

"You wouldn't have to dream about it if you hadn't followed me," she pointed out to him.

Ashure pressed a kiss to her temple. "I'm where I should be. Besides, you don't honestly think I'd let you two have all the fun, now do you?" he teased before straightening and releasing an enormous yawn. "I'm tired. The Golden Dagger has volunteered to guard the hut while we rest."

"The Golden Dagger," Asahi repeated as he raised an eyebrow at Mr. Gryphon. "How many names do you have?"

"I get more all the time," Mr. Gryphon said with a wink.

Ashure grinned. "Yes. He mentioned 'Mr. Gryphon' was the most boring of the bunch," he teased. "I wonder who could have named him so?"

Nali smothered her laughter when she saw the pained expression on Asahi's face. She didn't know who was more annoying, the enchanted dagger or Ashure.

With a grandiose wave of his hand, Ashure called forth a hammock, complete with a frame, thick blankets, and a pillow. Nali smiled. If there was one thing she knew about Ashure, it was that he never traveled unprepared, and he liked his creature comforts.

"I'm afraid I can't give you anything as elaborate as Ashure's hammock to sleep on," Asahi ruefully commented.

She laughed. "I have a spell or two of my own. Besides, a hammock for one isn't as nice as it looks," she said. "Tell me about yourself and your grandfather."

He gave her a startled look, then relaxed in his chair, silently staring into the flames. She could see that he was thinking. She continued eating while she waited for him to respond.

"There isn't much to tell—at least about me. I never knew my mother. From the few arguments I overheard, she was a student at the same university my father was attending. She and my father had an affair. Afraid her parents would disown her, she hid her pregnancy from them, had me, dropped me at my father's apartment, and promptly returned to Japan. Several years ago, I discovered she married an affluent older man, had a son, and was content with her life. We met once. She asked that I respect her wish to live separate lives. She does not want me to contact her again. My father was—" He paused and shrugged. "My father wasn't interested in being a father. He liked beautiful women, fast cars, and being anywhere that was away from home. He resented the expectations that came with being a good, dependable son and father. I know that deeply wounded my grandmother. After—after Aiko's disappearance, my grandmother doted on my father—giving him everything he wanted. Unfortunately, it was never enough and it was not always good for him."

Nali leaned over and laid her hand on his arm. "I'm so sorry your father could not appreciate what he had in front of him," she said.

He shook his head. "My father was a weak and selfish man, but he did one thing right. He took me to my grandmother. She died when I was seven—the same day that Aiko returned. Within a week, I lost both my grandmother and father, and gained a grandfather. Aiko—was a kind man, gentle and wise. I can't imagine what it must have been like when he first arrived in your world. I, at least, had the benefit of his knowledge to guide me, while he... while he found himself in a strange world without his wife or young son," he murmured.

"Did he ever tell you how he came to be here?" she curiously asked.

With a slight smile, he said, "Yes. The best way to share it is to tell the story as he told it to me. It all began a little over seventy years ago. My grandparents owned a small restaurant outside of Yachats. One morning, he set off before sunrise in his fishing trawler, hoping to catch enough to support the coming week's menu. Aiko said the ocean was as calm as a lake, not a ripple marred the surface. He had thrown the last line out when the water beneath the boat swirled with color. He said the ocean opened up, and before he knew what was happening, he and the trawler were sliding through a dark hole. Aiko clung to the trawler, terrified at first, then fascinated as the trawler slid through a funnel of water. All around him, he could see the marine life going about their business as if nothing was amiss. But the water began to change the farther he went until..."

"Until... what?" Nali demanded, leaning forward in her seat.

"Until his trawler popped out the other end of the funnel like a bobber at the end of a fishing line, and he found himself near a cove in another world," he said with a smile.

Nali smiled too and waited to hear what happened next.

"Aiko said he waited three days and three nights, hoping the funnel would return. He was afraid to leave his trawler, worried it would disappear," he explained.

"What did he do after the three days?" she asked.

"On the fourth day, driven by thirst, he anchored the trawler, dove over the side, and swam to shore. As he emerged from the surf, a beautiful young witch stepped out of the woods. Her name was LaDonna Fae, and she was looking for a way to sneak off the Isle. She promised she would help my grandfather if he would help her," he said.

"Why would LaDonna need help?" Nali asked with a frown.

Asahi chuckled. "I asked my grandfather that same question. He said she was betrothed to a much older wizard and wanted to live a little before she settled down. So they set sail that very evening—traveling far and wide for years across the Seven Kingdoms," he said.

"This must have been centuries before the Great War and the aliens," Nali reflected. "Did he tell you about their adventures?"

"Yes. He wrote them down in his journal," he replied.

Asahi retrieved his grandfather's journal from his bag. Over the next hour, he shared the adventures of Aiko and LaDonna. With her dinner pouch empty and her stomach full, she placed the dinner accoutrements aside and listened with rapt attention. Several times, Nali wiped away a few tears that escaped from her eyes.

By the end, she was crying for the little boy and her heart was breaking for the old man plunged into an era he didn't understand. Yet, she was thankful for the turn of events that had allowed Aiko to return to his own world so he could be there for Asahi. Listening to Asahi's story made her think of Ashure's magic mirror—the engraving on the back of it—and her own life.

"I buried him next to my Baba and father. That day, I promised him I would find a way to the Seven Kingdoms no matter how long it took," he finished.

"And you kept your promise," she said with a smile.

He gave her a small smile in return. Then his expression shifted to show his resolve. "I've decided I won't be returning to my world," he stated.

Nali took a breath to respond, but before she could, Ashure sleepily commented, "Like she would have let you go back after a story like that—not to mention after you two...." He poked his head out from his hammock to waggle his eyebrows suggestively, sending them a devilish smile that paired well with his wildly mussed hair.

"Shut up, Ashure," Nali and Asahi growled at the same time.

Ashure's snort of laughter as he disappeared inside the hammock again made Nali shake her head. She didn't know how Tonya put up with him. Well, she did, because she knew Tonya loved him. It was impossible not to love Ashure—spirits and all.

Nali bit her lip and smiled at Asahi, sending him a heated look. They both rose from their seats at the same time. Breathing deeply, Nali checked out his physique as she remembered the previous night. One night would never be enough with him. When he touched her, she came alive.

"I'll make our bed while you clean up. You can put all the trash in the fire. The magic will absorb it and convert it to energy," she said.

"I have a thermal blanket in my bag if we need it," he offered.

She shook her head. "I've got this," she reassured him.

Nali tried to keep her focus on what she was doing and not on Asahi. It was difficult. Every movement he made was pure grace, power, and discipline. He was meticulous in everything he did.

She forced her attention away from him and to the wide, long bed. She suspected this hut had once belonged to a huntsman. They were slightly smaller than trolls, each had the same grouchy personality as the goblins, and loved the forest as much as the fairies. While their name made it sound like they were hunters, they were a gentle, solitary race of herbivores who preferred staying out in the woods instead of indoors.

With the whisper of a few simple spells, she created a moss mattress, goose-down feather pillows, colorful silken sheets, and a thick duvet. She looked up when Asahi stopped and admired her handiwork. She quietly laughed at his perplexed expression.

"A few enlargement spells on items already here or those we brought can go a long way. There were pieces of moss from the old bedding. After multiplying and expanding them, we have a mattress. With magic, I can make covers out of a handkerchief from my bag and pillows from feathers left by geese that once nested here," she explained.

"I wonder if I could learn magic," he mused.

She tilted her head and looked at him. "I don't see why not. If you would like, I could teach you some," she offered.

"That would be nice. I need to brush my teeth," he said, looking around for his bag.

"Try this," she suggested with a smile and captured his hand. He frowned when she dropped several blossoms into the palm of his hand. She took one of them and slipped it between her lips. "Place one in your mouth. It has a minty flavor and will fizz for a moment. When it finishes, your teeth will be clean. I picked them from a bush I saw outside when we were cleaning out the hut."

He lifted a flower to his mouth and slipped the fragile petals between his lips. His eyes widened in surprise when the petals dissolved into a refreshing effervescence. He ran his tongue over his front teeth in appreciation.

"I remember my grandfather talking about this, but I never understood how it could work," he admitted.

"What do you use in your world?" she asked.

"An old-fashioned toothbrush with toothpaste," he said.

"We use that here if the bushes are not available. They are fragile and don't last for long. I need to freshen up before I retire," she said with a wave of her hand toward the bathroom.

A flash of lightning and the rolling sound of thunder made her look over at Ashure. His eyes were closed, but she doubted that he was asleep. The Gryphon lay on his chest polishing the dagger with his tail.

She walked to the bathroom and opened the door. It creaked loudly, and she grimaced as she pushed it shut.

"This place definitely belonged to a huntsman," she mumbled, an expression of distaste crinkling her features at the very crude toilet and pump fountain that poured into a bucket used as a sink.

Suck it up, Nali. You've been in worse places, she thought, fruitlessly trying to remember where that place might have been as she filled the bucket and washed her face.

CHAPTER 16

 aldier:
The Hive

Phoenix yawned and slowly opened her eyes. She snorted a laugh when Stardust wiggled underneath her, causing her body to move like she was floating on water. She rolled over onto her stomach and buried her face against the soft, golden body of her symbiot.

"I guess you're feeling better," she murmured.

She looked out of the cave and gently bit down on her bottom lip. Guilt swept through her at the thought of worrying her parents, her sister, and the others, but she knew if she had tried to explain, they would have prevented her from coming. She rubbed her cheek against Stardust.

"There is so much pain, Stardust. I have to help," she whispered aloud.

The symbiot shifted, flowed out from underneath her, and stood up. Phoenix giggled when she found herself staring into the eyes of a floppy-eared dog that resembled the one her mother had loved as a child. She squealed and turned her head when Stardust licked her on the cheek with a long golden tongue. With a lengthy sigh, she caressed her symbiot's muzzle.

"Thank you," she murmured.

Stardust stepped aside and sat down. Phoenix straightened and affectionately smiled at the golden dog as it shook its head and scratched behind its ear, the movement causing its large ears to flop back and forth. Then her stomach growled, and her smile faded. She was so hungry and wished that she had brought something to eat with her.

She reached out and scratched Stardust behind an ear. "You're going to trip over them. You always do when you're in this form. Come on, we better get going. We're in a heap of trouble, and I don't want Mom and Dad to ground us forever. Plus, the sooner we get home, the sooner I can get something to eat," she said.

Phoenix stood and wiped the dirt from the seat of her dark blue pants. The fire was barely smoldering in the pit. A quick survey of the area reassured her it would be safe to let the fire burn out. She and Stardust had used everything that was flammable close by, so there was no chance of it spreading.

She swallowed as she stared into the dark tunnel. Scared—that was what she was feeling. Instead of taking a step forward, she backed away.

Pl—ease, help... me.

The broken, whispered words echoed through her mind. She couldn't tell if it was a man or a woman, only that it was someone who needed her, someone who was begging her not to give up on them. She touched Stardust's head with one hand and covered her pounding heart with the other.

"I... I'm not ready," she said in desperation, her voice barely audible.

This was part of her destiny, Phoenix could feel it, but it wasn't supposed to be this soon! There was a cold lump in her stomach, and she was very much afraid that if she started on this path, she would never see her family again.

She turned to leave but froze when she heard a heartbroken sob. She stood at the Hive entrance, her eyes closed, as she focused on following the mental thread. In her mind's eye, she envisioned the winding path through the tunnels leading to the enormous cavern. A river of gold flowed through the center. She sensed she needed to follow the river.

Phoenix opened her eyes and stared out at the driving rain. Yes, she was afraid, but she couldn't abandon someone who was in trouble. That wasn't who she was.

"Take me to the river, Stardust," she quietly instructed the symbiot.

~

The Isle of the Monsters:

Huntsman's Hut

When Ashure stepped into the hut, Nali was placing her small bag on the ground next to Asahi's black duffle bag, and Asahi was tossing the remains of their breakfast into the magic fire.

"I've saddled the Fire-breathers, and they are ready to go. Last night's storm didn't faze them a bit." Ashure grinned with pride as if they were already his. "I swear you are teasing me with perfection, Nali. After this is all over, you should allow me to purchase a few of them lest I go mad with envy," he said.

"If we make it through this, I'll think about it," she grudgingly replied.

Ashure did a quick jig and grinned. "Finally!" he said, rubbing his hands together.

Nali helplessly smiled at his antics for a moment before a stern expression disguised her amusement. "I said I'd think about it, not that I would agree," she retorted with a shake of her head.

With sparkling eyes, Ashure replied, "Never you fear, my lady, I know very well that you strike a hard bargain." He touched a finger to the side of his nose in a knowing gesture.

Nali looked down at the map spread out on the table in front of her and allowed another genuine smile to curve her lips, this one a little bittersweet. "Well," she murmured, "I love them all." Ashure's expression softened, and she cleared her throat. "Let's move on. We have an alien to kill."

Asahi moved close behind her and looked over her shoulder at the map. "How far do you think it may have traveled?" he asked.

She shook her head. "I'm not sure. A lot depends on how far it got yesterday before the storm—assuming the storm would even affect it," she replied.

"It's likely that the entity is weak at the moment. It left a significant amount of its body matter behind at the Daktyloi's home. If it followed the canyon, it would take even longer," Ashure reflected.

"Especially if it needed to stay in the shadows," Asahi added.

"Nali, I think we—you—should try the Goddess's Mirror again since my mirror is lost," Ashure suggested.

Nali looked up from the map they were studying, frowned, and shook her head. "It is too dangerous. Besides, the Goddess's Mirror doesn't work like your mirror. Sometimes it shows me what I request, but it is just as likely to give me confusing, random images," she said.

"I, for one, do not want a repeat of it coming through the mirror to kill us—or when it found out where we were and tried to bury us in zombies and fire bugs," Asahi pointed out.

"Is it not our goal to battle and defeat this alien? What other choice do we have? We have guessed a likely location the alien may head toward, but we cannot be sure," Ashure argued.

Nali focused her attention on the map again. "You're right," she quietly agreed, her stomach clenching at the thought.

"I'm right?" Ashure repeated before he grinned. "Of course I'm right! Asahi, call the Golden Dagger."

Asahi nodded and pulled the dagger from the sheath. Mr. Gryphon yawned and shook his head, then glared at him with mild irritation.

"What is it now? I was recharging," the gryphon grumbled.

"Our apologies, Mr. Gryphon," Nali briskly replied. "I'm about to use the Goddess's Mirror to see if we can locate the alien, and I need your help," Nali diplomatically informed the lion.

Mr. Gryphon's mane fluffed up, and he stood at attention on the dagger's hilt. "Anything for you, Empress," the lion announced.

"Flattery—nice, Nali," Ashure murmured with an impressed nod.

"Ashure, are you ready?" Nali asked.

Ashure gave her a brief nod and pulled out his enchanted sword. For a moment, his mind went back to when he had received this from Magna, the fearsome Sea Witch. After his and Tonya's wedding, they had gone to see her family, and then popped over to Yachats for a quick visit because he couldn't dismiss the nagging worry that Nali might need help in her battle. No one knew the alien creatures' reasoning better than Magna did—and the first of these aliens would never have been destroyed without her help.

It had taken some fast talking—and Tonya's help—to get around Gabe and Kane. Magna's husbands were *very* protective of their pregnant wife. In the end though, Magna made the sword and gave it to him. He was still in awe of the changes in her appearance since she had been freed from the alien's possession. Centuries of imprisonment had changed her, but there was a reason that no other had survived the alien for a fraction as long as she had—and now her indomitable strength would be turned against the last of these alien invaders. Ashure hoped he would make her proud.

Nali looked at Asahi. He bowed his head, the dagger and Mr. Gryphon ready for whatever might happen. She lifted her hand and called forth the Goddess's Mirror.

"Goddess's Mirror, come to me." A cloud of gold appeared in front of her. It swirled and formed into the mirror. She reached out and wrapped her fingers tightly around the handle. The clear glass reflected her image, and she noticed what the two men must see as well—her worried expression. She drew in a deep breath, held it for a fraction of a second, and released it. "Show me the alien," she instructed.

Immediately, the image in the mirror changed. Energy flooded Nali's limbs, and she felt light on her feet, poised to move quickly and be fierce—ready for battle. The air in the room suddenly felt icy, and the shock to their lungs made it difficult to breathe.

Nali recoiled when the image became clear. A blood-soaked meadow, a river running red, and dozens of slaughtered unicorns littering the once pristine meadow of their mountaintop home. A sob caught in Nali's throat, devastating pain and shock holding her rigid.

Only a single, strong certainty consoled her. An instinctive knowledge came from her affinity and experience with this mirror. "This is the future, not the present or past," Nali reassured her companions in a choked voice. "This is the future," she repeated grimly.

The image shifted to the sad conclusion of a fight between the alien and Xyrie, the oldest and most powerful of the unicorns. The entity wrapped its dark body around the wildly struggling unicorn, and one of its black tentacles snapped the horn from Xyrie's head as if it was nothing more than a thin twig on a tree. Xyrie went limp, her eyes suddenly clouded, and she became still in death.

Darkness obscured the outer rim of the image. For a moment, Nali thought the scene was about to end. It wasn't until she observed the swirling colors in the background that she realized a portal had opened. Through the portal, they could now see a cavern in another universe. It felt both foreign and familiar to her. It was the same cavern the mirror had shown them before, the one with the river of gold, only this time, the river was turning black, and a wave of the same aliens they had been fighting on this world began emerging from the river. There were too many of them to count, wave after wave, a seemingly endless army of them, and after they took form, they began stepping through the portal. The alien they were hunting dropped Xyrie's body and stood to receive them, the horn of the unicorn still in its grasp.

The mirror flitted through more images. One by one, lush worlds filled with abundant life came into view. In each of them they saw the aliens destroying everything, each world became a bleak, lifeless husk.

"That's Earth," Asahi murmured, watching the annihilation of the next world.

Swarms of the aliens covered the blue and white marble. There was no sense of time given to Nali as the wielder of the mirror—only a sense of certainty that this is what would happen if they continued on their current course of actions. When the distinctive Isles of the Seven Kingdoms appeared in the mirror, Ashure's curse startled the group. The scenes increased in speed, showing one Isle after another falling under the onslaught of the alien invasion before everything vanished, and all Nali saw was her own reflection.

"Are we too late to stop it?" Ashure asked grimly.

She swallowed and shook her head. "No, we are not too late. This is what will happen if we do *not* stop the alien," she replied in a strained voice.

"At least we have confirmation of where the alien is heading. We can stop it before it harms Xyrie and the other unicorns," Ashure stated in a harsh tone.

"We need more help," Nali said, looking at Ashure speculatively.

His answering smile was mostly sardonic—she hadn't even wanted *his* help, after all—but his expression also conveyed a hint of his turbulent emotions. She had hoped to do this with no deaths except possibly her own. Yet, even with Ashure and Asahi inviting themselves along, the mirror had clarified that they must do something differently than they had planned. The risk of the alien possessing more people would just have to be mitigated somehow. Right now, Ashure didn't have an answer to that riddle, but perhaps someone else would.

"What do you propose?" Asahi asked.

She straightened. "Ashure should take an Adze and ask the rulers of the other kingdoms for their assistance," she replied.

Ashure whistled in approval. "Well, I'll admit that I like this plan much better than the one where you said, 'I need to do this alone'. So, what is an ass?"

She rolled her eyes and shook her head. "Not an ass—an Adze," she corrected.

"Will I want one when this is over?" he asked, rubbing his hands together.

"Why don't you ask me that question when this *is* all over?" she suggested sweetly.

An uneasy expression crossed Ashure's face. "This isn't like a Bogleech, is it?"

"No-oo, they are much worse if you do not take care. I'll summon one," she said, walking over to the door.

"Can't you just open a portal?" Ashure called behind her.

She shook her head. "I can't open portals. I can only open doorways for myself around the Isle, you know that," she answered as she pulled the front door open and stepped outside.

"What the heck could be worse than a Bogleech?" Ashure muttered under his breath.

Asahi cleared his throat. "The Adze is a vampiric dragonfly that can take over a person if it bites them," he answered.

Ashure looked at him with his mouth hanging open. "You're shitting me, right? Why haven't I heard of them before?" he mused.

"Where did you learn that phrase?" Asahi asked in surprise.

"Tonya," Ashure replied with a brief grin.

"Ah… yes, I thought it sounded a bit too human—and no, I'm not shitting you. My grandfather saw one in action at the market on the Isle of Magic," Asahi remarked before looking up when Nali peered through the doorway.

"I've found one," she called out with satisfaction.

"For once, I'm not all that excited," Ashure muttered before he reluctantly headed for the door.

CHAPTER 17

$\mathcal{A}$ sahi rolled his aching shoulder as he stood back near the hut's door and listened to Nali as she told Ashure how to control the Adze. The creature looked like an enormous dragonfly. On each side of the mammoth red and green body were twin sets of translucent wings and three legs.

The large, oval eyes were four feet long and half as wide. Thick hairs stuck out along its face, body, and legs. From the top of its head to the ground, the Adze was approximately six feet tall. Its wingspan was fifteen feet, and the length of its body was around ten feet. All-in-all, it looked like a flying truck.

"Whatever you do, Ashure, hang on and don't make it mad," she warned for the third time.

Ashure gave her an impatient glare. "I've got it—hang on, don't make it mad," he repeated.

"I've asked the Adze to take you to Drago. He and Orion are the most likely to be able to assist us right now," she replied.

Ashure leaned down from where he was sitting in front of the first set of legs and caressed Nali's cheek. He smiled when she covered his hand with her own.

"I'll be back before you know it," he promised.

She nodded. "Meet us on the mountain as quickly as you can," she ordered before stepping back.

"We will," Ashure promised. Then he gently nudged the dragonfly with his foot, and with a loud chain-saw sound, it lifted off and sped away.

Asahi stepped forward and wrapped his arm around Nali's waist, and together they watched Ashure disappear over the treetops. Nali leaned back against him and sighed.

"He'll be fine," he reassured her.

She absently nodded. "It's not him that I'm worried about. It's what we saw in the mirror. If we don't destroy the alien, it will destroy every-thing, all those worlds—gone," she replied in a soft voice.

She slowly turned in his arms, smiling gently at the tender look of concern in his eyes.

"We'll just have to make sure that doesn't happen," he responded.

She leaned into him and kissed him sweetly. "Yes, we will," she answered. She pulled away and turned to the horses. "If we ride hard, we should be at the foot of the mountains by mid-afternoon."

"You lead, I'll follow," he said.

The fire-breathing horse lowered its massive body so that Asahi could mount it. Wincing when a shaft of pain ran through his shoulder, he waited until the beast stood before he reached up and gently massaged the area.

It had been bothering him since the alien knocked into him after it emerged from the Goblins' underground tunnel. Today the tenderness was particularly uncomfortable. When the beast underneath him bolted forward after Nali, Asahi quickly gripped the horse's long mane.

For the next hour, they followed the river. Then Nali turned northeast into the forest, and their wide path eventually became a road. The horses picked up speed on the even surface, their hooves sending up tiny sparks as they struck the gravel-strewn road. Admiration for the powerful creatures and their Empress suddenly made Asahi feel incredibly lucky to be here with her. He was glad Nali did not go ahead on her own, and he was grateful that she had sent someone for reinforcements.

His thoughts turned to what he knew about Drago, which wasn't much. His grandfather had only seen a handful of any dragons during his travels. Most of his grandfather's information came from what LaDonna had told him. Asahi suspected the tales must have been exaggerated. There was no way Drago, the Dragon King, could be as fierce as told in the stories his grandfather had shared—not with what he knew about Carly Tate! How could a bank teller handle the King of Dragons?

Asahi leaned to the right when he saw several carts heading in their direction—and in no time they passed the travelers. The excited shouts of children in the back of the cart made him look over his shoulder. They were standing and gawking at the Empress and her huge, incredibly fast, fire-breathing horses. It wasn't long before their steeds left the awed travelers far behind.

He returned his focus to the road ahead of them. The forest was thinning, and through the trees, he noticed a mountain range, its tall and jagged peaks capped with snow. It was beautiful. On the slope below them, the white-water river flowed into a long, narrow lake that contained quite a few rocky, tree-covered islands of various sizes and shapes.

Asahi reined his mount to a walk and followed Nali as she guided her mount off the road. Their horses cautiously descended the steep slope, then stopped on a grassy knoll.

"What is it?" he inquired.

She glanced over her shoulder at him. "We will have to travel by boat the rest of the way."

Asahi's horse knelt, and he slid off. He unstrapped their bags from the saddle and asked, "What about the horses?"

"They know the way home," she replied as she caressed her mount's jaw.

She secured the reins on the saddle and he did the same. When Nali gave the two fire-breathing horses a quiet command, they whinnied, then turned and retraced their steps toward the path above. Asahi watched them for a moment before he turned back to Nali.

"How will we find a boat?" he asked, picking up the bags and securing them across his back.

"There will be one," she replied with confidence.

Asahi smiled and didn't question her further. If she said there would be a boat, there would be a boat.

They set off down a narrow path that looked more like an animal trail than a footpath. It zigzagged downward and straightened as the ground flattened out near the lake.

It wasn't until they rounded a rock outcropping that Asahi saw a faint wisp of smoke rising from the chimney of a cozy-looking hut. He counted five boats turned upside-down along the rocky shore and one pulled up on the beach. The sound of animals drew his attention toward the hut. A boy who appeared to be about eight years old was tending to the sheep that were grazing nearby.

"Father! Father, we have company," the boy excitedly called as he ran to the hut.

The door opened, and a man who seemed to be about Asahi's age stepped out. The man jerked back a step in surprise, then he hurriedly brushed his beard with his hand and wiped off the front of his shirt. Given the way he hastily chewed and swallowed, they must have interrupted him while he was eating.

"Empress, I was not expecting...." The man cleared his throat and began again. "Welcome to my home, Empress. 'Tis a great honor to be in your presence." He bowed low, then stood up straight with a curious smile.

"Greetings, Micco. How is Jeanetta?" she politely greeted.

"Fine... she is doing very well, thank you for asking. She's taken our daughter to visit her sister on the Isle of Magic," he replied.

"That is nice." She smiled. "I have need of one of your boats," she said.

Micco nodded. "Anything that you need, Empress," he eagerly responded, starting toward the boats on the beach. "Bishop, come help me," Micco ordered.

"Yes, Father," the boy said, flashing a smile at them.

"I'll assist you," Asahi said.

He followed the man and the boy down to the boats. In minutes, one of the boats was in the water. Asahi helped Nali into the boat and handed the bags to her. She stowed them in a long wooden box in the center of the boat.

"This is the sturdiest boat I have. She'll handle well for you. There is a tarp in case it rains or you need protection from the sun. All you have to do is pull the lever and it will unfurl. Jeanetta embedded a fine wind spell into the sail. You'll fly along the lake," Micco said with an expression of pride.

"Mother's spells are powerful," Bishop boasted.

Nali chuckled appreciatively. "Then we will fly across the water like one of my airships," she said.

"Oh, the ones with the Thunderbirds? I saw them once when we went to the Palace City. Mother took me down to the docks so I could watch them," Bishop breathed out with envy.

"The next time you come to Palace City, let me know, and I will arrange a tour of one of my ships for you. You can also visit the aviary where we raise the Thunderbirds," she offered.

"Oh, Father, can we go tomorrow?" Bishop implored, looking at his father.

Micco laughed and shook his head. "Not until your mother and sister return. Who would mind the boats and the livestock?" he pointed out.

Bishop looked disappointed for a moment before his expression brightened. "Mother and Sophie will be home in two weeks. That isn't long to wait," he said.

"No, it isn't long," his father agreed.

Micco gave the long oar to Asahi and held onto the bow rope as Asahi stepped over the side, then tossed the rope to him and pushed the boat out into deeper water.

"With the Goddess's blessing, I'll return your boat in a few days," Nali called out.

"Safe journeys, Empress," Micco replied.

Nali spun the wheel of the twenty-foot boat, turning the bow to the north. Asahi pulled the ropes, raising the sail. Memories of sailing off the coast of California with his grandfather came to mind as he did the task.

The sails filled the moment he tied off the rigging, and Asahi held onto the mast as the boat shot forward through the calm waters.

He moved to the stern of the boat where Nali was standing at the wheel, and remarked, "That is some spell his wife cast on the sail!"

Nali smiled. "Jeanetta is descended from the Isle of Magic and the Isle of the Sea Serpent. She has a special affinity for magic and water," she explained.

He looked back at the hut. It was now a speck on the horizon. "Where is Micco originally from?" he asked.

She grinned mischievously. "Micco's a changeling. His and Bishop's appearance were an illusion to make you more comfortable. Most changelings live on the islands in this lake or along its banks like Micco," she said.

"That is how you knew there would be a boat available," he surmised.

She nodded absentmindedly, her focus fixed ahead, and it was then that Asahi noticed a movement along the shore of a nearby island. A surge of excitement swept through him. He held his head still, remembering what his grandfather had told him about the best way to see a fairy—don't look directly at them.

All of Asahi's attention was on his peripheral vision as they passed the island—and the blurry movement became clear. Two teenage girls stood ankle deep in the water, their skirts tucked in at the waist, staring at them with curiosity.

"I always thought fairies would be smaller," he mused.

"There are many types of fairies," she responded.

I still have much to learn, Asahi thought. He looked thoughtfully at Nali.

Her gaze remained focused on the water in front of them. This gave him an opportunity to study her profile. He would never tire of looking at her. The memory of her body intimately pressed against his, his arms wrapped around her, and his hand cupping her breast was enough to cause his cock to harden.

This physical reaction to a mere memory was a first for him. He usually prided himself on his self-discipline, but now he wanted to embrace his lack of it. He understood that this battle may not go well and that one of them, if not both, could perish.

Asahi slid his arm around her waist, and the troubled look in her eyes disappeared. She gave him a pleased smile, and he pressed a light kiss on her lips.

"We will win this war, Nali," he quietly vowed.

Moisture clouded her eyes for a moment before she blinked it away. Taking a deep breath, she locked eyes with him.

"Asahi," she breathed. The space between them became charged with the depth of their emotions. Then she looked away and shook her head. Instead of saying more, she affectionately rubbed her cheek against his and held him close.

A sense of contentment swept through Asahi. The emotion in her eyes when she looked at him was all that he needed to know. She was falling in love with him. It was an emotion that he understood all too well—because he felt the same way for her.

CHAPTER 18

aldier:

Royal Palace

Creon Reykill paced back and forth in the living room of his family's apartment in the palace. Fear knotted his stomach. Outside, it was growing dark, and his youngest daughter still had not returned home. He stopped pacing and turned to his oldest twin daughter.

"Spring, when was the last time you saw Phoenix?" Creon asked.

He kept the worry out of his voice as much as he could. Spring wiped a tear from her cheek, sniffed, and twisted her hands in distress. He walked over to her and gave her a comforting hug.

"Late this morning. We were in the gardens working on a fresh flower bed. She—she said she was going for a flight and would search for some more seeds for my garden," she said.

They both turned when Carmen strode into the living room. "Stardust is gone, too. Nothing else is missing," she said in a strained voice.

Creon knelt to be eye-level with his daughter. "Spring, it is important that you remember. Did your sister say where she was going?" Creon gently coaxed.

Spring shook her head. "No," she replied as she wiped another tear from her cheek.

Carmen walked over and wrapped her arms around her daughter's thin shoulders. Creon's heart melted at the sight of his mate and their oldest daughter. They looked so much alike with their blonde hair and delicate features. He covered Carmen's hand with his own when she looked at him with fear and worry on her face.

"We'll find her," he promised.

"There *was* something else," Spring suddenly remembered, looking at him with a troubled expression.

Carmen stepped around Spring and stood next to Creon. She still clung to his hand, and they both looked at Spring with the wild, desperate hope of parents with a missing child. Spring was worrying her bottom lip with her teeth. The uncertainty on her face tore at him. She was always very protective of Phoenix.

"What is it, sweetheart?" Carmen encouraged.

"For the last few days, Phoenix has been acting different," she confessed.

Creon frowned. "What do you mean, honey?" he asked.

Spring clasped her hands together and held them to her chest. "She's been really distracted. I kept asking her what was wrong, but she always said that everything was alright—but, I know that isn't true. Sometimes... sometimes I can see what *she* sees, what she does—when I'm not actually there with her," she admitted, bowing her head.

Carmen's soft gasp of surprise echoed his own. They had wondered if their twin daughters would have the same type of connection that the fabled Valdier Twin Dragons did. Now they knew.

"What did you see?" Carmen asked.

Tears coursed down Spring's cheeks. "I heard a voice—begging for help. I didn't think it was real. It woke me up last night. I thought it was Phoenix. She.... Phoenix was muttering in her sleep. She kept telling whoever it was that she would help them," Spring said in a barely audible voice.

"Who needs help? Where was this person?" Creon urgently demanded.

Spring shook her head. "I don't know. The voice was so faint, and I only saw a glimpse of the cave before Phoenix woke up," she said.

Carmen gently gripped Spring's arms. "What did the cave look like? Try to remember, honey. Any little detail can help us find your sister," she encouraged.

Spring closed her eyes. A tiny frown furrowed her dainty brow as she concentrated on the memory. She licked her lips before she spoke in a halting voice.

"It... it's on an island with lots of rocks. The... the cave is dark... and cold. I saw... there were stairs leading up to a doorway, but... but there was nothing on the other side. It was a doorway to nowhere."

"What else did you see, Spring?" Creon murmured.

Spring opened her eyes and stared into his. "A river. There was a river, only it wasn't like any river I've ever seen before," she whispered.

Creon got a queasy feeling in the pit of his stomach. He took a deep breath, lifted his hand and cupped Spring's cheek while Carmen tenderly stroked her hair.

"What was different about the river?" he asked.

Spring stared at him with wide, confused eyes. "It was made of gold—just like Little Bit, Stardust, and Harvey," she answered.

"Creon," Carmen whispered, her own eyes filling with tears.

He shook his head and stood. "Stay with Spring," he said.

"What are you going to do?" Carmen asked in a tight, emotion-filled voice.

He caressed Carmen's cheek with one hand and Spring's with the other. A sense of resolve filled him. He wouldn't let anything happen to his family.

"I'm going to bring her home," he promised.

Isle of the Monsters:

Lake of the Sirens

"Asahi, can you take the wheel?" Nali asked nearly an hour into their journey.

"Of course," he replied.

She stepped aside when he reached for the wheel. Unable to resist the urge, she slid her hand across his lower back when she moved away. Heady pleasure coursed through her at the smoldering look in his eyes.

A movement in the water next to their vessel reminded her of why she wanted Asahi to take over the steering. She crossed the deck to the bow and sat down. Holding onto a thick cleat, she leaned over and looked into the clear water. Dozens of Water Sirens danced in the boat's wake.

She closed her eyes and listened to what they were saying. The whispered words sounded like a song. Their almost childlike voices were threaded with worry and fear.

"The darkness is coming, Empress."

"Where did you see it?" she asked.

"It has taken over one of the giant eels at the mouth of the lake. Even as we speak, it moves along the bottom of the lake, heading for the Mystic Mountains," the sirens responded.

"Warn the changelings," she instructed.

"They know and have taken refuge. We will try to slow it down," they replied.

"Be careful. Do not let it near enough to touch you," she warned.

"We will be careful, Empress," they promised.

Nali watched the sirens swim away from the bow of the boat and disappear back into deeper water. Haunted by the images of blood and death revealed in the Goddess's Mirror, she stared at the mountains ahead of them. She was afraid—not for herself, but for her people, for her world, for the many worlds out there that would perish if they failed.

She brushed her hand across her cheek. Looking down at her fingers, she stared at the moisture. Another droplet landed on her palm, and she realized that she was crying.

She took a shuddering breath and curled her fingers into a fist. She looked up in determination at the mountain shrouded in clouds. They would reach it in another couple of hours.

"Return as quickly as you can, Ashure. I need you," she whispered into the wind.

∾

Isle of the Dragons

. . .

Ashure wobbled on the Adze's back for a moment before he straightened. He pressed his booted feet against its side to keep from sliding off, so of course, the damn thing tried to buck him off again. If he survived this flight, he was going to have a serious talk with Nali about her transportation choice.

He breathed a sigh of relief when he glimpsed the Isle of the Dragons' jagged mountains ahead. Now, if only he could get this infernal creature to land without trying to kill him. His butt hurt, his back hurt, his head pounded with the same cadence as the rapid beat of the creature's wings, and his arms ached from holding on so tightly. To top it off, he was covered in salty sea spray because the huge bug was flying too close for comfort above the rolling ocean waves. Also, the constant wind was seriously irritating his skin.

As they neared the cliffs, the Adze suddenly changed direction, climbing in an almost vertical flight path up the cliff's sheer rock face. Ashure uttered a loud curse, wrapped his arms around the dragonfly's neck, and held on for dear life. He yanked his right arm back when the flying vampire tried to bite him, making him almost lose his seat —again.

They crested the top of the cliff and kept flying higher. It wasn't until the Adze swerved to the left that Ashure realized it was aiming for a balcony near the top of the palace. He gaped in alarm when he noticed Drago's tall frame standing in the precise spot where the evil vampire-devil dragonfly was heading.

"Mercy, this beast *is* trying to kill me," he muttered a second before the dragonfly suddenly stopped in midair, flipped up its backside, and sent him flying.

For a second, Ashure almost wished he had a way to capture the look of stunned disbelief on Drago's face. Unfortunately, he wouldn't have had the time even if he wanted to take a photo of the moment. He imagined his own face reflected the same shocked surprise.

"What—?" Drago hissed as the breath was knocked out of him.

Ashure winced as he collided with Drago, and the impact slid them across the floor. In the few moments before Drago recovered his wits, Ashure debated whether he was grateful for this development. On the one hand, being this close to the enraged King of Dragons would probably not be a pleasant thing; but on the other hand, the fearsome dragon-shifter had softened his landing!

"Hi, Carly!" Ashure greeted, flashing her a smile from his perch on top of her mate as they slid past her and through the balcony doors.

"Ashure?" Carly called in disbelief as she followed them into the room.

Drago loudly grunted when he came to a sudden stop. Ashure looked down at Drago and grinned. He was alive!

"Get off of me," Drago growled.

"Thank you, my friend, thank you for saving me! I could kiss you for that," Ashure passionately declared, as he patted his chest over his thundering heart.

"I'd have to kill you if you tried. Now move," Drago retorted.

This time, he was the one who did the grunting when Drago gripped his arms and roughly pushed him aside. Ashure rolled and hit his skull on the bedpost. Sitting up, he rubbed his head and added the spot to his growing list of aches and pains.

"What the hell are you doing here?" Drago demanded, rising to his feet.

Ashure looked up at Drago, his demeanor suddenly grave. "Nali sent me. We need your help," he said.

The irritated expression on Drago's face instantly changed to one of concern. He held out his hand. Ashure gripped it, wincing when he was pulled off the ground with a single swift yank.

"What happened?" Drago demanded.

Ashure looked at Carly before returning his attention to Drago. "It's the last remaining alien still free. It has found a way to destroy all of our worlds. We need the rulers of the Seven Kingdoms, and we are running out of time," he cautioned.

"Then it is a good thing that Orion is already here," Drago grimly replied.

~

Thirty minutes later, Ashure stood in the Dragon Palace's great hall. Drago had departed with a gruff comment that he needed to get something and would return as soon as possible. Ashure turned when he caught the sound of approaching footsteps. A moment later, Orion entered the room alongside Theron, Drago's Second-in-Command.

"Ashure, Theron said you were here on an urgent matter," Orion said by way of greeting.

He grimly nodded. "The alien is on the Isle of the Monsters. Nali needs our assistance," he said.

"When did it appear?" Orion asked.

Ashure pursed his lips before he reluctantly answered. "The morning of my wedding," he admitted.

Surprise swept across Orion's face before he concealed it. "Tell me everything," he said.

Ashure explained everything that he could, including Nali's reluctance to ask for help and what the Goddess's Mirror had revealed to them. He was finishing the story when Drago reappeared carrying a large round metal hoop.

He raised an inquiring eyebrow when he noticed cobwebs clinging to the other man's long black hair. Drago impatiently reached up and brushed them away, then held the hoop out to Theron. Ashure frowned when he caught sight of the etchings on it.

"Is that a...?" he breathed.

Drago gave him a sharp nod. "A Time-Space hoop," he said.

Ashure looked from the hoop to Drago's face. "Where did you get one of those? I thought they were destroyed by the ancients a millennium ago," he said.

"So did I," Orion muttered.

Drago shrugged. "I found it when I was a boy in the ruins of Arkla, the original stronghold of the dragons," he said in a nonchalant voice.

"You should have left it there, Drago," Ashure said.

"I've heard they were unpredictable, and that is why the Time Wizards destroyed them. Do you know how to use it?" Orion warily inquired.

"Well enough to not get us killed—I hope," Drago replied.

Ashure shook his head and held a hand up. "Oh, no. I'm telling you, those things are a lot worse than unpredictable. They were created with dark magic that pulls its power from the twisted recesses of a wizard's soul. I've heard tales of young men using them, only to come out the other side with their manhood shriveled. I'm telling you, a bunch of dried-up old wizards who couldn't get it up anymore probably created them out of jealousy. I promised Tonya I'd return to her. I want to do that with all my body parts intact and working," he snapped.

"Don't be such a wuss," Drago growled.

Ashure shook his finger at Drago. "I know what that means. I'm married to a human too. I'm not a wuss. I'm cautious—especially when it comes to my 'man-love.' Neither of you has anything to worry about. You two already have kids. I don't. I need to consider all the little pirates Tonya and I might have one day," he defended, unconsciously dropping his hand to cover his crotch.

"He's a wuss," Orion dryly said, looking at Drago.

"It was more fun when you two were trying to kill each other," Ashure muttered.

Orion snorted and shook his head. "How does it work, Drago?" he asked.

"With a lot of luck and the right spell. All we need to do is get to the Isle of Magic. Marina can help us from there," Drago replied.

Ashure warily watched as Drago turned over the Time-Space hoop and read the etchings inscribed on it by the ancient Time Wizards. His stomach nervously clenched when the center went from crystalline to solid black.

I think riding a vampire-dragonfly and facing an evil alien may be the least of my worries, he thought a split second before Drago moved in close and dropped the hoop over the three of them.

CHAPTER 19

*I*sle of the Monsters

Nali took over the helm. With a quiet command, she ordered the enchanted sail to slow their speed. A heavy fog swirled over the water, and she knew it would stay that way until they reached land. They would complete the rest of the journey at a frustrating crawl.

"What is this?" Asahi asked, standing beside her.

She spun the wheel to the left, and the bow veered a fraction of a second before an enormous boulder came into view. The boat passed within mere inches of the massive rock that would have demolished the vessel if they had hit it head on.

"Furl the sail. The current will take us from here," she instructed.

He nodded and hurriedly released the rigging holding the sail up. The gentle lapping of water against the hull sounded loud in the thick vapor enclosing them. Once again, Nali marveled at the fact that

Ashure had navigated these treacherous waters without dying when he was nothing more than a child.

She nodded to Asahi when he rejoined her. "This is magic. The fog is alive. You'll see shapes, hear voices, but you must not believe them. The things you perceive as real are not. They are created by spells that will try to pull you from the boat. If you fall into the water, you'll drown," she cautioned.

"What is it protecting?" he murmured, gazing around them.

"The Gateway to the Goddess," she softly replied.

He frowned. "Will the others be able to get through safely?"

She nodded. "Ashure knows what to do."

"He's been here before," he guessed.

"Yes, a long time ago. Trust me, this is not a journey that you forget," she said, turning the wheel to avoid another enormous boulder.

~

They had only been in the fog for about twenty minutes, but the harrowing journey already seemed much longer. Asahi had taken to monitoring the sides and using one of the long oars to push away from the rocks.

After turning back to warn Nali of another small boulder ahead, he froze in shock. She was gone!

"Nali?" he called into the fog.

"It's all your fault!" a man growled at him.

Asahi recoiled at the familiar voice.

"Father?" he said in a hushed whisper, shock evident on his face.

Hinata angrily stepped out of the fog as if he had been behind a curtain. Asahi stiffened in disbelief.

"If you hadn't been born, I could have left without feeling guilty. I could've had a life!" his father shouted.

Asahi shook his head. "Whatever you are, you aren't real," he replied in a tense voice.

The angry visage of this father disappeared like a puff of smoke. Asahi took a deep breath of the cool mist. The sudden appearance of his father, even though he knew what he saw wasn't real, had shaken him.

"Asahi," his grandfather's soothing voice came from the mist.

Asahi shook his head and closed his eyes. This wasn't real. His father and grandfather were dead.

He opened his eyes, startled when an icy hand on his shoulder sent a chill through him. In front of him stood a youthful version of his grandfather. Aiko looked much the same as the day he had reappeared.

"You are not real," he forced out between gritted teeth.

"Come with me, Asahi," Aiko replied in a mesmerizing voice. "Your Baba is waiting for us. She misses you."

Asahi involuntarily leaned toward the ghostly apparition, his mental resistance wavering. Aiko's hands multiplied, changing from two to four, then six. They gripped his arms, hands, and shoulders, but he stumbled on something when the phantom of his grandfather pulled him forward. That moment of distraction allowed his mind to clear, and he looked down at the obstacle near his feet.

Rope. I'm on a boat... with Nali. Nali!

He needed to focus on her. She had warned him this would happen. He shook his head to clear it and gripped the boat's gunwale.

"You are not real," he repeated.

The figure dissolved in front of him. He swayed when the boat veered to the left and he quickly gripped the rigging that held the mast in place. All around him, ghostly figures from his past moved in and out of his periphery. It was as if the fog were accessing his memories, trying to find the one that would entice him the most to let go of reality.

"Asahi, help me!" Nali implored in a desperate, terrified voice.

He instinctively turned in the direction of her voice and gasped in horror when he saw her being devoured by the alien. The liquid enemy was moving up her legs to her waist. She held her arms out to him.

"Asahi, please… save me," she choked.

He reached for her only to realize that he was leaning out over thin air. The boat's edge caught him at the knees, and he lost his balance. He exhaled quickly in alarm, twisted, and grabbed the rigging. The rough rope slipped in his grasp, causing a painful rope burn. He gritted his teeth and held on as the upper half of his body tipped over the side.

"Asahi, let go, boy," his grandmother pleaded with bewildered hurt. "Come back with us."

A wave of calm washed through him, and he focused on the rope he was holding. Then he swung his left arm up and captured a second rope. His muscles strained as he pulled himself up and swung one leg over the side.

He was precariously hanging by one leg outside of the boat, however, the ropes were supporting the majority of his weight, and he almost lost his grip on them when the boat suddenly rocked. He looked at the bow of the boat when he heard wood scraping against rock. Nali had steered away from it, but there were only a few inches between the boat and the boulder. If he hung suspended where he was for much longer, it would crush him.

Asahi pushed his legs against the hull enough to get some leverage, then he used his weight to fall into the boat. He lay panting on the deck and watched as they glided past one of the largest boulders they had passed so far. His stinging palms reminded him that he was still alive and that they were not out of this yet.

"Asahi, are you alright?" Nali called out.

He gritted his teeth and slowly rose to his feet. He flexed his fingers before he turned in the direction of her voice. The fog thinned for a moment, and he spotted her. She was standing at the helm and was holding one arm out to him. Relief swept through him when he clasped her warm, solid hand.

"I'm fine. How much longer before we get out of this?" he asked.

She tightened her grip on his hand. "Not too much farther. Stay close to me. It worried me when I couldn't see you," she answered in a tense voice.

He released a strained chuckle. "I was trying to make sure that Micco will get his boat back in one piece," he teased.

He scanned the fog-enshrouded deck. The ghostly figures continued to move in and out of his sight, but they appeared to be wary of coming too close to Nali.

Nali shivered, so he stepped up behind her and rubbed her arms. She leaned back against him, and he wrapped his arms around her waist. They remained silent, each lost in their own thoughts, as the current pulled them closer to their destination.

∾

Isle of Magic

. . .

Ashure slowly opened his eyes and clutched his crotch to make sure his cock was still there. He sighed in relief when he confirmed that it was. He just hoped it was still in working order. If it wasn't, he would have a lot of explaining to do to Tonya—after he killed Drago, of course.

His relief turned to horror when he took in the devastated state of their surroundings. Beside him, Orion lowered his trident and barked out a warning to be ready for battle while Drago stepped out of the Time-Space hoop and shifted into his dragon form. Ashure quickly pulled out his enchanted sword.

"What happened here?" Orion murmured.

Ashure slowly turned in a circle. Smoke still rose from the remains of huts and shops in the village. The grotesque remains of the villagers lay scattered amidst the ruins. Ashure and Orion stepped out of the hoop.

"Orion, watch out!" Ashure yelled when three black shapes emerged from the shadows.

The creatures were dogs, but the alien's liquid form rolled over their bodies. Orion and Drago turned in unison. Orion struck the closest animal with his trident while Drago released a superheated breath of dragon fire on the other two.

The alien-controlled animals screeched with fury and pain. Ashure surged forward, staying out of Orion and Drago's line of fire, and struck each creature with the enchanted sword. Each flash of brilliant light nearly blinded him as he pierced their bodies.

He stepped back and warily looked around. Everything was dead or dying. The trees that remained standing were drooping as if in sorrow.

"The attack has begun. We are too late," he said, his voice reflecting his shock.

Tonya....

"I have to get back to my kingdom," Ashure said, his voice rising with panic.

"Ashure behind you!" Orion shouted.

He twisted, bringing up his sword as Marina's father, Ariness, stepped out from behind an overturned cart and aimed a long wizard's staff at him along with a shouted spell. Fiery explosions rained down—in the area *next* to Ashure—causing the tangle of thorny vines that had been reaching for him to hastily retreat into the shadows.

"My lords, you are alive," Ariness said in a trembling voice.

"Ariness, what happened?" Ashure demanded.

"It isn't safe here. The spell won't scare the entity away for long. Come with me. Those of us that survived the initial attack have built a temporary stronghold," Ariness said. A glaze of fatigue and despair coated the wizard's eyes, and his shoulders sagged with exhaustion.

Orion and Drago warily looked at Ariness before they motioned for him to go ahead of them. Ashure followed the old wizard, with Orion and Drago close behind.

"Ariness, I don't understand. What happened? How can the alien have spread so quickly?" Ashure demanded.

Ariness glanced over his shoulder before refocusing on the path ahead of him. "Quickly? We've been under siege for over a month," he replied.

"A month!" Orion exclaimed.

Ashure's stomach twisted. How could this have been going on a month with none of the other kingdoms knowing about it? Surely King Oray or Queen Magika would have sent a warning when they returned from his and Tonya's wedding celebrations.

He swallowed. Seeing this kind of devastation in the mirror and in real life were two very different experiences. He wondered if, because they had intended to save time by using the portal, the thing had instead stolen time from them.

Ariness stopped and pointed his staff down the path, searching the area carefully before he nodded. Ashure frowned, trying to understand if there was a threat ahead of them.

"We placed a concealment spell around the area. The aliens can sense our magic and use it against us. They have already killed most of us. When I create an opening, we must move quickly," Ariness instructed.

"I'll go last," Drago stated with a menacing growl.

Ariness nodded. *"Open concealment,"* he intoned.

A powerful ball of changing colors glowed at the end of his staff for a moment before it shot outward. Ashure, Ariness, and Orion sprinted forward with Drago, still in his dragon form, following closely. They were almost to the entrance when Ashure heard a loud buzzing noise behind them. Glancing over his shoulder, he glimpsed a swarm of black insects approaching them, bringing with it a sense of déjà vu from the Daktyloi hut.

Drago twisted and released a long fiery breath of dragon fire at the swarm. A vine erupted out of the ground in front of Ashure. He quickly sliced through it just as Orion blasted another vine. They were running out of time.

"Drago, get your ass in here," Ashure yelled, swinging the blade through more vines.

"Go!" Drago roared as the swarm engulfed him.

Ashure stumbled back in shock when he caught the look of fury and resignation on Drago's face. The Dragon King's eyes and body glowed with his dragon's internal fire. Orion grabbed Ashure's arm and pulled him through the opening a split second before Drago's body ignited into a fireball of super-heated dragon fire.

Through the concealment, he and Orion stood in stunned silence as the tiny flakes of red-hot ash floated to the ground. Drago had destroyed the alien-possessed insects and vines, but killed himself in the process. The King of the Dragons was dead.

CHAPTER 20

 he Hive:
Valdier

Stardust, wait up for me, Phoenix breathlessly called through her connection with her symbiot.

Ten minutes earlier, she had finally given up trying to keep up with Stardust in her two-legged form and shifted into her dragon. It was actually easier because her eyesight was better, and she now had four legs instead of two. Unfortunately, there was not enough room for a dragon to fly, not even one as petite as she was. She followed the swiftly moving glowing symbiot as it weaved in and out of the labyrinth of tunnels.

No worry, we almost there, her dragon said.

We should stick together! Phoenix's unease filtered into their connection, and her symbiot slowed down enough to let her catch up. Even with her symbiot close by, she worried that they were about to face something unknown and scary alone. Maybe she should have told her family about the voice. She could have convinced them to come with her—but even she thought it sounded weird.

What would I have said? That I'm hearing a voice calling to me, asking me for help? She sighed.

She was already so different from the others. No one else saw Aikaterina when she came to visit. The thought of the beautiful alien that the others believed was a Goddess sent a wave of sadness through her. It had been so long since she'd last seen Aikaterina.

We here, her dragon murmured.

They paused in the entrance to an enormous cavern. It was just like the one she had seen in her dreams. She shifted into her two-legged form and walked around, exploring the cavern in awe.

Twin pillars, carved with images of different star systems and symbols, graced each side of the entrance. She studied each pillar in wide-eyed amazement. Her heart pounded when she realized that she actually understood what the symbols meant. She didn't know how or why, but she knew that they were star charts to other worlds.

Stardust padded on silent feet beside her as she ambled along the wide path. Massive slabs made of granite and limestone bordered the cavern. Along the walls were more pillars. Each pillar engraved with what appeared to be different star charts and symbols, also had a flat surface on top. The flat surfaces looked like platforms.

"Gateways," she whispered as a vision of golden figures standing on them formed in her mind.

She absently stroked Stardust's golden head and stepped around a large rock. She gasped when she saw a river of gold in front of her. A shiver of awareness ran through Stardust.

"This is where you came from," Phoenix murmured.

Stardust looked at her. Images flashed through her mind. It took her a moment to realize that they were Stardust's memories. She looked at the river.

"This is the river of life for the symbiots," she said with awe.

Fascinated, she walked over to the river's edge and sank down onto her knees. She stared at the moving gold liquid for several minutes before she bent forward and ran her fingers through it. Warmth surrounded her fingers, and she giggled at the pure joy she felt in the golden flow.

"I can feel the energy," she breathed, looking up at Stardust.

She gasped when she looked behind Stardust and saw a stairway carved into the rock at the far end of the cavern. A wide platform with an arched doorway stood at the top. She pulled her hand away from the river and rose to her feet. As if in a daze, she walked toward the steps.

The voice in her head was soft and faint at first. It grew louder the closer she got to the platform. She paused at the bottom of the steps and stared up at the arched doorway.

She studied the archway as she began climbing the steps. Stardust walked beside her. When she reached the top, she didn't stop. Knowledge flooded through her mind, and she swept her hands outward with a silent command. The ornately carved doorway opened, and beyond it, a vast universe filled with many worlds was laid out before her.

Phoenix kept her gaze fixed on a single faint glow of gold. Like a beacon in the night, the pulse of golden light called to her. Shifting into her dragon form, she crossed through the doorway and disappeared.

∾

The Isle of Magic

Ashure stood with his fists clenched at his sides until he felt Orion's hand on his shoulder.

"We need to find out what happened here," Orion murmured.

Ashure swallowed and nodded. He turned away from the ash that fell like snow beyond the confines of the concealment field. Unfamiliar emotion threatened to choke him when he saw the small encampment.

"This is all that is left of the residents?" he asked with disbelief.

Ariness nodded. "Yes. The aliens attacked the palace city first. The fight was over in a matter of hours. There were hundreds of thousands of the aliens. The palace forces were vastly outnumbered and quickly overwhelmed. Then the creatures swept across the Isle like a tsunami. My son, Isha, was killed in the initial attack. Mike and Marina barely made it back," Ariness stopped and wiped a hand across his face.

"Where are they?" Orion asked.

Ariness stared straight ahead. "Marina is very ill. Cornelia and Erin are with her. Mike was... wounded," he said, hesitating on the last word.

They followed Ariness to an open tent. Mike was sitting on the edge of a cot with his shirt open. An older woman was mumbling and holding her hands over a blackened area on his skin. He was extremely pale, sweat beaded on his face, and his eyes were glazed with pain. Ashure stopped in the opening and put his hand out, preventing Orion from entering.

"He's infected," he warned in a low voice.

Ariness nodded. "Yes. So far, we have been able to contain the spread within his body, but we won't be able to do so for much longer. Its cells are multiplying at an exponential rate," he replied.

"Ashure, Orion— Where are Drago and the others? Did they make it?" Mike asked through gritted teeth.

"Drago died battling the alien," Orion quietly replied.

Pain flashed through Mike's eyes before he closed them. He shook his head before he opened his eyes again and looked back at them. White lines of pain creased each side of his mouth.

"What about the others?" he demanded.

"We don't know. None of this makes any sense," Ashure confessed.

"What's there to fucking make sense of? The aliens have won," Mike harshly replied before leaning back.

"I've done all I can to stop the spread. The creature has connected with his cells and the magic can no longer distinguish between his body and the alien," the old woman said.

"How long do I have?" Mike muttered.

"A few hours at best, most likely less," she replied.

"Fuck!" Mike whispered, closing his eyes and leaning back against the post on the backside of the cot.

"King Ashure, you said that none of this makes sense. I'm afraid I don't understand. One of your men said that the Isle of the Pirates fell nearly two weeks ago, and that Lady Tonya—" Ariness said before he pursed his lips together.

Tonya's name sent a flare of panic through him. "What about Lady Tonya?" Ashure demanded, stepping closer to Ariness.

Ariness stared back at him with troubled eyes. "She was killed when the palace was destroyed," he said.

Ashure staggered back several steps as if he had been struck a mortal blow. His mind rebelled at the thought of Tonya's death. It couldn't be true.

"Who—who told you that she was—that she had died?" he hoarsely demanded.

Ariness turned and stared at a fire pit across from where they were standing. Ashure's eyes scoured the crowd outside the tent for his second-in-command. His attention locked on Dapier's drooping shoulders. The perpetually good-natured pirate looked old and hollow-eyed.

Ashure pushed his way past Orion and strode across the grounds. Dapier looked up, his eyes briefly widening before he lowered them with a hunching of his shoulders.

"Where is she? Where is Tonya?" Ashure demanded, reaching out and grabbing the front of Dapier's dirty shirt.

Dapier slowly lifted eyes filled with tears and sorrow. Ashure shook his head in denial and released Dapier's shirt as if he had been burned. He wanted to howl in pain and grief, but he swallowed it and backed away.

"I'm sorry, Cap'n. I tried to save her. Them aliens were attacking. Lady Tonya was right behind me when the wall crumbled. She pushed me out of the way. She said... she said... to tell you—she wanted me to tell you that she loves you and that she'll be waiting for you always," Dapier's voice was barely a whisper by the time he finished.

Blood rushed to Ashure's head, and he swayed. Bending over, he placed his hands on his knees to keep from falling. How was all this possible? He had only been gone half a day. The alien had not even made it to Mystic Mountain when he left this morning. How could it have caused so much devastation in such a small period of time?

"Ashure," Orion called behind him.

He slowly straightened, turned, and faced Orion, Mike, and Ariness. It was over. Mike would soon be dead, and this small encampment would not be able to last much longer.

He had lost everything. He slid his hand under his long coat and gripped the hilt of his dagger. There was nothing left for him to live for. He took a deep, shuddering breath.

Tonya, he whispered, remembering her lying in their bed with a small, sexy smile on her lips, her eyes warm and sleepy. *My love.*

He turned the dagger in his hand so that the blade was pointed at his chest. The pain was too reminiscent of the time when he had held her in his arms after Bleu shot her—only this was magnified a million times because he knew there was no hope of ever seeing her again. There was no Magna to slow down time this time.

"Ashure, no!" Orion called out.

Ashure opened his eyes as a new thought occurred to him, and he parted his lips with the first stirring of hope. "Time—we need to change the time," he whispered.

"Ashure, don't let Tonya's death be in vain," Orion urgently said, gripping his arm.

Ashure's eyes met Orion's, and he slowly nodded. "Time, Orion. There is another way," he said, his voice growing stronger and louder.

"What?" Orion asked with a confused expression.

Ashure waved the dagger in the air at the encampment. "Time, Orion. Drago's Time-Space hoop! The magic—that is why this doesn't make sense. We never made it to the Mystic Mountains to help Nali. That is why this is happening. We need Drago's hoop. We need to go back into the past," he exclaimed with growing excitement.

Ariness frowned. "You have a Time-Space hoop?" he repeated in disbelief.

"*Yes!*" Ashure said triumphantly.

"Where is it?" Ariness asked with growing excitement.

Ashure looked at Orion again. Ashure turned and looked back the way they had come. They had left it back in the village—forgotten during the attack.

"We don't know how to work it," Orion pointed out.

Ariness grimly nodded. "You may not, but I do," he said.

"It won't do us any good if we can't get to it," Ashure said.

"Where is it?" Mike asked this time.

"In the village," Ashure replied with a grimace.

CHAPTER 21

*I*sle of the Monsters

Asahi jumped out of the boat with the bow rope when he heard the hull scraping the lake's rocky bottom. He waded ashore and secured the rope around a large boulder. Nali looked around before gazing up at the steep cliff ahead of them. The sheer stone wall rose thousands of feet into the air. From this vantage point, clouds shielded most of the mountain from view.

She walked over to the boat's starboard side and flipped a rope ladder over the gunwale for Asahi to climb back into the boat. He gave her a wry grin of thanks. She stepped back when he pulled himself over the side.

"This looks like a dead end. I assume this is the mountain the mirror showed us," he said.

She nodded. "Yes."

He tilted his head back and looked up as far as he could. The skeptical expression on his face made her smile. She wrapped her arms around his waist and hugged him.

"It's a long way to the top. You should ask Ashure about that one day," she teased.

He looked down at her in surprise. "Ashure? He climbed to the top?" he asked.

She chuckled and nodded. "When he was nine. He almost died on his little adventure," she said.

He looked up at the cloud-shrouded peak again. "Nine! Incredible," he repeated.

She laughed and shook her head. "I think you mean incredibly lucky. The mountain only allows those who are true of heart to ascend it," she said.

"True of heart? You mentioned that before. What exactly does that mean?" he asked with a frown.

"Those that seek nothing in return. Legends passed down from one Empress to another say that after the Goddess created the Isle of the Monsters, she stood upon the highest mountain and marveled at the beauty and diversity of the creatures here. She didn't see them as ugly or something to fear, but unique and precious in their own way. To help protect them, she gave them three things," she explained, facing him.

"An Empress to protect them," he guessed.

She smiled and tilted her head. "Yes."

"The Goddess's Mirror to help her do so," he added.

She nodded. "And…."

He frowned and looked up at the mountain again. She loved the way he became still as he processed information.

"And a way to communicate with her in times of great need," he finally said, looking down at her.

"Yes, though I don't know if there has ever been a time greater than now," she murmured.

She slid her hands up his muscular arms until they rested on his shoulders. He gripped her waist. The warmth of his hands through the thin material of her blouse sent a shiver of awareness through her. She gazed up at him, her heart filled with emotion.

"I'm falling in love with you, Asahi Tanaka," she said as she ran her fingers through his hair.

He turned his head and pressed a kiss on her palm. "Then I am the luckiest man alive. From the moment I saw you land in the forest, there was never a doubt in my mind that you were the woman for me," he confessed.

She met his lips halfway. *This is what pure magic feels like,* she thought when he tightened his hold on her.

Her heart hammered when he slid his hands over her hips. Their kiss changed from passionate to almost desperate. The turmoil of the last few days and the fear of what the future held intensified the depth of their emotions. Nali never wanted their kiss to end.

He traced her bottom lip with his tongue and trailed soft kisses across her cheek to her neck. She instinctively tilted her head to give him free access to the slender column of her throat. All the while, she pulled at his neatly tucked shirt.

She groaned when she slipped her hands under the loose shirt and touched his warm skin. Pure pleasure coursed through her as she caressed his flesh. It would be so easy to forget where they were and the danger bearing down on them.

"One day—" she breathed.

She closed her eyes and sent out a fervent wish for them to have a future together. He paused, his lips still pressed against her neck as if he heard her unspoken request. He hugged her tighter. A sigh of regret slipped from her. She should have kept her worries to herself.

She looked deep into his eyes when he tenderly cupped her cheek. A sense of calm settled over her. She pressed her cheek against his hand when he caressed it with his thumb.

"That day will come soon," he vowed.

Nali nodded, her throat closed with a foreign emotion. She gave him a fierce hug before she released him. He touched one of her long curls as she stepped away.

"We need to be prepared in case Ashure doesn't make it back or he comes back alone. You have Mr. Gryphon, but the dagger alone will not be enough to protect you. The Water Sirens will do everything they can to slow down the alien and will help us as much as they can once it gets here," she said.

"Can the alien inhabit the Water Sirens?" he asked, warily scanning the water.

"I don't think so. The alien would have to inhabit each molecule of water. That would be an impossible feat since the sirens would merely dissolve and scatter," she explained.

"Well, that is at least one small positive, I guess," he wryly replied.

"One," she agreed.

"How do you suggest we prepare a defense?" he finally asked.

She studied their surroundings. There wasn't a lot they could do. Their best defense was the magic contained in the mountain.

"We need to get to higher ground. I'll find an area large enough to set up our base camp," she said.

"I'll gather our equipment," he replied with a nod.

"Asahi—thank you," she murmured.

He tilted his head. "For what?" he asked with a flash of surprise.

She lifted a hand and caressed his cheek. "For not listening and going the other way when I told you to," she answered.

She turned away from him and focused. The familiar transformation swept through her, changing her flesh from silken soft to hard granite. Long, powerful wings swept out behind her. She bent her knees and pushed off the boat's deck. Soaring upward, she sought a place where they would take their first stand against the alien. Hopefully, they would not be alone.

~

Isle of Magic

After discussing a strategy to retrieve the Time-Space hoop, Ashure warily scanned the area outside the dome. Ariness walked over and stood in front of him and Orion while Mike brought up the rear. He glanced briefly at Orion and saw the same expression of apprehension and determination on the Sea King's face. Shadows were rippling among the dead and dying foliage.

"I will create a shield, similar to the one around the dome, that will protect us until we get to the village," Ariness promised.

"The amount of magic needed to maintain it will drain you, Ariness," Orion cautioned.

Ariness looked at them with tired, sad eyes. "Yes. Mike and I both know that we will not be returning. The only hope for our world will rest on your success," he replied.

"Ariness, are you positive you can work the hoop? It was my understanding that only a Time Wizard can properly control them," Orion asked.

Ashure grimly nodded. "We found out the hard way what happens when a novice uses the hoop," he added.

Ariness's smiled sadly. "Then it is a good thing that you have one with you," he commented before turning away and lifting his staff.

Ashure tightly gripped his sword when the transparent shield morphed outward. They stepped through the opening and paused, giving the magic time to reseal behind them. Cocooned in a bubble, they cautiously advanced down the path.

Behind him, Ashure heard Mike's labored breathing. He looked over his shoulder with concern. The entity's dark essence ran under the skin on his neck like spider webs.

"Mike," he murmured, slowing down to walk beside him.

"I'm good. I'm good," Mike hissed between clenched teeth.

He tried to wrap an arm around Mike's waist, but Mike shook his head. Ashure frowned when Mike staggered a few steps away from him. It was clear the man was on the verge of collapsing.

"Don't!" Mike yelled. "Sorry, I didn't mean that to come out so harshly. Cornelia and the healer warned me that their magic would only contain the alien for so long. I don't want to risk it infecting anyone else," Mike explained in a strained voice.

"We will make this right," the Pirate King swore.

Mike's eyes darkened with emotion. "I hope you do. I would really love to hold my wife and son," he said.

Pain flashed through Ashure when he thought of Tonya. He understood exactly what Mike was feeling. The thought of never holding Tonya again was more than his mind and heart could handle.

He looked around at the dying landscape. There was no future in this timeline. He turned his focus on Ariness. The old wizard held the key to a different future, hopefully a better one. If Ariness unlocked the door, Ashure would do everything in his power to ensure that both he and Mike made it home to their families.

A low howling sound penetrated their protective bubble, and the alien shadows in the village multiplied, blindly creeping closer to the group, unable to pinpoint their exact location.

"They know we are here," Ariness stated.

"It's because of me," Mike said through clenched teeth. "The alien that's taking over my body is... reaching out to warn them."

Ariness nodded. "We won't have much time. I cannot maintain the magic shield when I work the spell to activate the Time-Space Hoop. Mike, you must use your connection with the alien to keep it at bay," he instructed.

Mike nodded. "Let me know when you're ready," he said.

Ashure looked warily at Orion. There weren't a lot of choices available. This would be their only chance of changing a devastating future for not only the Seven Kingdoms but countless other worlds, including Earth.

Ariness gave a sharp nod, and they weaved their way through the debris to the center of the village. Ashure saw the Time-Space hoop lying along the cobblestone road. He flexed his fingers around the hilt of his sword. Orion did the same, holding his Trident at the ready.

Once the hoop was within the protective bubble, Ariness stopped. He jammed his staff down between the stones but continued to hold onto it. Ariness's pallid complexion shocked Ashure when the old wizard twisted around and faced them. The man looked as if he had aged a century since they'd left the encampment.

"Step into the hoop and lift it above your head," Ariness instructed.

Ashure picked up the hoop. He frowned when Ariness placed a hand on Orion's arm and shook his head when the Sea King paused outside of the circle. Orion stiffened for a moment before he stepped back.

"What is it?" Ashure demanded with a frown.

"You must go alone," Ariness said.

Ashure stared at Ariness with a frown before he looked at Orion. "I don't understand. Why?" he asked.

Orion touched his arm. "Mike cannot hold off all the aliens by himself. Ariness must focus on the spell, and out of all of us, you must be protected at any cost. If the alien were to control you, it would control the Cauldron of Spirits—which contains some of the most dangerous criminal magic known to any world. I will assist Mike," he said.

Ashure stared in silence at the men in front of him and knew that they were sacrificing their lives so he could succeed. The alien had grown too powerful, already taking the life of one of their group and countless others. As things were, there would be no surviving this attack for any world, it was do or die. He nodded and sheathed his sword. Stepping back, he lifted the Time-Space Hoop above his head.

"Now," Ariness murmured, removing his hand from the staff.

The protective bubble evaporated, and shrieks of rage sounded from the possessed entities surrounding them when they were finally able to see the small group of men. Ariness lifted his hands and began chanting the spell to control the Time-Space Hoop. The silver etchings on the hoop began to glow in a specific sequence, but Ashure focused his attention on the battle.

Black discolorations now covered Mike's skin, and the human man flung out gestures in various directions like a desperate conductor, sending out commands to the attacking forces. Orion used his Trident to send powerful bursts of energy through the vines that were hungrily reaching for them.

Ashure cried out in denial when one vine pierced Mike's chest, lifting him off the ground. The memory of Ross Galloway's body flashed through his mind. Deep down, he knew that this time the Goddess would not interfere. If Mike was to have a second chance at life, Ashure would have to be successful in changing the past.

Orion's shout drew his attention, and he watched in horror as Orion sliced through the long stinger of an enormous scorpion that was rising from under the cobblestones. Large stones tumbled aside as the unnatural creature snapped its pincers. Orion blasted one off, but he was unable to get a clear shot at the scorpion's body. The scorpion grabbed Ariness around the waist with its other pincer and lifted the old wizard off his feet.

"Now, Ashure!" Ariness choked out.

Ashure dropped the hoop. The sights and sounds around him were forever burned into his memory. Blood seeped from Ariness's mouth as the scorpion crushed him. Orion roared a fierce battle cry as more scorpions appeared faster than even he could blast them. In that split second before he disappeared, he knew a hell far worse than even the deepest level of the Cauldron of Spirits. He briefly closed his eyes as he spun backward. He hoped the world he was going to would be much better than the one he had just left behind.

CHAPTER 22

 aldier:

The Hive

The storm was raging with gale force winds by late evening, but three powerful dragons cut through the wind and driving rain, intent on reaching their destination.

How much farther, Zoran? Creon asked, thankful of the connection between the dragons that made mental communication possible.

Not far, Zoran replied.

Creon cast a worried look at the dainty dragon flying beside him. Carmen had refused to stay home, so they had left Spring with Abby, Zoran's mate.

We are almost there, he encouraged.

The white dragon with shimmering scales edged with red, pink, and purple nodded her head. Admiration for his mate filled him.

How could Phoenix have made it through weather like this? Carmen's thought whispered through his mind.

He didn't answer, but breathed a sigh of relief instead when the Hive's rocky cliffs came into view through the swirling rain. The wind intensified as they neared the island. The thought of his tiny daughter facing such a journey—even with Stardust by her side— threatened to choke him with fear. He reminded himself that both of their daughters had their mother's indomitable strength and determination.

There is a cave near the foot of the mountain, Zoran said.

Waves crashed against the rocks as they swooped through the tall stone pillars rising out of the ocean. Carmen followed Zoran while Creon took up the rear. His dragon banked around another tower of rocks and under a natural bridge created by the relentless force of the waves. He veered again and lowered his head against the force of the wind. Zoran glided into a landing near the mouth of a cave. Carmen landed next to him with Harvey beside her. Creon's solid black dragon shifted a moment before he landed, lightly stepping forward into the cave.

He steadied Carmen when she shifted to her two-legged form. Goldie transformed from Zoran's armor into her four-legged form, and Zoran shifted too. The group stared out at the driving rain in silence.

"Goldie, light, please," Zoran said.

Goldie's body began to glow, illuminating the entrance to the cave. Creon looked around the area, stopping when he noticed a small firepit.

"Creon... she was here. I recognize the way she built the fire ring. Paul taught Trisha, Ariel, and me how to make one just like it," Carmen exclaimed with relief.

He strode over to the pit and knelt on one knee. Carmen followed him. She handed him a thin piece of partially burned driftwood. He took the stick and poked at the remains of the fire before he held his hand over the ash.

"It's still warm," he said.

He threw the stick into the fire pit and rose to his feet, pulling Carmen close to him. A shudder of relief ran through both of them.

"Let's find our daughter," she urged, kissing his neck.

He nodded, sliding his hands down Carmen's sides before he stepped away. Zoran placed a hand on Creon's shoulder in brotherly support, then took the lead. Carmen slid her hand into Creon's as they followed Zoran deeper into the Hive.

Isle of the Dragons:

A month earlier

The Time-Space hoop worked differently this time. Instead of dropping through a narrow tunnel, there was a dizzying perception that the world around him was turning backward on its axis. Ashure felt like he was being ripped in two. He saw a shadow of his former self standing in the Time-Space hoop in the village before he turned to dust. At one point he crossed the same thread of time and saw Drago, Orion, and himself passing through the portal.

The spinning slowed as he approached Drago's castle. He was suddenly thrust forward when he reached the point where he and Orion were waiting for Drago to return from his hoard. He sucked in a breath when he merged with his previous self in the great hall of the Dragon's Palace.

"Ashure, Theron said you were here on an urgent matter. Are you alright?" Orion asked, steadying him when he swayed.

Ashure held onto Orion and stared at the other man. Emotion threatened to choke him when he heard children's laughter and Carly, Drago's mate, calling out a warning to Roo, their daughter, to be careful.

"Yes," he finally forced out.

"What's wrong?" Orion demanded.

"The alien is on the Isle of the Monsters, and Nali needs our assistance," he replied, feeling a sense of déjà vu as he repeated what he had said before.

"When did it appear?" Orion asked.

He shook his head to clear his thoughts. It was important that they did not make the same mistake twice. Ashure cleared his throat.

"The morning of my wedding," he admitted.

Surprise swept across Orion's face. "Tell me everything," he urged.

"I'll tell you, but there is… more to the story," he cautioned.

He quickly ran through what he had told Orion the first time. His voice faded when Drago walked in carrying a large round metal hoop. Fear gripped him for a second when he saw the hoop in Drago's hand. Before Drago could say a word, he strode forward and ripped it out of the other man's hands.

"What are you doing?" Drago snapped in surprise.

"I watched you die a few hours ago," he harshly replied. He held up the Time-Space hoop and looked back and forth between Drago's stunned face and Orion. "I watched you both die. Everything was gone—you, your families, the Kingdoms… Tonya. The alien destroyed… everything."

His voice faltered as he remembered the devastation. He closed his eyes and breathed deeply to regain control of his emotions.

"What are you talking about?" Drago demanded.

He inhaled a deep breath and slowly released it. "We've used this already. We ended up in the future—a month from now—on the Isle of Magic. The alien creatures had already destroyed all but a few survivors. Ariness was leading us back to the last stronghold when we were attacked. There were too many of them." He looked at Drago. "You ignited the dragon fire inside you to give us time to escape. The few survivors there were from every Kingdom. Dapier told me— Tonya was killed. Mike was infected."

"How did you get back?" Orion asked in a somber tone.

He turned to Orion. "Ariness is a Time Wizard. He can control the Time-Space hoop. You and Mike held off the aliens long enough for him to activate it and send me back to this time," he explained. "None of you survived."

Ashure looked down at the hoop in his hand. It was far too dangerous to use, he knew without a doubt.

"What should we do?" Drago murmured.

Ashure thought for a moment. "I have the power of the sword that Magna gave me, and we know the entity cannot survive the combined power of Orion's Trident and your dragon fire. We three will have to be strong enough to aid Nali," he said. "We must, there is no other option."

Orion stepped up beside him and placed a hand on his shoulder.

Drago nodded grimly in agreement. "Oh, we'll be enough," he promised.

Ashure held out the Time-Space hoop to Drago. "Please do something with this thing. It is far too dangerous in the wrong hands," he said with a slight shudder of distaste.

"Done," Drago agreed, taking the hoop and tossing it into the air.

Ashure retreated several steps when Drago suddenly shifted into his dragon form and blew a long, fiery breath at the hoop. The hoop turned a brilliant yellowish-red and then burst into glittering flakes of molten ash. Shards of smoldering metal dotted the carpet, causing several spots to ignite.

Orion hastily pointed his Trident at the spots, and summoned water, quickly putting out the fires. Ashure wiggled his nose when the smell of smoke and wet wool hit his nostrils. This wasn't exactly what he had meant when he asked Drago to do something about the hoop. He had expected Drago to return the hoop to the safety of his hoard. They all turned and looked at the doorway when they heard Carly suddenly yell.

"Drago! You'd better not be burning the palace again," Carly growled from the other room.

Drago shifted back to his two-legged form. "It was just a small one, love," he replied with a grimace.

"So, what's the quickest way to get to Nali?" Orion asked.

Drago grinned. "Well, I *do* have one more thing that might work," he admitted.

"Really, Drago? You couldn't have used portal stones before trying to use that manhood-shriv...." He paused when Drago glared and glanced meaningfully at his child who was watching with wide eyes. "Before you decided to use the Time-Space hoop?" Ashure amended.

"I didn't think about it, alright? Besides, do you have any idea how much gold these damn things are costing me? At least the Time-Space hoop was already mine," Drago growled.

"Mommy says you aren't supposed to talk like that in front of us. I need five more big coins, Daddy," Roo informed her dad with a pleased expression.

Orion's muffled snort of laughter was contagious. Ashure rubbed a hand across his mouth to hide his grin when Drago muttered under his breath again about never doing a business deal with dragons. The fact that Drago was dealing with his own daughter made all of his grousing even more hilarious.

"Three, four, five," Drago counted, dropping the coins into the bag Roo was holding out.

"One more," Roo said.

Drago frowned. "But—I gave you five gold coins," he retorted with a frown.

Roo tapped her foot and shook her head. "Yes, but six would be even better. I'll give you a kiss to go with the rune stones that Mommy bought me. A kiss from me is worth two gold coins, but I'll give you a discount if you pay up in the next minute," she bargained.

"Your mommy had no idea what these were when she bought them for you," he muttered.

Drago grumbled, but pulled another coin out of the bag at his waist and pressed it into Roo's outstretched hand. She leaned in and gave him an enormous hug and a big, messy kiss on the cheek. Ashure was surprised at the sudden wave of yearning that struck him.

"You have that look in your eye," Orion murmured near his ear.

"I do? What look?" he asked.

Orion chuckled and shook his head. "You'll find out about nine months from the time you get back to Tonya," he predicted.

Ashure winced when Orion slapped his shoulder. He shook his head and studied Drago and Roo. Kids? Him? Who would have ever imagined him as a dad?

"Thank you, Roo. Make sure you stay close to your mother until I return," Drago instructed.

"I will, Daddy. I love you," Roo replied, giving Drago another hug and kiss before she clutched her bag of coins to her chest. "That kiss was free."

"Thank you," he dryly laughed, with a shake of his head. "And don't tell your brothers about the gold," he called after her as she skipped out of the room.

Drago rose to his feet, holding his purchase from his daughter in his hands. Ashure and Orion both grinned at him when he looked down and scowled at the colorful assortment of magical stones.

"You know, Drago, Roo wouldn't make a bad pirate," he ribbed.

"Don't you even think of putting that idea into her head, Ashure. Six gold coins…," Drago groaned.

"Well, you got an extra free kiss out of it," Orion pointed out.

Drago looked up and grinned. "I did, didn't I?" he reflected.

Ashure and Orion both laughed out loud. The twinkle of pride in Drago's eyes at Roo's determined negotiations was easy to see, and so was his love for the dainty little girl. Ashure sighed, thankful for this carefree moment.

"Do you know how to use these?" he asked, nodding at the stones.

Drago snorted. "These are child's play," he retorted.

"Child's play—as long as you say the spell correctly so we don't end up in the middle of the ocean," Ashure pointed out.

Drago waved away Ashure's concern. "Between Orion and myself, we'll get the spell right," he said confidently.

Ashure stared at Drago. "Between you and Orion... You don't remember the spell, do you?" he demanded.

Drago shrugged. "Not all of it, but we'll figure it out," he replied.

"You could always ask Roo," Orion suggested with an amused grin.

"Are you crazy? She'll probably demand twice as much gold for the spell as she did for the stones. Besides, you don't think that carpet-bagger of a crook at the market would give a child the actual spell to a magic portal, do you?" Drago argued.

"I don't know. I wouldn't have thought a vendor would sell the stones in the first place, so who knows," Orion countered.

Ashure opened his mouth to make his own caustic remark when the sound of running footsteps drew their attention. A pink-cheeked Roo stared at them for a moment before she ran over to Drago and held out a message. Drago took the paper she was holding.

"I forgot you'll need the spell that goes with the pretty rocks. DJ heard Aunty Marina telling the words and how they work to Mommy after I showed her my rocks, and he wrote them down, but I can't read all of them yet so I haven't tried the stones, but I know they work because DJ and Stone use them sometimes at night to visit with Dolph and Juno. I'm not supposed to tell you about that because it is a secret— but I'm telling you because they refused to pay me the gold coin they promised they would if I was quiet! So I really don't need to keep their secret 'cause they didn't pay me," she breathlessly added before giving Drago a huge smile. "Love you, Daddy. Have fun on your trip!"

Drago stared after his daughter with his mouth hanging open. For once, Ashure felt sorry for Drago. It was obvious the man was going to have his hands full with Roo when she got older.

Older? Hell, she's running circles around him now! he wryly thought.

"Perhaps we'd better get going before she returns," he suggested in a light tone.

Drago absently nodded, handing Ashure the piece of paper with the spell. "Maybe you should do this, since you know where we are supposed to go," he offered.

"That might be wise," he chuckled.

Orion took half the stones from Drago. "If the boys can do this, so can we," he stated.

CHAPTER 23

*I*sle of the Monsters

Asahi stood on a flat edge at the top of the mountain and took in the panorama of the long lake. He didn't understand how the magic worked, but he could see through the clouds as if it were a two-way mirror. Far below, he observed Nali returning with their meager supplies.

He absently rubbed his aching shoulder as a shiver ran through him. For a moment, he worried that he might be getting sick. His concern intensified when a wave of dizziness sent him stumbling back from the edge. Shaken by the combination of symptoms, he closed his eyes and took deep, calming breaths while he waited for the dizziness to pass.

We must access the Gateway, a malevolent voice whispered.

Asahi frowned and rubbed his suddenly aching brow. The voice sounded eerily like the alien—only now it was inside his head. He stiffened when a vision formed in his mind. The scene was so clear it was like watching a movie on a big screen television.

The Water Sirens were creating rip currents in the lake to slow the alien's progress. Each time the alien would change direction, the Water Sirens altered the current. He watched as the eel split open and the alien poured out. Horrified at the sight, it took him a second to understand what was happening. He jerked when he felt a touch on his arm, and the image in his head disappeared.

"Asahi, what is it?" Nali asked with concern.

He opened his eyes and swayed. Nali grabbed his arm and steadied him. He lifted his hand to caress her cheek, but suddenly paused, his hand in midair. Both of them froze as they noticed the trail of black spiderweb-like veins on the back of his hand.

"I'm infected," he replied in a strained voice.

The certainty of his statement filled him with dread. Fear for Nali caused him to jerk away from her touch. He curled his fingers into a fist.

"How—when?" she demanded in dismay.

He closed his eyes again and thought about the last few days. He remembered feeling an intense pain in his shoulder when the alien struck him outside the opening to the goblins' underground tunnels. Now he realized that was when the alien infected him. The blow had been brief, but sharp—like the stab of a needle.

"My shoulder—I thought it was just a bruise. The alien must have injected me with some of its body matter," he said.

"Loosen your shirt, and let me look at your back," she instructed.

"Look, but don't touch me. We don't know—" He paused and then voiced his grim realization. "There's a chance it could have spread to you when we made love." He released a shaky breath.

"If that is the case, then we will deal with it," she replied.

He slowly unbuttoned his shirt and shrugged the fabric off of his shoulders, turning his back to Nali. The sound of her low hiss confirmed his fear. He flinched when she gently touched the heated flesh around the bruise.

"There are streaks feathering outward from where the alien struck you," she exclaimed. "What are your symptoms?"

He stepped away as he pulled his shirt back on, then turned and faced her, slowly buttoning his shirt. He ignored his slight discomfort. There were far more important concerns at the moment, like the images he had seen a few moments ago—and the whispered words.

"Before, all I felt was an ache in my shoulder. A few minutes ago, I experienced minor chills and disorientation. I also had a vision, and it felt as if I could hear the alien's thoughts," he said.

Nali's lips parted on a soft gasp. She took a step forward, ignoring him when he lifted a hand to remind her to keep her distance. Frustration and concern churned inside him at her stubborn disregard for the danger he now presented to her and their mission. She wrapped her hand around his and held it against her chest.

"What did you see? What did the creature say?" she demanded.

"It said 'we must access the Gateway'. A moment later I saw the eel split apart and the alien spilling out of it. I lost the connection before I could see what happened next. Nali...," he murmured, cupping her chin so that she was forced to look into his eyes. "I now pose a danger to this mission."

She shook her head. "Not yet. The entity left Medjuline without killing her. We'll find a way to remove it from you," she replied in a hard, determined tone.

"I hope it doesn't require that I run head first into a tree," he wryly mused.

He started to pull away from her when a movement over her shoulder caught his attention. She sensed his surprise and twisted around to follow his gaze. A small army of dark shapes was approaching the mountain. Asahi's rising concern dissolved when he heard Nali's strained, but relieved, chuckle.

"I knew Pai would find me," she murmured.

Together they waited as the hippogriff led an army of gargoyles to their mountain perch. Minutes later, Pai swept up over the edge of the cliff, followed by the gargoyles. The sight of the granite-like army caused Asahi's throat to tighten with emotion. For the first time in a while, he was infused with hope. The large group circled around before landing in the serene meadow that carpeted the extinct volcano's sunken crater.

"Now we only need Ashure and the others to arrive," Nali murmured, as if reading his thoughts.

"They will," he replied with confidence.

The words had no sooner left his mouth than a shimmering portal opened less than thirty feet from them. The first thing he saw was Ashure's grinning face. Asahi noted several other men behind the pirate. He was distracted from watching them appear from the portal, however, by Ashure's exuberant greeting.

"You don't know how glad I am to see you!" Ashure exclaimed with relief.

Asahi frowned when he noticed new lines etched around Ashure's mouth and the unexpected amount of emotion in the man's eyes. He started to raise his hand to shake Ashure's but then dropped it back to his side. He pursed his lips before he nodded to the group in greeting.

"Thank you for coming," Nali softly greeted.

Ashure wrapped his arms around Nali and hugged her as if he would never let her go. Asahi met Ashure's searching look. He raised an eyebrow in inquiry.

"Where's the alien? I'm ready to incinerate the damn thing," Drago demanded, studying the area with a curious expression.

"When are you not ready to burn something?" Koorgan, the King of the Giants, dryly replied, drawing chuckles from the group.

Nali pulled away from Ashure and reached for Asahi. He shook his head in warning, but she ignored him and grabbed his hand. He returned the contemplative and curious looks directed at them.

"Ashure, you outdid yourself," Nali said with a smile. "Asahi, let me introduce you to some of the fiercest warriors in the Seven Kingdoms."

He murmured a greeting to each person, keeping a respectable distance from them to ensure their safety. There were eight representatives from the other kingdoms, including Ashure. He was surprised when he recognized Ross Galloway.

"Ross," Asahi greeted.

Ross gave him a wry grin and said, "Welcome to Fantasyland, Agent Tanaka."

After Nali introduced a pair from the Isle of Magic, Isha responded, "Mike wanted to be here, but Marina is due to have their first child any day. My father and I will fight beside you."

"Thank you, Isha," Nali replied gratefully. "Ariness, it is an honor to have two such powerful wizards standing with us."

Ariness bowed. "I have seen what the alien can do, Empress. I will do everything in my power to protect the Seven Kingdoms and beyond."

Asahi didn't miss Ashure's grim nod of agreement, and he wondered what had happened during Ashure's trip. The unflappable pirate appeared more somber than he remembered.

"Pai has overseen the setup of a camp for us. He and a small squadron of my elite gargoyle soldiers will track the alien. I would like to share with you what we know—and coordinate an attack," Nali said.

"We will follow your lead, Nali," Orion replied.

Asahi sat along the outer edge of the group inside a tent. The interior was spacious and provided relief from the sun that had been burning his eyes and flesh. As the alien inside him spread, so did his sensitivity to light.

He silently listened as Nali shared what had happened so far on the Isle of the Monsters with the group around the large central table. Once again, he was impressed by her commanding personality. She relayed the information in a clear, concise tone and answered each question thoroughly. The only thing she had yet to share with the others was his infected state.

He tensed when Ashure walked over and pulled up a chair next to him. He curled his fingers into a fist when the alien particles inside him reacted to Ashure's presence. The alien appeared to be repulsed by Ashure. Asahi glanced at the sword Ashure was holding. Ashure casually laid the enchanted blade across his lap and sat back. It was then that Asahi realized that it was the pirate's blade repelling the alien, not the man himself.

"We have a good team," Ashure murmured.

He nodded in agreement. "We do."

"How long have you been infected?" Ashure suddenly asked.

Asahi stiffened. "How did you know?" he countered.

Ashure stood up and nodded his head toward the opening. "Walk with me," he quietly requested.

Asahi rose to his feet and trailed Ashure out of the tent. They walked in silence, heading for the tree line. When Ashure kept going, Asahi glanced at the camp behind them, and then followed Ashure into the forest that surrounded the clearing.

They were on a wide, moss-covered path that led into the densest thicket of the woods. It was a stark contrast to the bright clearing they had left. Out of instinct, Asahi rested his hand on the hilt of Mr. Gryphon.

"Where are we going?" he demanded.

Ashure glanced at him before waving his hand in front of him. "Hopefully to find an old friend," he said.

"An old friend? Up here?" Asahi warily repeated.

Ashure didn't answer. Instead, he continued walking. Asahi eyed the sword the other man still held.

"I climbed this mountain when I was nine years old," Ashure casually remarked.

"Nali mentioned it. It's a very impressive feat," he replied.

"This mountain has a magic of its own, you know. You must have noticed when you arrived," Ashure continued, glancing at him.

"Yes, I noticed," Asahi wryly responded, trying to understand where the conversation was heading.

Ashure smiled. "It is said that only the worthy can even *see* this old volcano. Everyone else passes by without even wondering what is here. I certainly wasn't looking for a mountain. I had stolen a boat from a changeling along the lake—I wanted to pretend I was captain of all the oceans, you see—and I was puttering around with little direction when I saw it: a mysterious mountain shrouded in the thickest fog I'd ever seen. I just knew I had to climb to the top. Of course, I had to get to the damn thing first," Ashure mused.

"How did you manage it?" Asahi curiously asked. "The Water Sirens nearly pulled me off the boat."

Ashure chuckled. "I stuffed cotton in my ears. I am, after all, half Sprite, so I knew a thing or two about their tricks. They pushed me around a bit and finally decided to let the mountain do with me what it willed. It is alive, you know, the mountain. The sirens believed a child as naughty as I would certainly be crushed by it. Those slippery beauties love their death and destruction, but who would ever *like* dealing with the decaying bodies afterward? No one, that's who," he said with a flashing grin. "So, they decided I was more trouble than I was worth, and they let me pass."

"But—the mountain didn't crush you," Asahi replied.

Ashure shook his head. "No, the mountain didn't crush me," he replied in a low voice.

"Why didn't it?" Asahi asked, intrigued by the tale of a young boy on a magical adventure.

"Who knows? I talked to it the entire time. Nali says the mountain didn't know what to do with me," Ashure chuckled.

"Why did you do it? Why did you climb the mountain? This mountain?" he pressed.

Ashure slowed down until he came to a complete stop in the middle of the path. He idly looked around the forest. Asahi studied the pirate's expression, trying to discern why the man was telling him this.

"I wanted to find where the Goddess lived," Ashure finally replied with a shrug, looking back at him.

"And did you?" Asahi quietly asked.

"I like to think I did," Ashure replied.

He was about to ask Ashure what he meant when he heard a soft snort to his right. He twisted around, automatically pulling Mr. Gryphon from his sheath, and gaped in surprise when he saw a group of animals emerging from the shadows.

Dozens of unicorns stood silently watching them. The alien inside him immediately reacted to the creatures. Asahi recoiled in alarm when the edge of his vision darkened as if he were looking through a spyglass. The entity's black tendrils beneath his skin snaked up his throat and feathered outward across his cheeks. He groaned and sank to his knees.

"What is going on?" Mr. Gryphon demanded.

Asahi clenched his teeth and took a deep breath as he fought for control. Ashure pressed his sword's glowing tip against Asahi's throat. The entity, sensing the danger, retreated. Asahi tilted his head back, locked eyes with Ashure, and waited.

"You still have control over it—good," Ashure commented, pulling the sword away from his throat.

Asahi grunted. "You could've just asked," he muttered.

"When did the alien infect you? Why didn't you tell me?" Mr. Gryphon snapped, whipping his tail back and forth in his agitation.

Asahi slid the dagger back into the sheath without answering. He wasn't up to dealing with the irritating lion at the moment. His attention moved back to the woods. The unicorns were gone.

"Were they real?" he quietly asked.

Ashure nodded. "Yes."

He stood up and brushed the dirt and leaves off of his trousers. "Why did you bring me here?"

Ashure grimly replied, "Because your connection with the alien may be the thing that saves the Seven Kingdoms—or dooms us all."

CHAPTER 24

*N*ali studied Asahi from afar as he stared out over the lake. She started walking in his direction, only to pause when Pai flew overhead and landed in her path. She softly sighed in resignation when she noticed the gleam in Pai's eyes. He wanted to talk.

"Pai," she greeted.

"Empress," the hippogriff gruffly replied.

"Did you find the alien?" she asked.

Pai grimly nodded. "As your human stated, the alien is no longer in the eel," he answered.

She frowned and looked at Asahi. Her heart ached for him. He had spent the rest of the day avoiding everyone—except for the brief time he had disappeared with Ashure.

She wrapped her arms around her waist. "The creature needs to inhabit a form. Magna told us that the alien cannot survive long on our world without a body," she informed him.

"We searched but didn't find it. There is a deep ravine that runs the length of the lake. It has many caverns," he said.

She nodded. "I will ask the Water Sirens. They should be able to help us," she said.

"I've ordered double patrols and stationed lookouts along strategic vantage points on the mountain," Pai said.

Nali stroked Pai's feathered cheek. "You must be exhausted, my old friend. Why don't you get something to eat and rest? We will need you strong and ready for the battle to come."

Pai pulled his head away and shook it. "I may be old, but I'll always be ready to defend the Kingdom and you, Nali," he groused.

She watched Pai turn and walk away. He had a slight limp in his back left leg. Emotion threatened to choke her when she saw Ashure step out of the tent with an enormous platter of fresh fish. She sent him a grateful smile when he winked at her before shouting to Pai. The pirate's thoughtfulness touched her.

"Hey, Pai, I saved you some dinner before Drago could hoard it all," Ashure cheerfully called.

Taking a deep breath, she turned on her heel and continued on her original path. Asahi didn't acknowledge her when she stepped up beside him. He stared at the darkening landscape in front of them.

"Pai confirmed that the alien is no longer contained within the eel," she informed him.

She stood beside him in silence when he didn't reply. The minutes ticked by as they stood like silent sentinels along the edge of the mountain. Below them, she could see the gargoyles patrolling the lake.

"Ashure told me that he traveled to the future—a future where we failed. He witnessed the beginning of the end," he finally said.

She faced him fully. "We won't let that happen."

"Mike Hallbrook was infected with the alien. Mike could control the alien to a certain extent before he was killed in battle," he continued.

She reached out and gripped his arm. "Asahi, I won't let it kill you. Medjuline—" she said.

"Was one rare case of the alien leaving her body without killing her. Can you name another?" he demanded. When he looked at her, his eyes were glittering with anger.

"Yes, I can. Magna survived for centuries before she could rid her body of its hold. I won't let it kill you. I can't lose you. I—love you, Asahi. I love you so much," she passionately replied.

She wrapped her arms around his waist and held him like she would never let him go. Fear and grief mixed inside her at the thought of losing him. She would do anything to save him—anything.

She took a shuddering breath and closed her eyes when he slid his arms around her and rested his cheek against her hair. A tear slid down her cheek, and she rubbed it away against his shirt, afraid he would think her weak for crying.

"I love you, Nali. I want us to have a life together when this is over," he murmured.

"We can do this. We'll defeat the creature," she responded.

"Ashure was adamant that we do—or else. If we don't, he promised he'd give me a personal tour of the Cauldron of Spirits," he said with a small, rueful smile.

She tilted her head back and looked up at him. "Over his dead body," she threatened, her eyes gleamed with a warning before she continued. "What else did he say?"

He looked back out over the lake. "That my connection with the alien could either save the Seven Kingdoms—or doom it," Asahi grudgingly shared.

"Do you think you could connect with the alien again?" she asked.

He thought for a moment before he nodded. "My grandfather taught me the power of meditation when I was younger. If I focus, I can connect with the alien again," he said.

"I don't want you to do it if it endangers you," she insisted.

He chuckled and shook his head. "I think we are beyond that," he murmured.

"What do you need me to do?" she asked.

He pulled away from her and stepped back. She watched in puzzlement when he loosened his belt and pulled off the sheath holding the magical dagger. He held the sheathed blade out to her.

"Hold this. Whatever you do, don't pull the dagger out unless it becomes apparent that the alien has more control over me than I can resist. If I present a danger to you and the others, you must use it to stop me. Promise me, Nali," he said, cupping her hand around the dagger. "I need your solemn promise."

"Asahi—" she whispered in horror.

"I would rather die swiftly than turn into a monster that would harm you or anyone else," he quietly replied.

He leaned down and brushed a kiss across her forehead. She briefly closed her eyes and tightened her grip on the golden dagger's leather sheath. Could she do it? Did she have the strength to harm Asahi?

"I—promise," she forced out.

Tears burned her eyes when he tenderly caressed her cheek with his knuckles. A rueful smile curved his lips, and he nodded to the dagger. She looked down at it.

"Do me a favor and don't pull Mr. Gryphon out unless it's absolutely necessary. His constant talking is annoying, not to mention distracting. Just don't tell him I said that or he'll never stop complaining," he said.

Her laugh was strained, but she nodded.

"Stand back," he advised.

She moved back, her worried gaze never leaving his face. He stood perfectly still for several minutes with his hands together in front of his broad chest. His breathing grew slower, deeper and more measured.

She watched in fascination as he gracefully moved in a fluid kata that looked almost like a dance. He traced measured, graceful arcs with his hands as if he were embracing the world. He moved one foot in a circle and the rest of his body followed. She parted her lips in awe. She could almost imagine the wind moving under his command. It was the most beautiful thing she had ever seen.

Goddess, please help me save him, she silently pleaded.

~

Valdier:

The Hive

Carmen released Creon's hand when they entered the mammoth cavern. Her heart pounded with fear and desperation as she surveyed the deserted interior. The soft golden light did not immediately reveal her daughter.

"Phoenix! Phoenix, sweetheart, where are you?" Carmen called.

"Phoenix!" Creon shouted from behind her.

Their voices echoed throughout the cavern. Harvey bounded forward along a wide path through the rocks. Carmen hurriedly followed the symbiot.

"Carmen," Zoran called to her.

She ignored him, breaking into a run. "Phoenix, where are you?" she urgently yelled again.

She rounded an enormous boulder and stumbled to a stop. In front of her, a wide river of gold flowed through the center of the cavern. She observed the river's flow, following it to the far end and a nearby staircase—where she saw the fading ghostly image of her daughter in dragon form as she flew through a portal at the top of the stairs. "Phoenix!" she screamed.

"Carmen, wait," Zoran hissed, grabbing her arm.

She jerked free and transformed. Creon was already flying toward the Gateway. Her tail struck Zoran as she lifted off the ground.

Creon, catch her! she pleaded.

The fire of a mother's love filled her, driving her dragon to fly faster than she ever had before. The Gateway was closing. Creon was almost to it when a roaring hum and a wave of gold surged up from the river. Long bands of gold shot outward, wrapping around Creon's dragon and pulling him away from the rapidly closing gateway.

A cry of rage erupted from Carmen along with a torrent of dragon fire. Out of the corner of her eye, she saw spears of gold shooting out from the river like deadly missiles. She attempted to evade them, and Harvey flew between her and the spears, roaring when the long, golden shafts struck him.

She was almost to the platform when Zoran grabbed her from behind. Twisting, she cried out in shock when she saw Zoran's larger dragon gripping her by the wings. The force of his midair tackle sent them spiraling downward. Zoran turned them at the last second, taking the brunt of their impact with the stone floor. They rolled across the floor, sliding several feet before they stopped.

Carmen's frantic gaze remained glued to the Gateway as it vanished before her eyes, leaving a solid wall of rock outlined by an arched doorway. She shook uncontrollably, and a well of pain rose inside her until she thought her heart would break. Her pain turned to fury when she looked at Zoran. With a loud bellow, she rolled to her feet and launched herself at him.

"Release me!" Creon ordered, struggling to break free of the bonds holding him.

He had transformed seconds earlier, hoping the move would allow him to escape, but the restricting bands merely adjusted as his body changed. The sound of Carmen's furious roar made him wince. He twisted around, trying to see her.

"I need to reach my mate. Please—release me," he said, acknowledging that fighting against the bands would be futile.

The symbiot gold bands slowly released their grip and flowed back into the river. With the Gateway now closed, there was no longer any need to restrain Creon or Carmen. He grimaced when Zoran's dragon crashed down the steps.

"Carmen!" he called in a loud voice.

He hurried over to his brother. Zoran shifted back into his two-legged form and groaned. Creon gave his brother an apologetic look.

"We should probably give her space," Zoran grunted out, rather stiffly rising to his feet.

"Look out!" Creon hissed.

He tackled Zoran around the waist and pushed him back behind the boulder as Carmen released a long, furious stream of dragon fire. They kept their heads down as the rock heated and glowed. She was out of control with grief.

"Can you calm her?" Zoran asked, peering over the glowing boulder.

Creon glared at Zoran. "How do you think Abby would react if you stopped her from protecting Zohar?" he retorted.

Zoran grimaced. "Let me rephrase the question. Is there *any* way to calm her?" he asked.

Creon's mate was formidable in a fight in any form, but her emotions always added fuel to her fire, enhancing her speed and power. Creon would be a deadly catastrophe himself if he let himself think about their lost daughter. Instead, he focused all his energy on the current problem. Carmen needed him.

Her dragon was now attacking the rock wall where Phoenix had disappeared. Long, bloodied claw marks coated the uneven surface. Her snarls reflected their combined grief, both Carmen's and her dragon's. If Creon didn't do something soon, he feared Carmen's dragon would completely take her over, and he would lose them both. Madness was an ever-present threat for dragon-shifters. He could feel it lurking in his own mind, contained by a lifetime of training.

He leaned his head back against the boulder and thought, then narrowed his eyes when he saw Harvey emerge out of the river and shake. There might be one thing that would calm Carmen's dragon.

Harvey, I need enormous eyes and bigger ears, he silently requested.

"Stay here," he ordered his oldest brother.

Creon slowly rose to his feet as the symbiot shimmered. Together they climbed the stairs to the platform. Carmen had already known the pain of losing a child before they met. He couldn't fathom the agonizing fear she must be suffering at the thought of losing another.

"Carmen," he called, slowly walking forward. "Love, look at me."

Carmen's dragon continued to tear at the wall. He jumped to the side when her tail swept back and forth with her distress. With a wave of his hand, he motioned for Harvey to go to her.

The symbiot trotted forward, stumbling on his oversized ears. He was in the shape of the old hound dog that Carmen had loved as a child. Carmen's dragon turned around and snapped at the symbiot in warning. Harvey immediately dropped and rolled onto his back, four paws extended. The dragon froze, her wild eyes narrowing at the sight.

"Carmen, come to me, love. Let me hold you," he murmured. "I need you, Carmen. Come back to me."

Her dragon looked into his eyes, her turbulent expression gentling slightly. He kept speaking in a quiet, soothing voice. Once he was close enough, he caressed her wing. She shuddered and shifted back into her two-legged form.

He slowly enfolded her in his arms, holding on tightly to his sobbing mate. Her petite frame violently shook with the intensity of her heartbreak.

They held each other close, drawing strength and comfort from their embrace. He ran his hands up and down her back while Harvey pressed close against her leg.

"We have to bring her back, Creon. She's our little girl. We have to find her and bring her back," she said in a tortured voice.

Zoran carefully came closer and said, "Only a Goddess can pass through the Gateway, Carmen. I had to stop you. If you had gone through it—I would have lost both you and Creon."

Creon looked at the King of Valdier over Carmen's head. "Thank you, brother," he said before he tenderly caressed Carmen's cheek. "We will get our daughter back. I swear I won't rest until we do."

CHAPTER 25

$\mathcal{I}$sle of the Monsters

Asahi let the rhythm of Tai Chi calm his mind and body. While researchers called it meditation in motion, his grandfather said Tai Chi unblocked and encouraged the flow of Qi, the energy force that flowed through the body and expanded outward. The movements helped balance the opposing elements that make up the universe. He believed his grandfather's version.

He controlled his breathing, pulling on his inner discipline, learned from decades of practice. It took him longer than usual to relax his mind. When he finally achieved the balance, the visions and the voice of the alien flowed through him.

The alien had abandoned the eel because of the Water Sirens, choosing instead to divide into narrow bands that looked like thousands of sea snakes. He felt a moment of disorientation when he connected to them. The slithering bodies blended with the dark grass on the bottom of the lake. The spread of the alien in this form made it more challenging for the Water Sirens to stop its advance.

You must stop it.

The sorrow-filled voice swept through his mind. It was barely discernable above the indistinct sounds resonating from the multitude of other creatures, but it still pierced through the noise, noticeably different because it was feminine. He followed it back to the source. It was a lone strand of the alien, larger than the rest, solid black, but with a touch of gold peeking through. It fell behind the others, appearing reluctant to follow.

He focused on it. There were two distinct voices coming from it. The first voice was familiar. It was the same one that he'd heard down in the goblin cave and later at the home of the Daktyloi. The second voice, the barely audible feminine voice, was filled with overwhelming pain and sorrow.

Who are you? he let the words form in his mind, unsure if the entity could hear him.

You must not allow it to reach the Gateway, the voice responded.

How can we stop it? he asked.

This one uses me, so the only way to stop it is—

Asahi stiffened when the black band encircling the gold screeched with fury. He remained focused on the vision, even as the entity in his body rebelled. Sweat beaded on his brow and intense pain surged until he felt like it would split him in two.

"Asahi, stop!" Nali's harsh cry pierced the agonizing pressure.

A powerful wave of fatigue hit him, and his knees buckled. He would have hit the ground hard if not for Nali's arm around his waist. He reached out and held onto her as he staggered.

"I'm alright," he slurred.

"No, you are not. Let me get you back to the tent," she replied.

He tiredly nodded his head. "This one is stronger than we thought," he mumbled.

"Then we must be even tougher," she said in a soothing tone.

"Nali... I love you," he murmured.

She tightened her hold on him and released a shaky breath. "I love you, too, Asahi," she replied.

He was vaguely aware of Ashure hurrying forward to help Nali get him into a tent. He closed his eyes when his head connected with the pillow and thankfully gave into the numbing darkness of exhaustion that engulfed him.

"Will he be alright?" Ashure asked a few minutes later.

Nali nodded and rubbed her arms. She gazed around the camp. Gargoyles sharpened their swords, ate, and murmured among themselves. Drago and Koorgan stood with another group, sparring with a variety of weapons. Gem and Ross sat by the fire talking with Ariness and Isha.

"Where's Orion?" she asked with a frown.

Ashure shrugged. "I saw him walking toward the river a few minutes ago. He's probably having a conversation with the fish," he said.

She looked back into the tent where Asahi lay sleeping on the wide cot. There were a few things that she needed to do, but she was hesitant to leave Asahi's side. She feared for his safety. On the cliff, it had been impossible to miss the alien inside him. When he had connected with the alien, its dark web had spread across his skin, turning his flesh darker than her own.

"Ashure, can you watch over him?" she asked in an emotion-filled voice.

"With my life, Nali," he vowed.

She withdrew the dagger from the waist of her trousers and held it out with trembling fingers. Ashure probably wouldn't need Mr. Gryphon, but if Asahi was to wake before her return, he might. She couldn't bring herself to ask Ashure to harm Asahi. If it came to that horrific point, she would be the one to do it. She had promised that she would.

"I'll be back as soon as I can," she said.

"Be careful," he cautioned.

She nodded. "I will."

~

Nali landed along the bank of the river and shifted from her gargoyle form back to her normal appearance. She raised an inquiring eyebrow at Orion. The Sea King stood in the middle of the river, holding his trident.

"Are you telling the fish a bedtime story?" she asked with an amused grin.

Orion chuckled and shook his head. "Yes and no. You can learn a lot from the water," he said, wading ashore.

She tilted her head. "And what did it tell you?" she curiously asked.

"That it is very wet," he dryly replied.

She laughed. "I would think the Sea King would have already figured that out," she teased.

He walked over and leaned back against a large rock, propping his trident against it. She marveled that his clothing dried as soon as he was out of the water. She walked over and leaned next to him.

"We know the alien is in the lake. The aquifers are connected and can span hundreds, sometimes thousands, of miles underground. The voices of the Water Sirens carry through it," he said.

She raised an eyebrow. "Thousands of feet up a mountain?" she asked in a skeptical tone.

He looked back at the river and nodded. "This was once a volcano. Trust me when I tell you that there is a lake under the crater that goes down thousands of feet," he said.

"If anyone would know, it would be you. Is it possible that the alien could attack us through the underground aquifer?" she asked.

"Anything is possible," he said.

"There is something else bothering you," she shrewdly observed.

Orion gave a brief nod and looked up at the stars. "I've been thinking about what Ashure told Drago and me—about what happened... what *could* happen if we fail. I'm not afraid of dying, but the thought of losing Jenny and our children...," he confessed, his voice trailing away as he found himself unable to express his horror.

She reached out and squeezed his arm in comfort. "We won't let that happen. This is a powerful place. The Goddess gave the Seven Kingdoms to us to protect. We won't give up without a fight—and neither will she. She will help us defend our world if we need her to," she said.

Orion nodded. "I hope you are right, Nali," he replied.

"I am. I need to check on a few things before the battle starts," she said as she stood up.

"I'll continue to monitor the situation from here. The Water Sirens are resourceful and love to gossip," he mused.

She chuckled. "Be careful they don't lure you away from Jenny," she teased.

"Never," he swore.

She laughed again before focusing on her transformation. The ripple effect of her hardening skin would be lost on most because it occurred so quickly. She spread her wings and pushed off the ground. Her night vision wasn't as good as that of a dragon, but it was good enough, especially considering that one moon was in its waning gibbous phase and the other a waxing crescent. Even the stars alone would have been enough on a cloudless night like tonight.

As she flew, her thoughts immediately returned to Asahi. She had to save him. She knew deep in her heart that any other option would be impossible to accept. Just the thought of her promise to him caused her physical pain.

Yet, the look on Orion's face and the intense grief in his voice reminded her that this was greater than herself or Asahi. This would be a fight for the survival of an infinite number of worlds and their inhabitants. In the large scale of the universe, she and Asahi—and even the Seven Kingdoms—were nothing but a speck of sand on a beach. The only comfort she could draw was that somehow, some way, the Goddess would not allow them to fail.

She took in the sights of her beloved mountain meadow and forests. This sanctuary was where the Goddess had given her into the care of the fairies. Under Xyrie's watchful eye and with the unicorn's great wisdom, the fairies had entrusted her to the Emperor and Empress of the Isle of the Monsters. They had been loving parents. Their deaths within weeks of each other had taught her that life was fragile.

She dipped lower, flying into the forest. Moonlight streamed through the canopy, illuminating her way from above while bioluminescent plants and insects lit her way from below. Soft, golden lights moving through the forest told her that she had found what she was looking for. She was relieved to know that Xyrie and the other unicorns were farther inland from the cliffs.

She glided under the tree limbs until she came to a thinning section of trees where the unicorns rested among the high ferns, and she landed close to a young stallion. He tossed his head, sending his long mane flying back and forth, then he respectfully knelt before her.

"Empress, the night birds told us you were coming," the stallion greeted.

She searched the area. "Where is Xyrie?" she asked, concerned when she didn't see the elder unicorn.

"Under the Great Willow," the stallion replied.

"Thank you," she murmured.

Nali looked toward the Great Willow, the oldest tree on the Isle of the Monsters. She folded her wings and they disappeared. She remained in her gargoyle form. Until her Isle was safe, it was best to remain ready for the battle to come.

While she had visited the Great Willow many times over the centuries, there was something different about it tonight. She lifted her chin when a tingle of energy caressed her face. The long, draping limbs of the tree were encased in a delicate golden glow.

"Xyrie," she called.

She swept aside the curtain of hanging limbs and stepped under the Willow's canopy. The old unicorn was lying at the base of the tree with her eyes closed. Nearly a dozen unicorns, ranging in age from a few weeks to a year old, raised their heads to look at her.

"Empress," Xyrie greeted.

She waved to Xyrie. "Don't get up," she said with a gentle smile.

Xyrie shook her head. "I don't think I could if I wanted to at the moment," the old unicorn replied with a soft snort.

It was true. Four juvenile unicorns snuggled close to Xyrie. Two of the foals rested their chins on her back while the other two lay in a tangled heap against her chest.

"Xyrie, I'm afraid. I need your guidance."

Asahi jerked upright, suddenly wide awake. A sound on his left caused him to turn in that direction. He automatically reached for the dagger by his side. It was missing.

"Asahi, how do you feel?" Ashure asked, stepping out of the shadows.

"My dagger—Mr. Gryphon—where is it?" he forced past his dry throat.

The Pirate King walked over to a table and poured water from a pitcher into a crystal cup. Asahi took deep, calming breaths to quiet his thundering heart.

Twisting on the cot, he swung his legs to the ground, and gratefully accepted the cup, drinking all the water in one long gulp. Ashure raised his eyebrow before he turned and retrieved the pitcher. Ashure refilled his cup two more times before Asahi was sated.

"Here is your dagger," Ashure said, holding it out to him.

"Thank you," he replied.

"How are you feeling?" Ashure repeated.

Asahi noticed concern and wariness in Ashure's eyes. He clutched the Gryphon dagger and stood up.

"I'm fine. Where is Nali?" he asked.

"She said she had some things to do. She will return shortly."

He watched Ashure take the empty cup from his hand and place it back on the table along with the pitcher—and then suddenly the memories, dreams, or whatever in the hell he was having, returned, surging through his mind.

Visions, he realized.

His connection with the alien was stronger. Asahi closed his eyes and focused. He swayed with the movements of the creature. It was moving through the narrow, boulder-strewn section where he had almost fallen overboard.

"The alien is in the lake near the base of the mountain. It has taken a different shape," he said in a voice devoid of emotion.

"What form?" Ashure quietly demanded.

"It's massive. I see dozens of legs, protected by a segmented exoskeleton. It reminds me of the prehistoric trilobites from my world, only this one has flat armor. It has spikes along its legs and a tail with three long spines," he described.

Ashure cursed loudly. "Well, that is fitting. It takes the lowest and smallest of life forms and turns it into a killing machine," he muttered.

Asahi opened his eyes and looked at Ashure. "It also has two long fangs," he added.

An expression of distaste crossed Ashure's face. "And it has added its own *modifications* to the evolutionary design," he interpreted.

"We need to warn Nali and the others. It will be here before dawn. The Water Sirens can no longer delay it—and, Ashure, it is mutating because of the imprisoned entity inside it. It has more strength now than we ever would have expected. I saw three, maybe four of the creatures functioning independently. The images blur together so it is hard to know for certain," he said.

Ashure reached out and gripped his arm. "Do the best you can to let us know what it is doing. We need to warn the others," he said.

He nodded. Looking down at the dagger, he rubbed his thumb over the hilt. He hadn't told Ashure everything. The connection was so strong now that he had almost lost himself within the vision. If it hadn't been for the fiery creature that had emerged out of nowhere... he wasn't sure what would have happened to him—and he wasn't quite sure what he had seen in those last few moments. He needed to make sense of the images before he tried to explain it.

Maybe it was another alien—drawn to the first one—but far more powerful. Powerful enough to kill our evil nemesis—including the piece inside of me? he wondered.

"Asahi, are you coming?" Ashure asked.

"Yes," he replied, lost in thought.

CHAPTER 26

*N*ali kissed Xyrie's forehead. "Thank you," she murmured.

"Is she going to kiss all of us, Xyrie?" a young foal sleepily asked.

"Hush now," Xyrie gently admonished.

Nali leaned down and pressed an affectionate kiss on the foul's forehead before she straightened and walked back the way she had come. She brushed the willow branches aside, paused, and looked back over her shoulder. Xyrie returned her gaze with a steady and confident one of her own.

Nali bowed her head in respect and stepped out from under the concealing curtain of willow limbs. When she stood outside, she drew in a deep breath, held it for a moment, and slowly released it. The visit had morphed from the need to warn Xyrie of the impending danger to a heart-felt need to share her fears and doubts with her sage counselor.

As usual when Nali visited, Xyrie listened more than she talked and asked questions instead of giving answers. Nali looked up at the sky.

Stars glittered through the canopy. A sudden desire to reach out and touched them filled her.

She unfolded her wings, spread them wide, and with a swift flap, she lifted off the ground. Soaring upward, past the forest's canopy, she flew higher and higher until the air grew thin and ice crystals formed on the smooth granite surface of her skin.

She looked down at the Isle of the Monsters. This was her Kingdom, her people, her home. From this altitude, most of the Isle was visible, so she took the opportunity to examine her vast kingdom. The massive lake glittered like diamonds in the moonlight. The wind blew white trails of clouds across the snow-crested mountains. Faint lights from various villages twinkled in the darkness like fireflies. She imagined she could hear the songs and laughter of her people carried on the wind. In the camp, she knew Asahi was waiting for her.

She reveled in the beauty of the night and her resolve was renewed. She pulled her wings in tight, pinning her arms against her side to increase the speed of her descent. Her fear about the threat facing their world diminished in the thrill of her freefall to the Isle below. It was time to end the alien's attack on the Seven Kingdoms once and for all.

An explosion suddenly lit the sky and illuminated the ground below. Almost as quickly, additional explosions reverberated through the air. In the glow of the bursts, Nali spotted the outline of four massive shapes climbing the face of the mountain. Her heart pounded with fear and rage. The attack had begun.

~

The Gateway

The vast power of the Gateway surrounded Phoenix. She marveled at the energy coursing through her. Unlike the portals she could create, this one was a long corridor whose walls, floor, and ceiling showed the universe.

She shifted back into her two-legged form. Stardust circled her, swatting at a comet as it passed by. She giggled when the symbiot tried to chase the tail of the comet as if it were a string hanging from a ball of yarn.

"Stardust, we mustn't touch anything," she gently admonished the curious symbiot.

Stardust stopped and stared longingly at the departing comet before returning to her side. Phoenix laughed and caressed her symbiot's head. Stardust had taken the form of a juvenile Werecat, except she'd forgotten to change her ears. Instead of the usual short ears, Stardust still had long droopy ears like Harvey.

Phoenix curled her fingers to keep herself from reaching out and touching the planets, colorful nebulas, and star clusters. They looked small, but she knew it was an illusion. All around her were unique star systems of varying shapes, sizes, and colors.

She didn't understand everything that was happening, but she knew she was witnessing the heartbeat of the universe. There were many planets that would never support life, yet there were just as many or more that would one day be just like Valdier and Earth with abundant life.

Mixed within the vastness, she noticed colorful threads connecting some of the worlds. She turned when she observed a flash of golden light, like a brief beacon in the inky blackness, then another and another. Tears burned her eyes as a subconscious awareness rose inside her—Aikaterina's people.

"There are so few of them," she murmured.

Help her, a series of voices called out, resonating in her mind.

"Who? Who am I supposed to help?" she asked, turning in a circle.

Help our sister, the voices replied.

She slowly turned. The corridor in front of her stretched out to a planet that looked eerily like Earth. It was a mirror image, connected to her mother's world by one of the colorful threads. On the mirrored planet, she noticed a faint golden glow fading in and out.

Fading—dying, she thought with dismay.

The alien who controls her must fail, the voices urgently called.

"But, why me? How will I know what to do?" she argued.

It is time.

"Time? Time for what?" she demanded, searching for the glitter of gold among the worlds.

There was no answer. Phoenix turned around and stared at the flickering golden light again. Even in the few seconds of conversation with the beings out there, the minute speck of light had become dimmer.

She closed her eyes and focused. "Aikaterina, what am I supposed to do?" she whispered.

Be yourself, Aikaterina's soft voice replied from far away.

Phoenix opened her eyes as the image that Aikaterina had revealed seared through her. Her body glowed with dancing flames, and her eyes blazed with a golden radiance. She was Phoenix. She was the Dragon Warrior Princess, chosen by the ancient guardians to help protect the star systems. It was time to be herself.

Isle of the Monsters

Nali landed near the edge of the cliff just as Drago transformed and plunged off the edge with a dozen gargoyle soldiers. Ross and Ashure stood on either side of Asahi with Koorgan on Ashure's right. She didn't see Orion, but she could hear Ross's loud curses.

"Why the hell isn't it working?" Ross demanded, peering over the edge of the cliff.

"What is wrong? What isn't working?" Nali asked.

They all turned at the same time. "It's Gem. The power she emitted destroyed the last alien. It isn't working this time," Ashure replied.

"Asahi...," she gritted out with dismay, her eyes locked on his face.

"I'm in control," he promised her.

The spider-like webs ran up his throat and along his cheeks now. His eyes held a haunted expression but they were clear. She reluctantly returned her attention to Ashure.

"Drago is laying down some dragon fire, but it doesn't look like it slowed those things down either," Ross commented.

"I wonder if smashing it with a rock will work," Koorgan suggested with a grim glint in his eyes.

Asahi frowned. "It would take an enormous rock to do that," he observed.

"I'll find the perfect one," Koorgan promised before he bolted toward the edge of the cliff.

"What is he—? Is he suicidal?" Asahi exclaimed in shock.

Nali grabbed Asahi's arm when he stepped closer to the edge. "He'll be alright," she reassured him.

"Koorgan always had bigger balls than brains—literally," Ashure muttered.

Together, they watched as Koorgan twisted around and faced them as he flung himself over the edge and began to grow. Asahi's shocked intake of breath reminded Nali of the first time she had seen a giant enlarge. Koorgan's hand, now with a palm spread of close to twenty feet across, gripped the edge of the cliff before he began descending along the sheer wall. Asahi pulled away from her and walked over to the edge to peer down at Koorgan.

"Now I understand why he's called King of the Giants," Asahi mused.

"It looks like he's found a rock," Ross commented.

Nali was about to comment when she noticed Asahi suddenly stagger. She reached for him only to stop when he shook his head. His eyes swirled with—gold.

"What is it?" she murmured.

"You must stop the alien before it reaches the Gateway," Asahi urgently instructed with a feminine voice and inflection that didn't sound like him at all.

"Asahi? Are you—you?" Ashure warily asked.

Asahi turned and looked at Ashure. A smile curved his lips, and to Nali's shock, the alien's black spider webbing turned to gold under Asahi's skin.

"He is here, but I needed to communicate with you. There is only one way to stop this creature," the entity inside Asahi answered.

"Who are you?" Nali demanded.

"I am Aminta. I could only inject an infinitesimal amount of my energy into this body, I am sorry, but I *can* give you information."

"What are you?" Ross asked in a guarded tone.

"What I am is no longer important. The creature's composition used to consist of a bacterium that lives and grows within the DNA of its host, but a portion of it mixed with me and the remains of a genetically mutated symbiot. It feeds off our energy. I am too weak to stop the mutation," she explained.

"How do we destroy it?" Ashure demanded.

Aminta glanced up at the stars. "Someone is coming. She can destroy this abomination once and for all. Make no mistake, you will *all* be needed to battle this enemy. Kill its various forms, make it condense into a single body with a fraction of its power left—that is *vitally* important. You must hold it off until the visitor from Valdier arrives to deal the final blow. It cannot be allowed to reach the Gateway. If it were to access the River of Life, I fear it would be unstoppable. Every spark of life in this universe would eventually be consumed."

"What about Asahi? If we defeat the creature, what will happen to him?" Nali quietly asked.

Aminta looked at her, and Nali saw the answer reflected in Asahi's possessed eyes. Tears filled her eyes, and she silently shook her head.

"No—I won't lose him," she said in a raw voice.

"This has never been done before: dual essences within a human like this. I have claimed him for the side he wishes to fight for, but the creature still sees him as one of its own resources in this war. What happens next, it will hurt him. I wish I could give you hope, but I simply don't know if he can survive this."

Nali leaned heavily on Ashure when her knees threatened to collapse, and he wrapped his arm around her waist. She regarded Asahi's calm face, past the thin veneer of Aminta's control. The gold faded until she was staring into Asahi's brown eyes.

"Nali," Asahi hoarsely said.

She pulled away from Ashure and wrapped her arms around Asahi's waist. Closing her eyes, she held him. All around her, she could hear explosions, Drago's roar, and Koorgan's booming curses.

"Empress, our forces have retreated to the second level," Pai said.

Nali opened her eyes, pulled back, and stared into Asahi's eyes. She slid her hand up his chest and caressed his face. He wrapped his hand around hers and held it against his cheek.

"Go. Aminta and I will connect with the alien," he said.

She nodded and reluctantly turned toward Pai. "I will assess the situation," she replied.

"We'll help Asahi," Ashure said, waving his hand at Ross.

"Thank you," Nali murmured. She nodded to Pai. "Let's kill these things."

CHAPTER 27

*B*efore reaching out to the alien, Asahi linked to the Goddess inside him, bringing to the fore a strong desire to join forces—and knowledge flooded his entire being. The scene they had witnessed in the mirror made much more sense now.

The entity that had shattered Aminta's original form was a tainted symbiot. Symbiots, Asahi learned, were the living gold companions of the Valdier, a dragon-shifting species. These golden companions were healers and shapeshifters, and they were born in the River of Life that contained the essence of the species many believed to be Goddesses. The symbiot that had attacked Aminta, however, had been perversely altered by the power-hungry Valdier outcast, Raffvin Reykill. Together they had waged war on the Goddesses in the sacred cavern.

To survive the tainted symbiot's attack, Aminta had mixed her essence with that of the mutated symbiot. Luckily, she was able to section off enough of her mind to force her new self through the Gateway, away from the river of symbiots and inadvertently back in time—any centuries back in time.

That version of their enemy had the potential to be powerful and destructive, but when it encountered a meteor that contained the alien bacteria, it became something even worse. Weakened by the battle, they could not fend off the bacteria that seeped into their merged remains.

The bacteria had quickly spread, evolving and engulfing what remained of them to become something new—a dangerous and dark liquid parasite. The joining of the bacteria and Raffvin's tortured symbiot had produced a need to destroy and consume any and every living being they encountered. Aminta had unwillingly supplied the tainted symbiot with her species' immense power and the knowledge of the worlds she had encountered.

Thankfully, she was again able to encapsulate a small portion of her essence, holding on to her sense of self. She had hoped that one day she would grow strong enough to reach out for help from another of her kind.

In the meantime, the evolving entity had divided into more parts. The meteor had become a living ship, formed from the majority of Aminta's essence. With her knowledge of the star system as a guide, it had proceeded to the nearest planet with life—The Seven Kingdoms.

The meteor ship had crashed into the ocean near the Isle of the Sea Serpent. Two smaller portions had remained behind with Aminta's depleted form, while the other aliens spread out, searching for new and more powerful hosts to inhabit. The first one had discovered Magna. The others had worse luck, overtaking weaker inhabitants of the Seven Kingdoms and burning through them quickly. The possessed Magna had caused so much chaos that no one even noticed the trail of the other aliens, assuming it was more of Magna's carnage.

The last two had accessed more of Aminta's memories, eventually recognizing the power that lay beyond the gateway in this world—the power found in the River of Life. They then spent a long time preparing for this war to reach the Gateway. The mountain itself was the biggest obstacle. The aliens could not access it until Aminta had grown stronger—because she was pure of heart.

When it was time, all the aliens in the Seven Kingdoms except the one imprisoned in Nali's palace had merged and began their assault. Many hosts had died along the way, but at last, now the merged alien was on the mountain. Asahi reeled with the sudden knowledge. He felt as if he had lived centuries in just a few seconds.

"Asahi, are you with us?" Ashure asked, touching his arm.

He looked at Ashure with a start before he nodded. "Yes. Aminta was sharing her memories with me," Asahi quietly replied.

"Learn anything useful?" Ross asked.

Asahi hesitated, his mind whirling. "I'm not sure. No—the plan is still the same," he somberly answered, closing his eyes.

I cannot do anymore to help you until the alien inside us is destroyed, Aminta instructed.

He pulled Mr. Gryphon from the sheath. The lion yawned and shook himself as he came to life, then he looked over at Ashure and Ross, twisted around on the hilt of the dagger and glared up at Asahi.

"Well, you took your sweet...," Mr. Gryphon said in an annoyed tone before he looked into Asahi's eyes, snapped his jaw shut, and bowed his head in respect. "My apologies, Goddess. How may I serve you?"

"Goddess!" Ross and Ashure exclaimed at the same time.

"I want you to kill the alien inside me, Mr. Gryphon," Asahi quietly requested.

Mr. Gryphon bowed his head again. "As you command, Goddess," the lion replied.

Mr. Gryphon wrapped his claws around the hilt and fluttered his wings as he lifted the dagger from Asahi's open palm. The lion carefully scanned Asahi like an MRI machine, searching for the exact location of the alien hidden deep inside his body. Then the golden gryphon suddenly lunged forward, burying the magical dagger deep into Asahi's heart.

Asahi gasped and stiffened at the blow but surprisingly felt no pain. The tip of the golden dagger pierced the black matter of the alien. The magic contained within the blade glowed, blossoming outward, and spread throughout Asahi's body.

Asahi vaguely heard Ashure and Ross cursing. Inside him, the dagger's powerful magic combined with Aminta's unique energy and surged through him. Spider veins of gold rippled along his skin, and his blood cells mutated.

Aminta's calming words flowed through him. *Do not be afraid.*

I'm not afraid of death. All I ask is that you protect Nali and the worlds endangered by the alien, he replied.

I will do my best, Asahi, Aminta vowed.

Asahi sensed Aminta's resolve to keep her promise but knew that she was still so very weak from her ordeal. He looked down at the cliffs below, searching for Nali in the light from the explosions. Like a beacon in the night, he saw her. She was his precious warrior.

I love you, Nali, he thought as Aminta took over his body.

Nali ducked under a cascade of falling boulders as Koorgan struck one of the alien trilobites. Three of her elite soldiers were trapped and needed assistance. She raised her sword and struck the trilobite when it swung its spiked tail in their direction. Her sword caught between the joint of two spikes, embedding it in the alien's flesh. The force drove her back into the cliff wall.

She grunted from the impact and fought to prevent the spike from piercing her granite flesh. She turned her head and saw her three gargoyles. One of them was wounded.

"Get him to safety," she ordered.

"Thank you, Empress," one soldier said.

She braced her feet against the cliff and pushed off. Her sharp blade sliced through part of the alien's tail. Surging forward, she whirled and sliced through the rest of the tail when the alien swung it back toward her.

The severed tail tumbled down the cliff face, bouncing off rocks before landing nearly a thousand feet below. She shielded her eyes when Gem materialized near the severed portion of the alien and released a brilliant burst worthy of a supernova.

They had discovered the only way to kill the damn things was to dismember them and then let Drago and Gem incinerate the pieces. If they didn't immediately destroy the part, it would regenerate, leaving them to fight even more of the damn things. Fortunately, they had discovered that fact after the first piece fell. Unfortunately, the hard shell on the alien trilobite was almost impossible to penetrate.

Nali looked up. One creature was almost to the mountain top. Pai and six gargoyle soldiers were attacking it. She uttered a loud cry of warning when one poisonous fang, concealed under the trilobite's armored head, suddenly unfurled and struck out at a young gargoyle. Pai saw the movement and flew between the gargoyle and the alien.

"Pai, no!" she screamed.

Grief and rage thundered through her when the fang pierced Pai's chest. She channeled her emotions into her wings' powerful strokes. Soaring upward, she swung her sword and severed the fang.

Pai fell—right off the edge of the cliff. Nali followed him, shifting into an enormous eagle, and plummeted along the mountain's cliff face.

She gently closed her massive claws around the venerable hippogriff and spread her wings, sweeping upward and away from the battle. Tears blinded her as she circled back to the mountain top. She needed to find Xyrie.

Ashure and Ross looked up as she flew overhead, but Nali didn't see Asahi with them. Her heart hammered in her chest. She had to trust that they would keep their promise to protect Asahi until she returned.

She focused on where she was going. Ahead in the long meadow, Nali glimpsed Xyrie emerging from the trees. The unicorn was alone.

Nali glided lower until she was only a few feet above the ground. She lifted her wings, spread her feathers, and hovered near Xyrie. As gently as she could, she lowered Pai to the ground and released him.

The moment she did, she transformed and dropped to the ground. Her booted feet landed on the soft grass that Pai loved to curl up and nap on, and she sank to her knees beside him.

She trembled as she tenderly caressed the bloodstained gray feathers on his face. His breathing was shallow and uneven. She was afraid to remove the fang for fear he would bleed out.

"Pai, you stubborn old hippogriff. What were you doing in the middle of the battle? You were supposed to coordinate from a safe distance," she lovingly chided.

"What... fun... is... there... in that?" he faintly responded, opening his eyes and looking at her.

A tear slipped down her cheek, and she caressed his beak. "Not much, I guess," she admitted.

Pai took a shuddering breath and turned his beak into her palm. She sobbed when he went limp in her arms. Tears freely coursed down her cheeks. She lowered her head and pressed a kiss against the hippogriff's brow.

"Please, Xyrie, help him," she begged, not looking up when the unicorn stopped next to them.

"There are some things even a Goddess cannot heal," Xyrie gently replied.

With a broken heart, Nali protectively held Pai's head and looked up at Xyrie. The elder unicorn looked back at her with a sad expression. She took a shuddering breath and tilted her head back to stare up at the sky. Dawn was breaking, and the stars were fading as the colors of morning filled the heavens.

She bowed her head. "Return to the universe, my dear friend," she murmured. She closed her eyes and whispered a spell.

Colorful light surrounded Pai's body as he faded away. His essence swirled with the colors of dawn before rising into the sky. Nali opened her eyes and watched as Pai's essence returned to the Seven Kingdoms. With a heavy heart, she rose to her feet and tiredly looked back toward the cliff. The sounds of battle still raged.

"I want you and the unicorns to go to the old fortress. Call my house-elves and have them seal the gates," she instructed.

"I have already instructed the other unicorns to go there," Xyrie replied.

Nali looked at the elder unicorn, her dear friend and mentor. "I want you to go too, Xyrie," she said.

Xyrie shook her head. "Nay, Empress. My place is here, protecting you and the Kingdom," the unicorn firmly stated.

Nali shook her head. "You saw what happened to Pai. I can't lose you, Xyrie... or Asahi," she stated.

"I will do what I can to help you, Nali. Trust in those who stand beside you," Xyrie replied.

She bowed her head, knowing that Xyrie would not budge on her decision. "I must return to the cliffs," Nali said.

"I will go to the river," Xyrie replied.

"Xyrie...," Nali muttered in frustration before she shook her head.

"Go, Nali," Xyrie gently ordered with a toss of her head.

Nali called forth the form of the gargoyle, hardening her flesh. She harnessed her rage and grief. She would not lose any more of the creatures under her protection. Pai's death would be the last, she vowed to herself.

She lifted off the ground, soaring back to the cliffs. In the growing light of morning, Nali surveyed the scene below. Koorgan and the gargoyle forces hammered at the remaining two alien trilobites. Gem's blinding power and the blue-white flames of dragon fire consumed the alien fragments that were ripped or cut off.

On the cliff, Ariness and Isha had formed a massive magical shield to prevent the trilobites from breaching the top. Nali's heart thundered when one trilobite rose above the barrier and unfurled both of its fangs. It struck out toward Isha.

Ross tackled Isha, pulling him aside and rolling away as Ashure charged toward the creature. With his enchanted sword, Ashure jumped high into the air and pierced the underbelly of the trilobite, slicing it open. Nali dove, catching Ashure from behind as he fell.

The alien trilobite struck out with one of its fangs as it fell backward. She twisted in the air, grunting when the fang shattered as it hit her stone back between her wings. The blow, combined with the weight of Ashure, was enough to knock her out of the air.

She flipped over at the last second, wrapping her wings protectively around Ashure as they hit the ground and skidded several yards. Grass and dirt flew in all directions as she cut a deep rut in the ground before coming to a stop. She peered through her wings making sure it was safe.

"Tonya will thank you for saving my neck," Ashure said.

"It isn't safe yet," she replied, opening her wings and releasing him. "Where is Asahi?"

"Asahi—yes, well, things became a little complicated after you left," he nervously answered.

Nali pushed Ashure aside and stood. She wildly scanned the area. The trilobite Ashure had sliced open was turning to ash before her eyes. Isha, impressed with the success of Ashure's move, had retrieved the enchanted sword and was using the same move on the last creature— with the help of Koorgan who held it around the neck from behind. Koorgan tossed the mortally wounded alien off the mountain. Gem and Drago hovered nearby, ready to incinerate it. Yet, no matter where she looked, Nali didn't see Asahi.

"Where is he?" she demanded as she turned and faced Ashure, who was now standing.

"I'm not sure. The last time I saw him, he was headed in the direction of the river. He disappeared when the bugs came up over the cliff's edge," he confessed.

"I have to find him. The alien is still inside him. With the destruction of the others, the alien might…." She shook her head, unable to continue as visions of the dead Sea Stag formed in her mind.

"Nali, wait," Ashure said, touching her arm when she took a step away from him.

"What?" she snapped before she drew in a deep breath and slowly released it. "I'm sorry. Pai is dead, and I'm afraid of losing Asahi."

"I'm sorry about Pai. I know how much you cared about him. I… I think it would be best if I went with you to find Asahi. He… isn't the same. I can fill you in while we search for him," he hesitantly explained in a compassionate voice.

"It will be faster if we fly," she said.

"I was afraid you'd say that," he muttered.

Despite the tense situation, Nali smiled when Ashure turned his back to her and raised his arms so she could wrap hers around him. Stepping up behind him, she rested her chin on his shoulder.

"Thank you for being here for me," she murmured.

"Always, whether or not you think you need me. Now, let's go save your man," he said.

CHAPTER 28

The memory of the dagger in his heart made Asahi rub the aching spot. Fortunately for him, the magic that had killed the invasive alien had healed him. Aminta withdrew to the back of his mind once he had recovered his wits after being on the edge of death. Asahi only felt her through his subconscious now. There was a force pulling him away from the cliff, and he followed it, trusting that Aminta would not lead him astray.

"You were the one who told me to stab you," Mr. Gryphon growled when he noticed Asahi touching his former stab wound.

Asahi fought to keep from grinning at the irritated, defensive tone in the Gryphon's voice. If he didn't know better, he would have thought the animated dagger cared about him.

"I didn't say stab me. If it helps soothe your mind, I am grateful for your assistance," he said.

Mr. Gryphon sniffed loudly. "Good. I was just doing what I was told to do by the Goddess," he reiterated.

"I fully understand that, my friend," Asahi murmured.

The need to hurry increased the farther inland he walked. He knew he was getting close to something dangerous.

It comes. If it reaches the Gateway, the worlds are doomed, Aminta whispered in his mind.

"What is coming?" he asked.

He stopped when he observed Orion standing in a river. He frowned when he noticed a horse on the bank beside the Sea King. For a second, he wondered if he had stepped onto a western movie set. That idea burst when he glimpsed the horse's profile. There was a long horn protruding from its forehead.

Okay, more like the Lord of the Rings movie set, he amended.

The thought had no sooner flashed through his mind than a vision replaced it. It showed the alien's remaining portion that contained the rest of Aminta. It was smaller but more powerful than the others combined. It had used the other parts of itself as a distraction.

"Orion! Get out of the water, now!" he shouted.

Adrenaline flooded him, and he sprinted forward. A funnel of water lifted Orion out of the river and deposited him on the bank. Orion gripped the trident in both hands and pointed it at the water. Xyrie pawed at the ground as the water exploded around them.

The ground shook, and water gushed into the opening abyss beneath the river. Out of the widening gap, the head of a serpent appeared.

Orion pointed his trident at the beast and fired a burst of lightning. The energy bounced off the slick black scales. The creature released a menacing chuckle before it lunged.

Horror changed to astonishment when the unicorn stepped in front of Orion and lowered her head. The horn on her forehead glowed a brilliant incandescent gold. The serpent recoiled.

"Your tricks will not work now," the alien hissed. "We have found your weakness."

It will pull the ground out from underneath them, Aminta warned.

"Orion, get back! The ground...," Asahi yelled.

In the ensuing quake, Asahi stumbled backward. The unicorn turned and bolted across the meadow and into the forest. He cursed when he saw Orion fall into a fissure.

Bracing a hand against the ground, Asahi pushed off like a sprinter. He jumped over the widening gap, zigzagging back and forth as more appeared. The alien serpent emerged out of the destroyed riverbed. Asahi fell and rolled aside when it flew past him.

You must stop it, Aminta cried.

"I have to help Orion," he growled.

You must stop the alien from reaching the Gateway, Aminta frantically insisted.

"After I save Orion," he calmly replied.

"Asahi!"

The sound of Nali's voice caused him to jerk to a stop, and he searched for her. He was surprised to see she wasn't alone. He instinctively steadied Ashure when she released the pirate. She landed beside them with a rush of wind.

"There is another alien, I take it," Ashure said, looking at the gaping hole.

"Yes, it headed into the woods. Orion fell into the fissure," Asahi said, swaying.

"What is it?" Nali asked.

He wanted to close his eyes when she cupped his face between her hands. "We need to see if Orion is alive and stop the alien," he growled.

"I've got Orion," Ashure offered. "If there's a lake down there like he said, he'll be fine. He's probably talking to an antisocial sea monster hidden in the depths as we speak." Ashure handed his precious sword to Nali. "Take my sword; you'll need it more than I will. Now you two go save our worlds! I've seen what will happen if you don't."

Nali took the magic sword and nodded. With a flick of her fingers, a sheath with a strap formed around the sword. She slid the strap over her head and positioned it against her side.

"Three—we *three* will go save the world," Mr. Gryphon grumbled. "One of these days you people will stop forgetting your most important treasure like I'm some ordinary, dusty relic! I'm the Golden Dagger, and I can slay evil aliens just as well as any sword the Sea Witch can enchant. How many times am I going to have to save the day before I get any respect?"

"You have my greatest respect, Mr. Gryphon," Asahi reassured the golden lion before he turned his attention to Nali. "How fast can you fly?" he asked.

"Fast," she replied with a determined glint in her eyes. She stepped behind him and held him tight.

Taking a deep breath, Asahi realized that this might be the last time he ever felt her arms around him, and he was going to savor every second.

"Oh, this is going to be fun," Mr. Gryphon sassed. "Whatever you do, don't drop me!" he ordered as he crawled to the hilt of the dagger and wrapped his tail around it.

"I won't, my friend," Asahi quietly promised. He tightened his grip on the dagger as Nali lifted them off the ground.

They soared across the meadow and into the forest at a blinding speed. Asahi's breath caught in his throat as Nali skillfully negotiated the forest. She skirted around trees and under low-hanging limbs with the skill of a Peregrine falcon on the hunt. The alien serpent was less than a hundred yards ahead of them.

I have tried to slow it down, but now I haven't the strength to resist it, Aminta's faint voice murmured.

We will end this, Asahi silently vowed.

He didn't know if Aminta heard him. He could no longer detect her tiny spark inside himself. Nali's arms tightened around him, and he knew the final battle for their survival depended on what happened next.

"Fly over and drop me," he instructed.

"Are you crazy?" she hissed in disbelief.

"Completely," he replied.

She shook her head but swerved to intercept the alien serpent. "You've been hanging around Ashure for too long," she muttered.

"I concur!" Mr. Gryphon snapped.

"Be ready, Golden Dagger," Asahi warned.

Nali dropped them. He spread his feet apart and held the dagger with both hands as he fell. For a moment, he was weightless until his feet connected with the thick scales behind the serpent's head, which was nearly thirty feet off the ground. He buried the dagger to the hilt in the smooth surface of the serpent's skull and clung to the snake as it jerked.

Mr. Gryphon roared and blazed like a beacon as he poured every ounce of the magic held within his dagger into the alien. The serpent snapped its head back and forth, trying to dislodge the dagger. Asahi fought to hold on.

"Asahi, behind you!" Nali shouted.

Out of the corner of his eye, Asahi saw the serpent's tail curving around in his direction. He let go when the serpent shook its head again, and as he went airborne, he twisted and stretched out his hands. Nali swooped down and caught him in midair.

She dropped him near the ground. Twisting around and facing the serpent, she pulled Ashure's sword from the sheath. Asahi sprinted to the left, yelling, while Nali flew to the right.

The serpent swung its tail around and caught him across the stomach, knocking the breath out of him and lifting him off the ground again. Asahi clung to the tail and glanced up. Nali was deflecting the serpent's lethal strikes.

Between attacks, the alien hissed, "You cannot defeat me. I have unlocked the knowledge and might of the most powerful species in the universe."

Nali slashed the serpent's nose. Ashure's enchanted blade opened a deep cut, and the alien drew back with a loud hiss. Nali ducked when the serpent slammed into a nearby tree.

The impact nearly dislodged Asahi from the serpent's tail. He dug his fingers in between the scales for better purchase and looked up. Mr. Gryphon was frantically trying to pull the dagger out of the sticky black liquid pouring from the alien's head. With grim determination, Asahi began climbing the creature's back, while Nali kept the its attention on her and Ashure's sword.

"You will *never* succeed," she snarled. "Your reign of terror will end here and now."

"It is only the beginning," the alien gleefully hissed. "Nothing can stop me."

An idea formed in Asahi's mind. He could almost hear his grandfather chuckling. To kill evil, you need to cut off its head. Of course, Aiko had never mentioned evil being a giant serpent, most likely because his grandfather was terrified of snakes. Still, the words were apropos in this instance, and if it worked, he would have to light a candle in his grandfather's memory and thank him for all his years of guidance.

Let's hope I get a chance to do it, he thought as he climbed.

Nali swung the sword at the alien, slicing several deep cuts into its flesh. Despite the creature's claim that they couldn't destroy it, the magic in the sword was inflicting damage. Now, if she could only get close enough to do some lethal damage without becoming a morning snack!

She ducked and gritted her teeth when the serpent rammed the tree near her. The crack of snapping wood alerted her to the added danger she faced. She barely dodged a large branch that fell to her right. Quickly, she flew upward, threading her way through the maze of limbs falling around her. Her left wing collided with a branch, and she winced when the force of the impact sent her spinning out of control. She rolled, trying to miss a clump of branches, and bounced off a tree trunk.

She tucked her wings in, rolled in the opposite direction of the tree as it fell, and planted her feet on the trunk. With a tight grip on the sword's hilt, she ran up the falling tree, jumping over limbs. In her peripheral vision, she could see Asahi climbing the serpent's back near its head. She smiled.

"We know what you are. You are nothing but a parasite," she shouted, jumping the last few feet and taking to the air again once she was clear of the tree.

"No longer," the alien replied before breathing deeply. "You think I cannot sense the Goddess's power in you? I *know.* It will not save you or your world," the alien goaded.

"Yet, you are fearful. We stopped the others of your kind. You are the one who is powerless. You will fail just as the others failed—*parasite*," Nali retorted in a condescending tone.

While she antagonized the alien, the sun appeared over the horizon, and Asahi reached the base of the serpent's head. Nali called forth the Goddess's Mirror and lifted it into the air. The sun caught the polished surface, and she directed the blinding rays at the serpent.

The creature screeched in rage when an intensely bright beam of sunlight struck its eyes. Nali threw the enchanted sword to Asahi and held her breath. This might be their only chance to defeat the creature.

She was so focused on Asahi and the sword that the serpent's strike caught her off-guard. She cried out when it closed its powerful jaws around her. The mirror tumbled to the ground, disappearing beneath the branches of the fallen tree.

She braced her hands between the serpent's fangs and pressed her booted feet into the soft tissue of its jaw. She groaned when the serpent exerted pressure. Tiny fissures appeared along her skin, and her knees bent as she fought to keep from being crushed. Pain slashed through her when the serpent slammed its forked tongue into her stomach.

The alien's menacing laughter nearly deafened her. She winced as its fiery breath surrounded her. It was impossible to turn into another creature without making herself even more vulnerable.

"Asahi, if you are ready, now would be an excellent time," she muttered between gritted teeth.

"He's working on it. In the meantime, I have an idea, Empress," Mr. Gryphon cheerfully responded as he sailed into the serpent's right nostril.

Nali blinked in surprise. The alien shook its head, trying to dislodge the sudden irritation. It flexed its jaws, moving like a wave rolling to shore. It took her a second to realize that the serpent was about to sneeze.

She muttered a curse when Mr. Gryphon reappeared out of the serpent's left nostril, grabbed the back of her collar, and yanked her out of the creature's mouth with surprising strength. She shouted in alarm and rolled aside when the serpent opened its mouth wide and moved its head in her direction.

The serpent's head brushed the tip of her left wing as she turned and faced it again. In that instant, she realized that the alien's head was continuing to the ground while the rest of its body collapsed.

Plumes of black ash rose from the fallen creature, transforming into white mist as the magic sword did its work. Nali's heart pounded as she searched for Asahi. She laughed in relief when she saw him clinging to a branch.

"We did it!" she breathed, lifting a shaky hand to her cheek.

"I hope he remembered to retrieve my dagger," Mr. Gryphon commented, fluttering next to her ear.

Nali absently nodded, her rapt gaze never leaving Asahi's face. He was staring down at the ground. The branch he was clinging to was drooping dangerously. She quickly flew to him.

"Would you like a lift?" she teased.

He looked at her and smiled. "That would be nice. I appear to have developed a distressing habit of getting stuck in trees since I arrived— or at least since I met you," he confessed.

"Thank you for sending Mr. Gryphon to help me," she said, wrapping her arms around his waist and lifting him off the branch.

He held onto her and kissed her lips softly. She parted them and returned his kiss with a passion born from the fear of losing him and her love. A persistent and irritating noise next to her ear brought her back to the present.

"Can you two do that later? I'd like to find my dagger," Mr. Gryphon growled.

Asahi sighed. "I dropped it along with the sword when the serpent evaporated underneath me," he admitted.

"You dropped it! 'Go save the Empress. I'll protect the dagger' you said," Mr. Gryphon complained. "I'll be having nightmares for the next *century* of being inside that monster's nose. No offense, Empress," he quickly tacked on. "Of course your life was worth it."

"None taken, my dear, brave Golden Dagger," Nali replied with a smile.

She fought to keep from laughing when the tiny lion puffed out his chest, fluttered his wings, shook out his mane, and snapped his tail with delight at her compliment. Asahi's exasperated groan made her joyous laughter burst forth. Her relief and joy was too much to be contained.

"Mr. Gryphon, can you go search for your dagger?" Nali asked sweetly. "We'll join you in a few minutes."

"I save the day, he loses my dagger, and he's the one getting kissed," Mr. Gryphon grumbled as he disappeared through the branches below.

Nali ignored the lion's grumbling. Her attention was all on Asahi. She tilted her head, leaned in, and kissed him again.

"Do you have a license to fly and kiss?" he seductively murmured when she paused a breath away from his lips.

"I'm the Empress of the Monsters. Trust me when I say I can do a lot more," she breathed.

Their lips met again with fervent relief. They molded their bodies together as she softly landed. The second their feet touched the ground, she pulled away and began placing tiny kisses along his jaw.

"I... was... so afraid," she confessed, peppering his lips with brief kisses between her words.

He captured her face between his hands. "How do you think I felt when I saw you disappear into that snake's mouth?" he retorted.

He covered her lips with his again. She tasted his fear in that kiss. Their tongues tangled and their breathing grew heavy. She ran her hands across his back, trying to pull him closer.

"Hey, love birds, you need to see this!" Mr. Gryphon shouted.

Nali groaned when Asahi reluctantly pulled away. She rested her forehead against his and pulled deep, calming breaths into her lungs. A giggle escaped her when she saw the expression on Asahi's face.

"I hope he found his dagger because I'm ready to shove him back in his sheath," he stated.

"I know what you mean," Nali laughed.

"Nali! Asahi! You really need to come here," Mr. Gryphon insisted.

Asahi shook his head and looked at her with amusement. "We better go, or he'll never shut up," he said.

"If it helps, I know about this amazing little cottage nearby," she said with a suggestive gleam in her eyes as she turned away.

"I look forward to visiting it—with you," he murmured, wrapping his arm around her waist.

CHAPTER 29

*A*sahi held a branch aside so Nali could pass through. Mr. Gryphon's tone was becoming more animated with each passing minute. On a positive note, the lion didn't sound upset.

As long as it isn't more of the alien, he thought.

He tried to ignore the nagging feeling in his gut when he remembered his vision of the flaming entity. He must have misinterpreted the image. It seemed impossible that any piece of the alien could have survived. From his vantage point at the top of the branches, Asahi had an unobstructed view of what had happened to the alien.

He replayed the scene in his mind, searching for any pertinent detail that he might have missed. Nali had thrown Ashure's sword to him, and he had plunged it into the serpent's neck at the base of its head. A brilliant white light had burst from the sword, searing through the creature's body like spikes of lightning, creating a ring around its neck. The magic had spread, growing brighter and hotter as it ate away the alien's flesh until nothing remained but glowing embers. Even those dissipated when they hit the ground. There had been nothing left but ash. He was sure of it.

Yet, Aminta had been certain that someone would arrive from Valdier to destroy the alien. She had also been pretty certain that Asahi would die, though. Perhaps the fact that he had survived made all the difference. Perhaps something had happened to their fiery savior to keep her from coming to their aid.

Asahi paused when Nali put her hand out. They both stared at the sword embedded in the ground. He walked over and pulled it out. There was a long scorch mark running from the tip to the hilt as if a lightning bolt had struck it.

"This looks like it has seen better days," he dryly commented, holding it out to Nali.

She grimaced as she took it. "Ashure is sure to have a few choice words for me. He absolutely adores his swords. I'd say he was compensating for something, but unfortunately, I *have* seen him in the buff, so I know he isn't," she said.

"Really?" Asahi inquired with a raised eyebrow.

She scrunched her nose. "Let's change the subject, shall we? He's like a brother to me! Let's just say Ashure has kept the ladies purring with happiness for several centuries, and leave it at that," she replied with a shudder.

"Hello!" Mr. Gryphon called. "Are you two ever going to…. There you are! What took you so long? Wait, strike that question. If you two were having sex, I don't want to know," Mr. Gryphon growled.

"Did you find your dagger?" Asahi politely inquired.

Mr. Gryphon nodded. "Yes, and something else." He led them farther into the tangled tree limbs.

"Wha…? Oh, my," Nali breathed, stunned.

Asahi swallowed and gaped in awe at the beautiful woman rising from the ground into a sitting position. Her body was solid gold, like his vision of the aliens in the cave. He stepped forward when she turned and faced them.

"Aminta?" he quietly surmised.

The woman tilted her head, frowned, and looked around before returning her gaze to his face. She bowed her head uncertainly. He reached out and helped her to her feet. She swayed.

"I... Where am I?" she asked in a confused voice.

"You are on the Isle of the Monsters. It is part of the Seven Kingdoms," Nali replied in a gentle tone.

"The Seven Kingdoms.... I remember the alien creature that held me...," Aminta murmured, looking around again.

"Gone. Destroyed," Nali reassured her.

Aminta sagged against him. "Thank you," she whispered in an unsteady voice.

"You're welcome," Mr. Gryphon preened. "I helped with that, by the way," the Golden Dagger added rather self-importantly.

Nali touched Aminta's arm and looked at Asahi. "We should have Xyrie check her over to make sure she is alright," she suggested.

"I'll carry her," he said.

"Perhaps you should sheath yourself for a well-deserved rest after all your hard work, Mr. Gryphon," Nali suggested.

"Don't mind if I do," the lion said with a huge yawn. "Saving the universe is quite tiring."

Asahi shook his head and held his arm away from his side until Mr. Gryphon, clutching the hilt of the dagger, slid the blade into the sheath. Once he secured the dagger, Asahi swept Aminta into his arms. She held onto his neck and laid her head against his shoulder. He was shocked that this beautiful entity had survived, much less could stand, after everything she had been through. It boggled his mind how anyone could have survived after enduring such destructive evil.

"How far is it?" he asked.

Nali glanced over her shoulder and smiled. "Not far. I'm glad the alien didn't realize how close it was to the Gateway. If it had, we might never have been able to stop it," she confessed.

He silently agreed when they stepped out of the woods into a small clearing no more than a hundred yards from where they had destroyed the alien. In the center of the clearing stood a magnificent willow tree.

He had never seen one this large before. The branches of the giant willow draped to the ground. It stood nearly five stories high and probably measured a half-acre or more in circumference . Brilliant purple flowers, twinkling like fairy lights in the early morning light, were mixed in with the pale green leaves. In front of the willow stood the unicorn from the river.

Nali smiled and rushed forward, wrapping her arms around Xyrie's neck. A sense of peace swept over him at the sight. He couldn't imagine being anywhere but here, on this alien world, surrounded by mythical creatures, holding a Goddess, and following the most beautiful woman in all the kingdoms.

"I can stand," Aminta murmured near his ear.

"Of course. My apologies," he said, gently placing her feet on the ground.

"No apologies necessary, human. You have done everything I hoped you would," Aminta said gleefully.

Asahi frowned, looking down at the face so close to his own, and noticed black swirls mixed with Aminta's golden pupils. He attempted to let her go and move away, but thick golden bands wrapped around his arm.

"Nali!" he shouted in warning.

Nali turned and gasped. Asahi grunted when the golden bands wrapped around his chest and up his neck. He struggled to break free. It felt like he was being eaten alive.

"Release him, alien," Xyrie's voice commanded.

Aminta scoffed and shook her head. "Why don't you show them your natural form, *sister*. It is time, don't you think?" she mocked.

Asahi focused on slowing his breathing as the bands moved up to his jaw. He slid his hand down to his side, trying to reach Mr. Gryphon. Pain shot through him when the alien bent him backward.

"I can make this painful, or I can make it excruciating. Either way, I will enjoy it, human," the alien murmured near his ear.

"Kill it," he choked out.

"Release him," Xyrie ordered.

The quick breath Asahi inhaled was knocked out of him when the unicorn suddenly transformed. In its place stood an elegant woman made of gold.

"You cannot harm one of your own kind, Xyrie. It is forbidden," Aminta smugly replied.

"You are no longer one of us. The alien has contaminated the power that once belonged to you. I can kill it," Xyrie stated, taking a step closer to them.

Aminta raised an eyebrow. "Yes, you can, but are you willing to kill the human?" she asked.

Asahi felt the alien sinking into his skin. He knew what it was doing—and what it would do, not only to him, but to the worlds. One life or countless billions? There was no choice.

"Destroy it, Nali," he ordered in a strained voice.

"NO!" Nali pleaded, reaching for him.

He stiffened as a chill seeped over him. Mentally, he fought to retain control, detaching part of his mind behind a protective wall. The real Aminta within—the tiny ember that was left of her—sought to shield him from the pain as he was consumed.

"Stand aside, Xyrie," the alien ordered.

Asahi internally winced when he heard the words coming from his mouth. The sensation of being disconnected from his body was bewildering. Afraid of losing what little remained of himself, he focused on Nali.

"Release him," Nali ordered, her voice dropping to a growl in her fury.

She raised Ashure's sword and walked toward him. Tears glistened in her beautiful eyes. Asahi desperately wanted to erase the pain he saw there. For a brief second, he regained control of his body.

"Remember your promise, Nali. If I become a danger to you or your people...," he reminded her.

"Asahi...," she choked out in a raw voice.

The sword in her hands dipped, and he desperately wanted to touch her one last time. Instead, he curled his fingers into a fist of frustration. The alien was using his emotions—and Nali's—to manipulate them.

"I will always love you, Empress, but now it is time for you to save our worlds," he said in a gentle voice.

Tears coursed down Nali's cheeks. "I love you, Asahi," she whispered.

He didn't look away when she lifted the sword above her head. Her choked sob tore at his heart even as the alien tried to wrest control of his body to stop her from killing it once and for all. He lifted his chin.

The Gateway!

Asahi heard Aminta's faint voice but didn't process what she meant until he noticed that an area near the giant willow was beginning to glow. Nali must have felt the energy shift in the air because she paused. Xyrie's startled reaction to the forming gateway made him think the alien was responsible for what was occurring.

"Nali, kill the alien now!" he harshly ordered. With stark terror, he saw the blackness of space through the portal.

Nali swung the sword at his fierce command. Time slowed, stretching into nanoseconds. The alien howled with fury and desperately attempted to withdraw from his body. Aminta, equally desperate, clung to him.

From the Gateway a brilliant fireball struck his chest and passed through his body. The impact nearly lifted him off of his feet. He stumbled backward, flailing his arms to keep his balance before he sank to his knees. He took a deep gasping breath as he realized the flame that had passed through him had extracted the alien from his body.

The alien's bellow of rage forced Asahi into action. Though still dazed, he drew his dagger, twisted, and threw it with deadly accuracy. Nali swept past him as he collapsed in an exhausted heap. She swung Ashure's enchanted sword with a primitive war cry. The two magical blades pierced the malevolent being—one through the chest, the other in the center of its forehead.

Asahi forced himself to his feet and beheld the winged creature who had emerged from the Gateway. She looked like a phoenix—

No, a dragon, he thought as she spewed a dazzling torrent of fire. The small dragon was covered in flaming, black downy feathers and shielded with golden armor. He instinctively turned away and lifted his arm to shield his face from the flame, only to lower it when he didn't feel any heat. He stared in awe at the flaming bird-like dragon hovering above the shrieking alien.

"What is that?" Nali breathed in disbelief, dropping her sword and staggering back.

He wrapped his arms around her and pulled her close. She gripped his shoulders in shock. They both jumped and turned their heads, protecting their eyes, when a brilliant light engulfed the alien, temporarily blinding them.

Asahi carefully lowered his arm and straightened. He studied the alien's rigid form, forever frozen like the ash-covered mummified bodies at Pompeii. It looked like a plaster casting.

He tightened his hold on Nali when she tried to pull away from him. They looked at each other, then turned toward Xyrie, still shocked to see her as a woman made of living gold instead of a unicorn. She came closer and stood beside them, and then all of their attention was arrested by a young adolescent—a black-haired girl who suddenly replaced the bird-dragon. The girl stood with her feet spread apart, staring back at them with a wide-eyed and wary yet curious gaze. She gently caressed the head of a gigantic golden creature that resembled the golden Xyrie, only instead of a gold woman, it was a dog with long droopy ears.

The girl kept looking at them and then at the encrusted alien. She was clearly trying to discern if they were a threat. Asahi stepped in front of Nali and raised his hand.

"It's alright. We won't hurt you," he said in a calm voice.

"It's not me that I'm afraid you might hurt," the girl replied.

The sound of thumping and the cracking of the crust surrounding the alien drew their attention. Nali grabbed Ashure's sword from the ground. Asahi urgently waved his hand at the girl when she stepped closer to the alien.

"Stop!" Asahi warned.

"Will someone get me out of here?" Mr. Gryphon demanded from inside the crust.

"Mr. Gryphon?" Nali exclaimed in a shocked voice.

"Get me out of this pie crust!" the Golden Dagger growled.

A small golden paw appeared through a hole. Asahi hurried forward and began pulling pieces of the crust away. Mr. Gryphon stuck his head out of the opening and glared at him.

"If I wasn't an animated object, I would need therapy for this!" Mr. Gryphon yelled, trying to wiggle through the opening. "My dagger's stuck," he added with a grunt.

"Stand back," Nali said, lifting her sword.

Asahi stood aside as Nali smashed the hilt of the sword against the crust. Long cracks appeared, spreading outward. She hit it again and it crumbled. Asahi caught Mr. Gryphon in mid-flight. He held the dagger with one hand and cupped the exhausted lion with the other. He frowned when Nali grabbed his arm and pulled him back a step.

"Asahi!" Nali said with alarm.

Something under the pile of crust was moving. He gripped the hilt of the dagger, ready to use it. Everyone warily watched as a slender golden arm appeared.

"Don't hurt her," the young dragon-shifter said.

"Stay back," Asahi ordered.

The girl ignored him, stepped forward, and carefully uncovered the woman. He glanced at Nali and then at Xyrie, who was glowing.

"She won't hurt you," the girl said, helping the woman sit up.

"Who are you?" Nali whispered, staring at the young adolescent.

"Her name is Phoenix," the golden woman responded. "She came to help me. You heard my plea," she said with a smile.

"Aminta?" Xyrie murmured with concern, stepping forward.

"Xyrie, wait! This may be another trick," Nali warned, holding her arm out.

"No. The alien is finally dead. I'm no longer infected," Aminta said, rising to her feet with Phoenix's help.

"How can we be sure?" Asahi asked.

Aminta smiled at Phoenix and then looked at Asahi. She shimmered, turning almost transparent. When she held out her hand, there was something in it.

"The Goddess's Mirror!" Nali exclaimed.

"A gift given long ago to the Empress of the Monsters to help her watch over and protect the Seven Kingdoms," Aminta said, holding out the mirror to Nali.

Nali lowered her sword and took the mirror. In its reflection, Asahi could see Aminta giving the mirror to the first Empress of Monsters. The image shifted, and he saw Aminta watching over the creatures living in the Seven Kingdoms with the pride and joy of a loving parent. He looked at Xyrie when she spoke.

"Aminta is an ancient. She is among the few of our kind who still remain from the creation of time. When we thought she was destroyed, we vowed to do what we could to protect this world," Xyrie confessed.

"Why didn't you tell me? Why didn't you help us?" Nali exclaimed in shock.

Aminta shook her head. "It would be easy for us to solve the problems of all the realms we have created, but it would also be a disservice. We learned long ago that after we give birth to new worlds, it is best to restrict our presence as much as possible. I was visiting Valdier when I was attacked and severely weakened. I am sorry that this abomination used me against you," she said.

"My family defeated the man who hurt you," Phoenix reassured her. "I overheard them talking about it. My Grandma was there too, of course, 'cause she helps care for the river of symbiots. She's the Priestess of the Hive," Phoenix informed the residents of the Seven Kingdoms.

"The river... I saw what happened," Asahi quietly replied. He looked at Phoenix. "But she called *you* to help defeat the alien?" he said.

"Yep!" Phoenix smiled at him. "My mom is human like you, but my dad is from Valdier. Stardust is a symbiot. She's made from the same energy as Aminta. I think that's how I got the message."

The next question on Asahi's lips died when the ground trembled. Nali readied her sword while Phoenix shifted into a dragon and literally disappeared before his eyes. When he heard trees cracking and splitting, his first thought was that yet *another* part of the alien must have found them, so he was very relieved to hear Ashure's loud voice carrying through the trees.

"Koorgan, do you even know what the definition of stealth is? Sea Monkeys are quieter than you, and everyone knows how loud and annoying those damn things are!" Ashure complained.

"Believe me, I know. You put a whole shipload of the damn things in my bedroom on my wedding night," Koorgan's deep voice growled.

"What are you...?" Ashure exclaimed. "Koorgan, don't you dare.... Orion! Damn it! Get me out of this tree!"

"It is amazing that those two have survived this long," Xyrie observed with an amused sigh.

Phoenix's giggle drew Asahi's attention. She had reappeared and was looking at him with eyes shining in delight.

"They sound just like my family when we all get together," Phoenix giggled. "I better go home now. I have a feeling that I'm going to be grounded for a long, long time."

"I will escort you home, child," Aminta said.

Phoenix shyly nodded. "That would be cool. Do you know Aikaterina? She—" Aminta, Phoenix, and the oversized golden Basset Hound passed through the Gateway as if they were going for a stroll in the park, and the sound of their conversation was cut off as the Gateway closed behind them.

Koorgan, Orion, and the others—excluding Ashure, who was still yelling—appeared out of the forest.

"Where is the alien?" Koorgan growled.

"It was destroyed," Nali said with a grin.

"For good this time?" Gem inquired, solidifying next to Ross.

"For good," Nali replied.

"What about you, Asahi? Are you... alright?" Ross asked, looking at him with a wary expression.

Asahi thought about the question for a second before he dipped his head in response. "I'm more than alright," he asserted, wrapping his arm around Nali and pulling her close.

"Thanks to me," Mr. Gryphon interjected. "Don't forget that part."

Relieved laughter burst from everyone there. "Yes. Thanks to you, Mr. Gryphon," Asahi acknowledged.

The gryphon sniffed. "That's 'Golden Dagger'. I definitely need a new title after all of this," the lion proclaimed, with a wave of his paw.

"Maybe I should call myself the Magnificent Golden Dagger. That has an impressive sound to it, don't you think?" Mr. Gryphon asked.

Nali chuckled and leaned against Asahi. "I think you've created a monster," she murmured near his ear.

"The first of many, I hope," he pledged.

Nali's eyes flashed with desire. She reached up and tangled her fingers in the hair at his nape. He captured her upturned lips in a kiss that left no doubt he meant what he said.

He ignored the chorus of laughter and the sound of Ashure's aggravated curses still carrying from farther back in the trees. The only thing he focused on was the beautiful, passionate woman in his arms. If he remembered correctly, she had mentioned something about an amazing little cottage nearby.

CHAPTER 30

*N*ali sighed and leaned back against Asahi as they stood on the cliff above the lake and watched the last of her gargoyle soldiers return home. She vaguely wondered if maybe she had been a little too blunt about insisting that everyone leave. Her guilt melted away when Asahi kissed her neck.

"I'm impressed," he murmured.

She turned in his arms and slid her hands up his chest. "You don't think I was a little too...," she paused, trying to find the right word.

"Bossy?" he teased.

She leaned her head back and laughed. "I *am* the boss of them—but I was rude, wasn't I?" she asked with a wince.

"Not rude. Impatient, but I suspect they were just as impatient to leave, spread the good news, and hold their loved ones close. I know that's how I'm feeling at the moment," he responded as he leaned forward and kissed her.

She slid her arms around his neck, pressed herself against his hard body, and returned his kiss. She groaned with exasperation when a dozen shadows passed overhead. Reluctantly ending the kiss, she looked up and laughed when she realized flying horses had cast the shadows. They had returned.

"It was nice of Ariness and Isha to open portals for everyone," she commented.

Asahi chuckled. "I think everyone was grateful because it shut Ashure up," he agreed.

"I must see if I can find his missing magic mirror. Now that he knows it can act as a portal, I'm sure the only reason he wants it back is so he can torment Koorgan," she replied.

"Koorgan mentioned something along those lines. Apparently, Ashure has a long list of retaliations planned against Koorgan for placing him in that tree." He laughed, then sighed and looked thoughtfully out over the Isle of the Monsters.

He looked down when she caressed his cheek. "What is it?" she asked.

He captured her hand and pressed his lips against the back of her fingers. "There was always a note of reverence in my grandfather's voice when he spoke of your world. I heard it, but I never really understood it until now," he said.

She tightened her grip on his hand. "*Our* world. You belong here, with me."

He trailed his fingers down her cheek. "*Aishiteru*. I love you, Nali," he murmured.

She leaned forward and kissed him. "What do you say we go find that cottage I was telling you about?" she suggested.

"Walk or fly?" he asked.

"Fly... definitely fly. It's faster," she laughed.

Less than ten minutes later, Asahi's feet sank into the soft soil as Nali released her grip on him in front of a beautiful hut that looked like it was from a fairy tale. Smoke rose from the stone chimney. Nali touched down beside him. He was struck once again by her beauty. Her long, black curls fell around her shoulders. She briefly shimmered as she transformed. Her wings folded and disappeared from sight.

"I come here sometimes, when I want to be alone," she explained.

"It is beautiful—and peaceful," he said.

"Yes," she quietly agreed, stepping around him and opening the door.

He followed her, pausing at the threshold. He allowed his gaze to linger over the room, noting each detail. Near the door, was a square table with two chairs. It was set for two diners to share an intimate meal. Dark blue cloth napkins had been placed on the plates and a beautiful crystal vase held fresh cut flowers in the center.

A cozy fire burned in the fireplace. He blinked when a small creature with pointed ears suddenly appeared in front of him holding up a bowl of fresh fruit. Another one hurried over and whispered to it.

"You can leave the food for later. We would like to get cleaned up first," Nali instructed.

"Yes, Empress," the creature said with a quick bow.

"Elves?" he asked with a note of uncertainty.

"House elves. They are incredibly efficient," she said with a smile.

"I can see that," he said, watching them move about with amazing speed.

She turned and captured his hand. "I thought we should clean up before we eat," she suggested, walking toward an open door leading into a bedroom.

The suggestive look in her eyes left no doubt as to what was on her mind. He strode forward, grasped her wrist, and twirled her around, then pulled her back against him. His lips connected with her throat when she tilted her head sideways and chuckled.

"Let me help you," he said.

"Oh, yes," she breathed.

The sensual slide of Asahi's fingers along her wrist sent waves of pleasure through her. She loved the way he ran his hands across her skin. He didn't speak. He didn't need to. Every caress, every kiss showed his love for her.

Her heart thundered in anticipation when he trailed his fingers under the collar of her blouse, and with the precision of a tailor, slowly undid each button. Her body heated at the sensuality of his movements.

The soft material of her blouse slid down her arms. Nali swallowed when he carefully folded the fabric and placed it on the dresser, then gave her a heated look that she felt deep in her very core. The sexual tension between them was intensifying. She barely kept still as he slid his hands down her bare arms to the hem of her thin undershirt.

She thought he was going to remove it. Instead, he slipped his fingers underneath, caressing her stomach. He guided her to a chair in the corner of the room, and she sat down, watching as he silently removed her boots.

Gazing at his long fingers, she followed their movements as he unhooked each bootstrap with meticulous precision. Memories of his hands as they glided over her flesh, memorizing every inch of her, sent a shiver of awareness through her.

She touched a tuft of his hair that hung down over his forehead, smiling at the contrast between his strong, chiseled face and his tousled hair. His lips curved into the mysterious smile that drove her crazy, but he didn't look up from his task. He held her calf while he pulled off her boot and long stocking. She gritted her teeth to keep from groaning out loud when he placed both aside before doing the same to her other foot.

"You enjoy torturing me, don't you?" she murmured.

He smiled again in response, and her inner muscles clenched as she let him do as he wished to her. Each touch was deliberate, as if he were carefully unwrapping a special gift.

She took a deep breath when he rose to his feet and held out his hands. Their eyes locked as he unfastened the button on her trousers and slowly lowered the zipper. She tilted her head back as he gently blew on her neck and collarbone, sending tingles down her spine in sensual waves.

"Asahi," she whispered when he slowly pulled her trousers and panties off, his penetrating looks making her tremble with need. He had barely touched her and she was already incredibly sensitive, waiting for what he would do next. He stood, taking the time again to fold each item neatly, then picked up her stockings and placed the items on the dresser.

Impatient, she grasped the hem of her undershirt. When he gave her a sharp, silent look, she released it, moaning in frustration and glaring at him.

He walked back to her, leaned very close, his lips a breath away from hers, and caressed her hips with the tips of his fingers as he pulled her shirt over her head, leaving her naked. She parted her lips and swayed toward him, feeling his clothed erection against her. He took a step back, folded her undershirt, and started to turn away, but she reached out and gripped his arm, keeping him from moving.

"Leave it. The house elves will wash them," she said in a voice laden with desire.

He smiled and shook his head. He carefully folded the top and placed it on the pile of clothing. She waited for him to return and felt another wave of heat when she noticed the desire in his eyes as he lovingly looked at her curves and gleaming skin.

"Why?" she asked as she looked at the clothes and then at him.

He stopped in front of her, captured her hand, and lifted it to his lips. "A flower, especially one as rare and precious as you, should always be respected," he explained as he caressed her cheek. "It is an honor for me to undress you. I show respect to you by caring for your belongings. Plus…," he murmured near her ear as he slowly walked around her, "it builds the anticipation. I will worship your body, Nali."

A shaft of need, so sharp that it created a physical pain, ran through her. She closed her eyes and focused on the touch of his lips on her bare shoulder and his hands as he caressed her buttocks. A breathy moan slipped from her when he slid his hand across her stomach and cupped her breast. She opened her eyes and hungrily gazed at him.

"I… don't think I can take much more worshipping, Asahi," she confessed in a strained voice.

She reached up and began unbuttoning his shirt, savoring his warm skin as he unbuckled the belt around his waist and allowed his trousers to fall to the floor. She traced the muscles along his chest, down to his waist.

They moved like dancers across the floor, caressing each other as their bodies touched. Nali had never been so aroused nor so enthralled. This feeling was beyond physical needs. It was spiritual—a connection of their souls becoming one.

She tilted her head to the side when he trailed his lips along her neck. She lightly glided her fingers across his buttocks.

"I want to wash you," he murmured as he clasped her wrist.

She uttered a low, strained chuckle. "Oh, Asahi. You are tempting a monster to forget her control," she warned, the look in her eyes far more intense than her teasing voice.

"I wouldn't have her any other way," he murmured.

Nali waved her hand at the shower. Warm water flowed like rain from the ceiling. She wrapped her arms around Asahi's neck and their lips connected in a passionate kiss. They moved as one under the water's flow.

She feverishly glided her hands over his slick skin. Her heart thundered against her chest when he gripped her wrist and twisted her around, pressing her back against his chest. She instinctively tilted her hips back, pressing her buttocks against his engorged cock.

"My beautiful Empress," he murmured between kisses.

Nali splayed her hands against the wall of the shower and bowed her head. She could see the droplets of water clinging to her aching nipples.

"Love me, Asahi," she pleaded in a voice filled with need.

"Forever," he promised.

She turned around, lifted one slender leg, and curved it over his hip. Then she slid her hands along his shoulders, pulling him closer, and he bent his knees, bringing his throbbing cock to the entrance of her channel. She stared into his eyes as he gripped her hips and slowly impaled her.

"Yes," she moaned as he moved inside her.

Her taut nipples brushed against his chest as they moved. He tightened his grip on her thighs and buried his face against her shoulder, rocking back and forth, pushing ever deeper into her. She could feel each stroke of his cock as it filled her.

His heavy breathing teased her ears and brushed against her neck. She pressed her lips against his temple, cherishing the moment. Her lips parted on a loud gasp when he slid his hand up to her throat and tilted her head back so he could kiss her.

Their tongues tangled in a primitive mating union. She closed her eyes and lost herself in the ecstasy of the moment. Her arousal was building to a peak, and she thought she would burst into flames from the heat. She curled her fingers in his hair, then ripped her lips from his with a loud cry as her orgasm engulfed her.

Asahi tightened his hold on her chin and turned her head, capturing her lips again. He rocked his hips faster, and she clawed at him as his hunger reached a fever pitch. He pressed her back against the wall and grabbed her thigh, lifting her up. She wrapped her legs around his waist. The position drove his shaft so deep inside that she swore she could feel it touching her womb.

She tightened her hold on his neck when he stiffened and groaned. His cock pulsed with his release, filling her with his seed. She locked her ankles behind him and pressed her heels into his buttocks, pushing him even deeper as she relaxed between him and the wall.

Their kiss became tender as their release took the edge off their desperation. She melted against him, savoring the taste of his lips. He caressed her thighs with his thumbs. They finally broke their kiss and rested their foreheads against each other.

"*Aishiteru,* Nali. I love you," he murmured.

Tears of emotion burned her eyes, and she gave him a tender kiss.

EPILOGUE

he Gateway

Phoenix worried her bottom lip with her teeth. Curiosity filled her as she glanced back over her shoulder. She couldn't shake the memory of her dragon changing into some kind of fire and her ability to pass through the man's body. She blinked when Aminta gently laid a hand on her shoulder.

"You are very brave, Phoenix," Aminta said.

She looked up at Aminta. "I don't feel brave. At least, not all the time," she confessed.

"Nevertheless, you are. Aikaterina chose well," Aminta replied.

"What do you mean 'chose well'?" Phoenix asked.

Aminta stopped and waved a hand at the surrounding universe. Phoenix's eyes followed the movement. Her breath caught at the beauty surrounding them. Galaxies in all shapes and sizes, filled with the brilliant dots of numerous stars spread as far as she could see.

"The worlds are changing and they need guardians who are young and strong enough to help protect them. Long ago, the Elders of our kind had a disagreement. Some of us, like myself, Xyrie, and Aikaterina believed that seeding the universe was not enough. We believed that guidance was important, so we created Protectors. Those chosen by us to protect the star systems against threats," Aminta explained.

"What kinds of threats?" Phoenix asked with a frown.

"Before this? There were always disasters that could end civilizations, be they natural or due to the blind stumbling of mortals as they pushed their boundaries. However," Aminta took a bracing breath.

"*This* entity…the abomination that you just helped defeat, it is but one of many." Aminta sighed, and continued in an exhausted voice.

"They were released by a few dangerously radical believers of the same philosophy that Aikaterina, Xyrie, and I adhere to—that we should be more involved—but to go this far…."

Aminta pursed her lips angrily. "They wished to rally us all against a common threat," she said, "and so they irresponsibly *created* such a threat to the universe. We will be fighting for survival for a long time, Phoenix, and we need your help."

Phoenix looked at the vast space around them again. "But—what about Arosa and Arilla? And the symbiots?" Her hand dropped to Stardust and she caressed her symbiot's head. "Aren't they like you? Wouldn't they be more powerful than I am? I'm just a kid," she protested.

Aminta shook her head. "Yes, there are others like Arosa and Arilla, but we are still restricted by our laws. The symbiots are different. They were created to assist and give balance to those who need it," she explained.

"Why me? Why was I chosen?" Phoenix asked.

"That is a question only Aikaterina can answer," Aminta gently responded.

"What will happen to me now?" she wondered.

"For now, I will return you to your family," Aminta said.

Phoenix absently nodded. Her eyes were locked on a distant world. She rubbed her hand over her heart. Aminta laid a hand on her shoulder.

"Come, child. Your parents are worried about you."

Phoenix nodded. Her eyes widened with joy when a Gateway appeared before her and she saw her parents. Her lips parted on a cry and she surged forward.

"Mom! Dad!" she cried.

"Phoenix!" they exclaimed, their voices thick with relief and joy.

"Oh, Phoenix," her mom choked out, opening her arms. "You're home."

Phoenix rushed into their arms, happy to be home. She turned back to look at the Gateway. It was closed—and Aminta was gone.

"Where did you go? Why didn't you tell us? Are you alright?" her father hoarsely demanded, caressing her hair.

Phoenix looked into the worried eyes of her parents and gave them a rueful smile. "I should have told you. I'm sorry. I guess I'm grounded, huh?" she said.

"Only forever," her mom teased, gently kissing her forehead and clasping her hand.

"What happened? Where did you go?" her dad asked.

Phoenix drank in the sight of her parents, unaware that her eyes shimmered with the fire of her dragon. "My dragon has changed. She is amazing, Dad. I can't wait to show her to you. It all started when I heard a cry for help..." she began, excited finally to be able to share what had happened.

~

The Isle of the Monsters

Asahi drifted through the dream world. A part of him knew that he was dreaming, while another part wondered how everything appeared so real. His body, weighed down with exhaustion from the last few weeks of adventure and sated from lovemaking, remained wrapped in his lover's arms. His mind was a different matter.

He felt refreshed and alert. Vivid colors and strange images floated past him, and he turned around, taking in the amazing vision of stars, planets, and galaxies all around. The dream seemed real, yet when he reached out to touch a planet, his fingers passed through it.

"Hello, Asahi."

"Aminta," he replied, startled.

Aminta emerged out of the darkness, looking more like gold stardust than her last form. She solidified as she walked closer.

"Is this a dream?" he asked with a frown.

"Yes—and no. Our conversation is real. The surrounding universe is real," she said.

"You aren't going to send me back to Earth, are you? I refuse to go. My place is beside Nali," he growled.

Aminta laughed and looked at him with an amused expression. *"You have a lot of your grandfather in you,"* she mused.

Asahi frowned. *"You knew my grandfather?"*

Aminta bowed her head in acknowledgment. Asahi blinked in surprise when she waved her hand and a planet appeared. He recognized the blue and white marble as Earth. He glanced from the planet to Aminta.

"Yes, as well as Nali's parents. Many centuries ago, I rescued an infant from a dying world. I knew she was special. Her father found me when I was tired and worn down from a millennium of fighting with another of my kind. My opponent did not share the same faith in the worlds we seeded as I did. Nali's father gave me hope. In return, I gave him the gift of my blood should he ever need it," she explained.

"Why didn't you save her world? Her parents?" Asahi asked.

Sadness etched itself on Aminta's face. *"Alas, even as old as I am, I must live by the rules I helped create. Nali's world was created early, near a red star. I arrived too late to save her world. I tried to send warnings to her people, but they refused to listen,"* she answered.

Asahi watched in fascination as Aminta touched the swirling cloud formation of a massive hurricane, running her fingers through the thick clouds. The edge of the storm sheared off, as if a strong current had cut through it like a knife.

"What about my grandfather?" he asked.

"I saw him first as a young boy. He looked different from most people around him, and he suffered for it," she shared.

As the clouds floated away, Asahi saw Aiko as a young boy, standing on the beach and staring out at the ocean. Asahi's heart ached for the bruised and battered boy who refused to shrink from the older boys around him. The boys yelled that he was a monster, that he didn't belong there, and threw stones at him. Eventually tiring of their game, they left the little boy alone.

"He never told me this story," Asahi murmured.

Aiko picked up a colorful shell and held it to his chest. *"I wish I was a monster and lived in a magical world filled with magical creatures.* He sighed and kicked the sand. *One day—one day I'll sail across the oceans and find it, and when I do, I'll be happy."*

"You gave him his wish," Asahi softly said.

"Yes, but he knew he couldn't stay forever. He had left behind too much to live the rest of his days away from his family, and when he asked to return home, I granted him his last wish," she said.

"I needed him," Asahi confessed.

"I know," Aminta said with an understanding smile.

His throat tight at the thought of being torn away from the love of his life, Asahi said, *"I never want to return to Earth. My place is with Nali."*

"Do you have what it takes to be a monster, Asahi?" Aminta asked.

He looked at her with a startled expression, then glanced at the adolescent version of his grandfather, standing on the beach holding the shell against his chest. If he could have a wish, would it be any different?

"I wish I was a monster," he murmured, repeating his grandfather's words.

"Then, as a gift for saving my life, I grant your wish," Aminta softly declared.

Asahi was startled when Aminta swept a hand in his direction and gold dust engulfed him. For a moment, he thought of Peter Pan sprinkling fairy dust over Wendy and telling her to think happy thoughts. His thoughts immediately went to Nali. He remembered the flush in her cheeks as she carried him to the cottage, the rush of the wind against his face as she flew, and the beauty of the Isle of the Monsters from the air.

Asahi closed his eyes and wished he had wings so he could fly with her. Memories flashed through his mind–Nali talking with the Trolls, how the Goblins looked up to her, and how she had changed her shape so she could lift them out of the underground cave. He remembered the feel of her skin—hard, yet supple in her gargoyle form. Visions filled his mind of the way the sunlight and moonlight glistened on her beautiful face, her tender smile, the way she teased Ashure, and her tears as she grieved for Pai and the lost Sea Stags.

He loved everything about this world and wanted to be a part of it. He wanted to stand beside Nali as an equal and help her protect the monsters she loved. If he could have one wish, he would want to spend the rest of his life here, with Nali.

As the last thought swept through his mind, a tingling warmth flowed through him and soft feathers brushed against his back. He blinked in surprise when he looked over his shoulder and saw a pair of golden wings.

He looked at Aminta. She gave him a smile and bowed her head. He parted his lips in protest when she faded away.

"Asahi."

He woke with a start, pulled from the dream. He blinked when he saw Nali lean over him with a worried expression. She caressed his cheek with her fingers.

"Are you alright?" she asked.

"Yes. I—I had a dream," he replied.

She tilted her head. "A good one?" she inquired, leaning closer to him.

His gaze softened. "I dreamed about you," he confessed.

She ran her thumb along his bottom lip. "There is a legend that once you've experienced the caress of a monster, you'll never want to leave," she breathed.

"I haven't heard that legend before," he murmured.

She chuckled and rubbed the tip of her nose against his. "That's because I just made it up," she teased.

"Well, I believe it," he replied.

He wrapped his arms around her and rolled them so that he was on top. They fondly gazed at each other. She spread her legs when he pressed his hard cock against her.

"Caress me, Nali, my precious monster," he requested, pressing forward with a groan of pleasure.

It was dark outside by the time they finally got out of bed, driven by hunger. Nali sniffed the air with delight when she saw the wide variety of food on the table. She would have to thank the House Elves for their thoughtfulness.

"My compliments to your house elves. The food smells delicious," Asahi commented.

"The Elves are amazing cooks. I don't know about you, but I'm starving!" she moaned, lifting the lid off one platter.

He chuckled and brushed his fingers along her cheek. She nipped at his knuckles and gave him a wicked smile before lifting a steamed vegetable that looked suspiciously like broccoli to her lips. He took a quick bite of the other side.

"Delicious," he murmured.

She waved a finger at him. "If you keep that up, it won't be food we're eating," she playfully warned.

He softly kissed her lips. "I look forward to giving you something to eat—again," he said.

She shook her head. "You are playing with fire, Asahi. Remember that," she said.

He chuckled, sat down across from her, filled his plate, and began eating. "Speaking of fire, I wonder if Phoenix made it home safely," he said.

"I could try to find out. I wish we knew more about her," she confessed.

"Do you think the Goddess's Mirror would show her to us?" he asked.

"Let us see," she said.

She waved her hand. The Goddess's Mirror appeared, floating in the air in front of her. She held the mirror at an angle so they could both see the reflection.

"Goddess's Mirror, show Phoenix to me," she requested.

Their reflection swirled and distorted. They studied the scene that appeared in the mirror. Instead of Phoenix, they saw a large wolf standing on his hind legs with a very pregnant human woman in his arms. A small but beautiful cottage ringed with flowers was in the background. It reminded her of this one. They were lovingly gazing at each other while the creature's hand rested against the woman's protruding abdomen. The wolf's form shimmered and changed until he took on a human-like appearance.

"He's a monster," she breathed.

"The woman looks like you," Asahi murmured.

She lifted her hand and touched a strand of her hair. It was true. The woman had the same long, black hair with tight corkscrew curls and facial features as she did—though she had the man's long, slender nose.

The scene in the mirror dissolved, changing to another. This time the world was different. Smoke darkened the sky. The cottage and gardens lay in ruins. In the courtyard, the woman was looking up at fireballs streaking across the sky.

She lifted her eyes to the smoke-filled sky and roared in rage and anguish as explosions burst around the cottage. The man staggered forward, catching her when her knees collapsed. He tenderly cradled her in his arms as pain flashed across her face, and she placed her hand on her pregnant stomach.

The next scene shook Nali the most. Asahi cupped her hand and held the mirror steady when it wobbled. The woman lay on a pallet of blankets partially hidden by the collapsed roof. Shock, horror, and pain filled Nali when she realized the woman was dead. Beside her, the man held a newborn baby wrapped in a blanket. He removed a gold band from his wrist and kissed it. He gently unwrapped the baby and held the gold bracelet over the infant. Nali blinked when she realized that she was staring into her own curious eyes.

"We should have listened to the warnings. Our world here has ended. Please Goddess, I beg you to protect our daughter," he whispered.

The gold in his hand dissolved and flowed over the infant. Her dark brown eyes shimmered and changed to gold. The man wrapped the infant again and tenderly caressed the long curls of black hair peeking out from under the blanket. He looked over his shoulder and stood. Nali's heart ached when she saw the man's expression. A tear escaped and slid down her cheek at the intense mixture of emotions running through her. Grief, resignation, and acceptance filled her at the sight of the approaching pyroclastic flow.

She knew what it felt like to watch the end of the world approaching. Memories and emotions flooded her as the familiar sense of helplessness swept over her. She had felt the same intense emotions of grief, resignation, and acceptance the man was experiencing when she thought she had lost Asahi.

The image changed again. This time softening around the edges and focusing on one tiny spot—the baby. A gateway opened and delicate golden hands reached down to pick up the tiny infant.

"Xyrie," she breathed.

Xyrie smiled and locked eyes with the adult Nali watching in the mirror. "There are pleas we cannot ignore. Your father once came to my assistance. Aminta gave him the symbiot bracelet in return, to use if he should ever need help. She could not save your world, but she could save you. On the day your father asked her to protect you, another father asked for a child to love. Aminta knew you would fit in on this world and asked that I help keep an eye on you," she explained.

"Thank you," Nali murmured in a voice thick with emotion.

"What about Phoenix?" Asahi asked as the image faded.

"She is safe," Xyrie said in a far-away voice.

Nali stared at her and Asahi's reflection. She met his gaze and gave him a watery smile. He tightened his hold on her hand when the mirror vanished. Turning in her chair, she wrapped her arms around his neck and leaned her head against his shoulder.

He tenderly rubbed her back as she quietly cried. Her adoptive parents had shared how they found her, but they could never tell her where she came from—or about her birth parents. Their love had filled her heart, and she had accepted that the Goddess had brought her here because this was where she belonged. Now her heart ached for her biological parents, and it pained her to know that she would never meet them.

"I wish I could take your pain," Asahi murmured, kissing her temple.

She sniffed and sat back. Asahi picked up one of the cloth napkins and gently wiped the tears from her cheeks. She threaded her fingers through his and kissed him before leaning back. The love in his eyes warmed her and helped ease her pain.

"You do whenever you hold me. I love you," she whispered, tracing his face from his temple down to his chin. "Thank you."

"*Aishiteru*," he quietly replied as he kissed her fingers. "You never have to thank me."

She sighed when he turned, poured two glasses of wine, and handed one to her. It was then that she noticed an unusual glow in his dark brown eyes—a swirl of gold that she didn't remember seeing before. He smiled.

"What is that in your eyes?" she asked.

"I do feel different. The dream I had, it was not just about you," he confessed.

She lifted an eyebrow in inquiry. "What happened in the dream?" she asked.

He placed his cup on the table and rose to his feet. She tilted her head in curiosity when he held his hand out to her. With a tired sigh, she placed her cup on the table, slid her hand into his, and stood up. A small gasp slipped from her when he pulled her into his arms. The breath from his light chuckle caressed the skin near her ear.

"I dreamed that I could fly," he murmured.

Her lips parted in shock when a pair of beautiful golden wings slowly appeared out of Asahi's back and wrapped around her. She gazed up at him, trying to understand. He leaned forward and pressed a kiss against her parted lips.

"Aminta...," she whispered as she reached out and touched his soft feathers.

"A gift," he replied with a nod.

She cradled the back of his head and leaned forward, capturing his lips. Her heart swelled with love. He tenderly caressed her back, drawing a groan from her when his hands dipped lower. She tangled her fingers in his hair and looked up at him with a gasp.

"I want you, Asahi," she said, her voice growing desperate with need.

He laughed with happiness. His wings vanished into his back and he picked her up. She lovingly ran her hand along his shoulders, missing the beautiful golden feathers already. Tomorrow they would fly, but for the rest of the night, she would relish being in Asahi's arms where their love would soar.

Note from the Author

I hope you've enjoyed the adventures of the Seven Kingdoms as much as I have. For those that have read my series, you know that many of them intertwine with another. In this case, it is with the Dragon Lords of Valdier. Phoenix, one of my characters from the Dragon Lords and Dragonlings series, has captured my heart. Her journey is just beginning. If you have not read my Dragon Lords of Valdier series, I encourage you to discover this amazing world starting with Abducting Abby. A list of my series can be found below or on my website at http://sesmithfl.com/reading-list-by-series/

ADDITIONAL BOOKS

If you loved this story by me (S.E. Smith) please leave a review! You can discover additional books at: http://sesmithfl.com and http://sesmithya.com or find your favorite way to keep in touch here: https://sesmithfl.com/contact-me/ Be sure to sign up for my newsletter to hear about new releases!

Recommended Reading Order Lists:

http://sesmithfl.com/reading-list-by-events/

http://sesmithfl.com/reading-list-by-series/

The Series

Science Fiction / Romance

Dragon Lords of Valdier Series

It all started with a king who crashed on Earth, desperately hurt. He inadvertently discovered a species that would save his own.

Curizan Warrior Series

The Curizans have a secret, kept even from their closest allies, but even they are not immune to the draw of a little known species from an isolated planet called Earth.

Marastin Dow Warriors Series

The Marastin Dow are reviled and feared for their ruthlessness, but not all want to live a life of murder. Some wait for just the right time to escape....

Sarafin Warriors Series

A hilariously ridiculous human family who happen to be quite formidable... and a secret hidden on Earth. The origin of the Sarafin species is more than it seems. Those cat-shifting aliens won't know what hit them!

Dragonlings of Valdier Novellas

The Valdier, Sarafin, and Curizan Lords had children who just cannot stop getting into trouble! There is nothing as cute or funny as magical, shapeshifting kids, and nothing as heartwarming as family.

Cosmos' Gateway Series

Cosmos created a portal between his lab and the warriors of Prime. Discover new worlds, new species, and outrageous adventures as secrets are unravelled and bridges are crossed.

The Alliance Series

When Earth received its first visitors from space, the planet was thrown into a panicked chaos. The Trivators came to bring Earth into the Alliance of Star Systems, but now they must take control to prevent the humans from destroying themselves. No one was prepared for how the humans will affect the Trivators, though, starting with a family of three sisters....

Lords of Kassis Series

It began with a random abduction and a stowaway, and yet, somehow, the Kassisans knew the humans were coming long before now. The fate of more than one world hangs in the balance, and time is not always linear....

Zion Warriors Series

Time travel, epic heroics, and love beyond measure. Sci-fi adventures with heart and soul, laughter, and awe-inspiring discovery...

Paranormal / Fantasy / Romance

Magic, New Mexico Series

Within New Mexico is a small town named Magic, an... unusual town, to say the least. With no beginning and no end, spanning genres, authors, and universes, hilarity and drama combine to keep you on the edge of your seat!

Spirit Pass Series

There is a physical connection between two times. Follow the stories of those who travel back and forth. These westerns are as wild as they come!

Second Chance Series

Stand-alone worlds featuring a woman who remembers her own death. Fiery and mysterious, these books will steal your heart.

More Than Human Series

Long ago there was a war on Earth between shifters and humans. Humans lost, and today they know they will become extinct if something is not done....

The Fairy Tale Series

A twist on your favorite fairy tales!

A Seven Kingdoms Tale

Long ago, a strange entity came to the Seven Kingdoms to conquer and feed on their life force. It found a host, and she battled it within her body for centuries while destruction and devastation surrounded her. Our story begins when the end is near, and a portal is opened....

Epic Science Fiction / Action Adventure

Project Gliese 581G Series

An international team leave Earth to investigate a mysterious object in our solar system that was clearly made by <u>someone</u>, someone who isn't from Earth. Discover new worlds and conflicts in a sci-fi adventure sure to become your favorite!

New Adult / Young Adult

Breaking Free Series

A journey that will challenge everything she has ever believed about herself as danger reveals itself in sudden, heart-stopping moments.

The Dust Series

Fragments of a comet hit Earth, and Dust wakes to discover the world as he knew it is gone. It isn't the only thing that has changed, though, so has Dust...

ABOUT THE AUTHOR

S.E. Smith is an ***internationally acclaimed, New York Times* and *USA TODAY Bestselling*** author of science fiction, romance, fantasy, paranormal, and contemporary works for adults, young adults, and children. She enjoys writing a wide variety of genres that pull her readers into new worlds.

Printed in Great Britain
by Amazon

59652326R10180